DIZZY
A MAGICAL PLACE

BY ALAN A. ANDERSON

CONTENTS

ISBN Paperback: 9798329638073

ISBN Hardcopy: 9798329808261

AUTHOR'S NOTE

The language and scenes in this novel may offend some readers. However, to stay true to the subject matter, the actual slang, jargon, and scenarios are portrayed realistically.

Some people have the misconception that human trafficking occurs only in countries like Thailand, the Philippines, Malaysia, and Russia. However, that's not true. Human trafficking is happening everywhere. Human trafficking is the fastest-growing crime in the world. An estimated twenty thousand women annually are forced into the sex trade in the U.S. alone. It's an unsavory topic, to say the least. Sex trafficking will continue to grow until we are willing to pay the price and allocate the proper resources to stop it.

Please support the A21 Campaign, which aims to "abolish slavery everywhere, forever." It focuses on combatting slavery around the world through educational awareness and prevention, the protection of victims, and the prosecution of traffickers.

Dream of a world where every single person is free. A place where no one is forced into sex slavery to be beaten and raped over and over again. Please do your part to make this dream come true.

PROLOGUE

This story is told to us by an unknown narrator. However, the narrator is believed to be the ghost of a young Vietnam veteran who never got the chance to wed his high school sweetheart. A ghost who surfs through time and space, searching for something he never got...a ghost who has made Dizzy his favorite haunt for various reasons. He tells a story about a cast of characters, a lucky few, who have found unexpected love.

Some say that Dizzy, a Bangkok go-go bar, is a magical place. A place that has been anointed with enchanted dust. And not your Tinkerbell pixie dust, which allows you to float in the air, a ticket to Never-Never-Land. No, this enchanted silvery dust is more akin to the arrows of Cupid that spark desires, lust, and sometimes even love in the hearts of humans.

Dizzy was built during the Vietnam War era. When going to such an establishment, a GI, usually with a big shit-eating grin on his face, just like the MVP of past Super Bowl Games, would announce, "I'm going to Disneyland!"

1

The original owner of Dizzy wanted to name his bar "Disneyland" but was told he could not. Disney's tentacles reached all the way to Bangkok, and they would not tolerate such a copyright infringement upon their name.

Since the go-go bar's owner couldn't name his bar Disneyland, the name "Disneyland" morphed into "Dizzyland" and then to "Dizzy." From the go-go bar's original owner to the current one, the name *"Dizzy"* and its enchanted silvery dust have stuck.

1
NO REGRETS

How in the hell did I get here? JJ, the current proprietor of Dizzy, thought as he slowly sipped Wild Turkey on ice while sitting on his private upstairs balcony. However, JJ has no regrets. There was nowhere he would rather be, even though his heart was aching, nearly breaking.

He had fallen head-over-heels in love with a serial killer, a woman who was a victim of sex trafficking, who decided to commit evil to inhibit a greater evil. A woman willing to pay any price to fulfill her ambitions and dreams, even if it meant jeopardizing her life and those she loves. She is a woman to be reckoned with, the most powerful warlord in Cambodia, and JJ is completely taken by her. But no matter how much he's in love with her, at this very moment, he's angry with her. Yet, if she returned to his arms, that anger would dissipate quicker than a puff of smoke on a windy day.

JJ, a retired deputy police chief and a retired First Sergeant in the 23rd Marine Regiment reserves didn't come to Thailand to buy a go-go bar. He didn't come to Thailand to fall in love. *Hell no!* But it happened, and he didn't regret it. Not one little bit.

After his retirement, he began to reminisce about his days as a young Marine; at no other time in his life did he feel more alive. He thought that *no one who had never been in combat or worked the streets of Oakland could understand what it was like - the good, the bad, and the ugly.*

As a Marine, he saw combat in Granada, both Gulf wars, and Afghanistan. While in the Marines, he met his best friend, Clyde Frazer Jr. He smiled as he reminisced about their trip to Thailand long ago. The memory of that trip and the promise he made to himself at the end of it brought him back to Thailand.

There was no action down below. Dizzy was quiet and likely to remain so for a few more hours. Once the sun goes down, there would be plenty of action down below, action on crack cocaine. Then there will be seminude women in high heels, dancing on a raised platform to the beat of loud music and flashing lights. There will be gawking and hooting men voicing their approval. These gentlemen will buy these fine ladies their drinks and offer to pay their bar fines, a required payment before a patron can take a dancer out of a go-go bar, for very personal off-site services.

JJ heard a man below shout at a dancer on stage, "Come on, baby; take it all off! I want to see your lovely pussy." The topless dancer squatted down in front of the drunken man, shaking her head side-to-side and waving her index finger in front of her face. She blew him a kiss before standing back up and continuing with her dance, listening to the lyrics of the Duran Duran's song *"Rio."*

"Her name is Rio and she dances on the sand

Just like that river twisting through a dusty land

And when she shines, she really shows you all she can

Oh Rio, Rio, dance across the Rio Grande."

She danced as if alone in her own world, twisting and turning around a slim metallic pole, swaying to the beat of loud music, and just like Rio, she showed all she could.

After the dancer refused to grant the drunken man his wish, the man got up from his chair, dropped his drawers, and shouted, "If you don't show me that cute little pussy of yours, then by God, I'm going to show you the biggest pecker you have ever seen!"

This got the attention of Clyde. He swiftly jumped to his feet and started walking toward the man. "Sir, if you plan to stay in this bar, you have two choices," said Clyde,

"Choice #1 – Pull your pants back up, sit down, and act like a gentleman. Then the girl on stage, when she has finished her dance, might allow you to buy her a drink and pay her bar fine. If that happens, then you may show her your big pecker in the privacy of your hotel room.

Choice #2 – You can continue to be an obnoxious asshole, get your ass kicked, and spend a night in a Bangkok jail. It's your choice."

The drunk did the smart thing; he decided to take Choice #1. JJ just shook his head, thinking: *It's going to be one of those nights. It's way too early for this kind of nonsense.* With the distraction over and Clyde handling the drunken man, JJ went back to dreaming of the day when he would again have his love wrapped in his arms.

2
TIME TO LEAVE

Clyde hails from Jackson, Mississippi. He is not a light-skinned Black man. He is nearly ebony black. He is a muscular, good-looking man with a straight back and a lean frame. His grandmother raised Clyde in the projects.

Clyde is not a bigot when it comes to the color of a man's skin. This was surprising because, in the projects, he was taught by many of his peers to mistrust and hate Whitey. "Never trust a Honky. The Black man in America will never be free. They only want to keep us in chains!" Clyde felt that all sermons promoting racial hatred were evil, regardless of their source. Like Martin Luther King Jr, Clyde dreamed of the day when people wouldn't be judged based on the color of their skin, but rather by the contents of their character.

His grandmother was a hard-working woman who didn't take shit from anyone. She liked to say, "I don't gladly suffer fools." She got up at five o'clock every morning to go to work and didn't go to bed until after eleven. Sunday was her only day off. Sunday morning, she made sure that she found her way to church alongside Clyde, and they never skipped Wednesday's service. Clyde was the apple of her eye. The one thing that Clyde could always count on was his grandmother's love.

Clyde learned his work ethic from his grandmother, and he was very smart and did well in school. For the most part, Clyde stayed out of trouble on account of his grandmother. He loved her too much to intentionally hurt her, like getting into trouble. Unlike some of his friends, he had no trouble with the neighborhood police.

Women were Clyde's only vice; he loved women. They were his Achilles tendon. He was addicted to women, and he would do just about anything to get his fix. His grandmother repeatedly told him, "Boy, those girls will be the death of you." His grandmother's prediction nearly came true. Yet, like a cat, Clyde always landed on his feet.

Clyde found himself going on a date with the girlfriend of a local drug dealer named "Half-Dead." Half-Dead's drug of choice was not crack, meth, or heroin. It was Angel Dust. Angel Dust or PCP can be legally used as a horse tranquilizer. It can make a human user violent, giving the user a feeling of invincibility and supernatural strength.

Half-Dead had no problems ripping off other drug dealers, especially while he was high on Angel Dust. Living in the hood, with so many enemies, it was highly unlikely he would ever see his twenty-fifth birthday, hence his street name "Half-Dead."

Half-Dead's girlfriend, Sonia, was long-legged and cute. She had shapely legs like Tina Turner's, and like Tina, she knew how to use them to turn heads. Unlike Half-Dead, Sonia didn't smoke, consume adult beverages, or take any mind-altering drugs. Sonia lived in the projects with her mother.

Before meeting Half-Dead, Sonia stayed at home as much as possible. She quit associating with her friends and neighbors after the death of her brother, a victim of a drive-by shooting. She left her home only to go to work, and shop for herself and her mother.

Sonia met Half-Dead while in a small neighborhood in an Arab-owned market. She was buying a bottle of Morgan David blackberry wine. Her mother enjoyed drinking a small glass of blackberry wine just before going to bed.

While Sonia was in the store when a group of young Black women, former high school friends, started harassing her, asking her, "So now you think you're too good to hang out with us?" when Half-Dead walked in. Half-Dead told the group of women to beat it. They left without argument; they were afraid of Half-Dead and didn't want to risk an altercation with him.

Half-Dead walked to the counter and started talking to Sonia while she was paying for her mother's wine. "You know those women are waiting for you outside. Why don't you let me drive you home, and I'll make sure they don't bother you?"

Sonia looked at Half-Dead and liked what she saw. "Why, thank you. You are such a gentleman." At the time, she didn't know anything about Half-Dead. She picked up her bottle of wine and walked out of the store with Half-Dead, holding his arm.

Sonia smiled at the group of women waiting for her. Half-Dead glared at them; he was not smiling. In a deep, raspy voice, he told them, "Good night, ladies." The waiting women said nothing in return, as Sonia and Half-Dead strolled past them. They knew better than to cross Half-Dead.

When they met, Sonia had no idea how Half-Dead made his living, or that he was a borderline sociopath. Half-Dead liked wearing nice clothes. He didn't look or act like the street thug he was, except when he was high on Angel Dust. Sonia called him by his Christian name, "Samuel."

At first, Half-Dead treated her like all women like to be treated, with respect and kindness. In the beginning, he was good to her. He drew her out of her shell. She no longer stayed inside her house all day. She started going back to church. It was something she used to do with her mother, before her mother lost her faith, following the death of her brother. Since he was a victim of a drive-by shooting, Sonia nor her mother knew who was to blame for his death. They found it easier to isolate themselves instead of listening to the accusing voices in their heads.

Half-Dead didn't much like going to church. But at the start of their relationship, he went just to make Sonia happy. As time went by, Half-Dead stopped going to church altogether. In fact, he stopped doing many things that drew Sonia to him. He had love-bombed her and began to see her as his property. While lost in the thick of the relationship, Sonia continued to go, alone. The church had become her sanctuary, a place where she could forget all her outside troubles and worries. It was a place where she could forget all about Half-Dead.

On the Sunday, she met Clyde, Sonia regretted her relationship with Half-Dead. She learned Half-Dead was a drug dealer, and he was extremely jealous and violent. The only thing he seemed to be interested in, nowadays, was sex. It was something she no longer enjoyed nor wanted, at least not with Half-Dead.

After Half-Dead caught her smiling at another man, he nearly killed the man and gave her a black eye. He accused her of flirting. "I will not put up with that. You're my woman. Now act like it!" Half-Dead seethed. When she protested, he punched her in the eye.

She wanted to end the relationship right then and there but was afraid to. She didn't want to end up dead, like her brother. *If he kills me, then who will take care of Mother?* She now knew just how ruthless Half-Dead could be.

While at church, Clyde spotted Sonia, alone. Half-Dead wasn't with her. She wore a summer dress and red high heels, showcasing her delightful long brown legs. Like a heat-seeking missile, Clyde zeroed in on her. This was stupid on Clyde's part. He knew that Sonia was Half-Dead's girlfriend, but she was just too cute to ignore. Her long, bare legs were like green lights signaling him to his target. As he often did when it came to women, Clyde used the wrong head, the one between his legs, for his thinking. He stood tall and confident and decided to shoot his shot. "I see you here every Sunday, and for the longest time, I've been wanting to talk to you."

Sonia grinned lightly with her eyes, "You know I have a boyfriend, and I think you know who he is?"

Clyde nodded his head up and down but didn't appear to be intimidated. She wondered if he was fearless or just stupid. *HMM...maybe both?*

"I haven't seen him here lately. If I were your boyfriend, I would never think of letting someone as cute as you go to church alone. Do you mind if I sit next to you?"

She thought about it, taking her time, before giving her answer. "No, go ahead." She scooted over to make room for him on the crowded bench. He sat down and liked the feel of her hip up against his. He couldn't help but steal glances at Sonia's long, beautiful legs, which didn't go unnoticed. Being somewhat of a tease, she accidentally, on purpose, hiked her dress up a little to show more of her beautiful legs. Sonia was enjoying the effect she was having on Clyde.

When the service was over, Clyde turned to her, licked his lips, and said, "I would love to take you out to a movie tonight. How about it?"

Half-Dead had become very predictable. He would come over to see her three times a week for one sole purpose – sex, and never on Sunday, at least not at this time of the year, at the beginning of the football season. He would be watching football all day and well into the night.

The first thing out of Sonia's mouth was, "No, I got plans for the night." Then, a smile came to her face. Sonia loved going to the movie theater and hadn't gone out to watch a movie in a very long time. It was something she liked and missed doing. She turned around and looked at Clyde, "All right, but I get to choose the movie, and I would like popcorn and a large Coke."

Clyde replied, "Me too."

. . .

"The thing is... you are going to pay for everything," Sonia said. Do you have a problem with that?"

"No, not at all," he said, returning her smile.

Their only physical contact on the date was holding hands and a brief goodnight kiss, even though Clyde would have liked more. Sonia told Clyde, "I had a good time," and promised she would go out with him again.

One of Half-Dead's associates spotted Sonia and Clyde sitting together at the movie theater and told Half-Dead. When Half-Dead got Sonia alone, he shouted at her, "You fucking bitch!" In his rage, he punched her so hard in the stomach, that it caused her to vomit. "I'll kill you if I find out you are dating other men," and Sonia believed him.

Half-Dead felt Clyde had personally insulted him by going after "*My woman*," something he would not and could not tolerate. He would make an example out of Clyde. *That Nigga is gonna pay!*

Like most summer nights, after finishing work, Clyde headed for the local basketball court and played hoops with his friends. On the way to the court, Clyde ran into Half-Dead. They crossed paths in a housing project parking lot. It was getting dark, and no one was around. Half-Dead pulled out a pistol, holding it gangster-style, pointing it at Clyde's face. "So, Nigga, you think you can go after my woman and get away with it?"

With his hands outstretched in front of him, palms down, Clyde lied, "Really, man, I didn't know she was your woman. I meant you no disrespect."

"I don't believe you. Everyone knows she's my woman. You know Nigga, excuses are like assholes. Everyone has one, and they all stink."

Half-Dead then pulled the trigger on his cheap semiautomatic pistol, and it jammed. This was the second time in Clyde's life that his guardian angel had saved him. The first time was when he survived the car crash that killed his parents.

Clyde, a good defensive tackle on his high school football team, tackled Half-Dead. The back of Half-Dead's head landed hard on the asphalt, knocking him nearly unconscious. Clyde easily placed him into a rear-naked choke.

After Half-Dead lost consciousness, Clyde considered releasing the choke, but he didn't. Half-Dead was just too dangerous. He didn't release the choke until Half-Dead became fully dead. He then got up and continued his way to the basketball court, acting as if nothing had happened.

No one missed Half-Dead; it was good riddance. With no witnesses and Half-Dead having so many enemies, it would be difficult for the police to solve his murder. Clyde didn't need to worry at all. The police didn't seem to care who killed Half-Dead. No one mourned his death, which was especially true regarding Sonia; her stomach was still bruised from his punch. Half-Dead was twenty-three years old when he died. He never made it to twenty-five.

Killing a person can place a weight on your consciousness. How heavy that weight is... *depends*. A psychopath or sociopath feels nothing except maybe pleasure from killing. For others, the weight of killing a person can be as light as a feather or as heavy as a sumo wrestler sitting on your chest. It depends on the circumstances surrounding the killing and the type of person you are. It depends on whether or not you can justify the killing. Some can't justify killing another person, even in self-defense. Clyde felt no remorse for killing Half-Dead, but it did weigh on him.

Over the following years, Half-Dead would occasionally haunt Clyde's dreams; in these dreams, Half-Dead would speak to him, asking, "So

Nigga, you think you can go after my woman and get away with it?" But in his dreams, when Half-Dead pulled the gun's trigger, a round went off. It's a dream that never failed to wake him in a panic, with his heart pounding in his chest, shortness of breath, and beads of sweat forming on his forehead.

The next Sunday, Clyde saw Sonia in church. Begrudgingly, she moved over to allow him to sit next to her. She reneged on her promise and refused to go out with Clyde on a second date. "Clyde, it's not that I don't like you, but I'm not ready to jump into another relationship. Besides that, I'm twenty-two, and you are only eighteen." Sonia wanted an older man with a good-paying job and a car; Clyde had neither. Clyde did not take her rejection well and didn't like the direction his life was taking him.

He decided to take the advice of a local cop who had befriended him. The police officer was a former Marine and a Vietnam vet. A White cop who was surprisingly well-liked in the projects. A cop who got out of his patrol car and talked to people. He was honest and fair. Most importantly, unlike some of his White counterparts, he was colorblind, and everyone knew it.

He liked telling people, "When you are in a foxhole with another man, you don't care about the color of his skin. The only thing that matters is: can I count on this man having my back when shit hits the fan?" He had been encouraging Clyde to leave the projects. He told Clyde, "You don't have a future here. Why don't you become a Marine? Become someone you and your grandmother can be proud of."

Clyde was tired of his dead-end job and uninterested in attending college. So, two months after graduating high school, Clyde decided to join the U.S. Marine Corps. He told his grandmother, "I need to leave."

"Honey, I know you do."

. . .

13

His grandmother was sad to see him go but knew it was for the best. Two weeks later, he kissed his grandmother goodbye and headed off to Parris Island. Their parting left tears in her eyes. Until the day she died, she received phone calls at least twice a week from Clyde.

Clyde visited his grandmother whenever he was on leave. He was always eager to go home, to get a hug from her, and to enjoy her delicious home cooking. No one could fry chicken or bake an apple pie like his grandmother. Her fried potato cakes were enough to kill for.

In boot camp, Clyde stood out. He was squared away, and he had his shit together. Clyde became his platoon's guide, which earned him a stripe and his dress blues upon graduating from boot camp.

After graduation, his senior drill instructor came up to him and said, "Clyde, you're going to make one damn good Marine." It was the only time the senior drill instructor had paid him a compliment, just after he'd gotten used to him calling him "maggot."

3
HOLLYWOOD MARINES

Around the same time Clyde joined the Marines, so did JJ, but on the opposite side of the country. There are two Marine Corps Recruit Depots (MCRDs). Anyone living east of the Mississippi River went to boot camp at Parris Island MCRD, South Carolina, and those living west of the Mississippi went to boot camp at San Diego MCRD and Camp Pendleton, California. You do not become a Marine until you finish boot camp. And once you have finished, you're a Marine for life.

Marines who graduated boot camp from Parris Island liked calling the West Coast Marines "Hollywood Marines." Clyde enjoyed calling JJ a Hollywood Marine. It's said in jest because all Marines receive the same treatment and training in boot camp, regardless of which MCRD they attended.

If you have seen the first half of the movie *Full Metal Jacket*, you have some idea of what the treatment and training are like. Marine Corps boot camp is not a cakewalk; it's a rite of passage. It's a proud tradition that never compromises its values. "OOOOOORRRAAAAHHHHH!!!"

Like Clyde, JJ earned his first stripe, Private First Class, at the end of boot camp.

4

YELLOW FEVER

JJ and Clyde met as Regimental Surveillance and Target Acquisition Platoon members with the 1st Battalion. Both were Lance Corporals and Scout Snipers. At first, their opposing cultures kept them apart, but over time, they found they were more alike than different, regardless of their backgrounds. For one, they shared the same work ethic: both were young and gung-ho. They eventually became close friends.

There were still a few leftover Vietnam vets in their unit, but not many. The Nam vets loved to talk about all their fun on their Rest and Relaxation trips from Nam to Thailand and the Philippines Islands. After returning from Operation Urgent Fury, JJ and Clyde decided to see for themselves if Thailand or the Philippines were half the fun as the Nam vets made them out to be.

They didn't have enough leave to go to both the Philippines and Thailand. They had to choose – Thailand or the Philippines. A coin was flipped, and Thailand came up as the winner. They decided to take military flight hops to Thailand, where they planned to spend two weeks.

"I hope those Nam Vets are not exaggerating," Clyde said, slapping his hands together.

"We'll soon find out," JJ replied, stroking his chin.

Before leaving for Thailand, the Nam vets gave them one last bit of advice, "Protect yourselves against 'Suzie Rotten Crotch.' Make sure you wear rubbers." It's advice they took. They did not want to bring anything back from Thailand other than a few knick-knacks and good memories.

They were not disappointed; the Vietnam vets were right-on. The girls of the night, hot spicy food, Buddhist temples, white sandy beaches, and the clear blue seas, were unbelievably spectacular. And the Thai people were friendly. Clyde nearly overdosed on all the beautiful Thai women he met, and JJ contracted a serious case of what some folks like to refer to as "yellow fever," a strong attraction for Asian women. When the trip was over, JJ promised himself: *One day, I'm gonna return to Thailand. I love this place. It's magical. I know it's a place where my dreams can come true.*

5

BLUE JEAN BABY

When JJ's four-year enlistment ended, he left active duty and joined the Marine Reserves. He went back home to Antioch, California, and enrolled in Los Medanos Junior College, in Pittsburg, California, to pursue an associate degree in administrative justice. Also, with the rank of sergeant, he became a reserve member of the 23rd Marine Regiment.

On the other hand, Clyde decided to become a "Lifer," remaining on active duty until retirement. JJ and Clyde went their separate ways but continued to stay in touch; they maintained a lifetime friendship. And on occasions, they would vacation together.

Clyde had no desire to get married; he was married to the Corps, which didn't hinder him from getting his much-needed fixes. Nothing excited him more than being in bed with a beautiful naked woman, and for Clyde, the gangster of love, variety was the spice of life!

After getting his associate degree, JJ got his bachelor's degree in criminal justice at Hayward State University and then joined the Oakland Police Department. It did not take long for him to move up the ranks and become a detective.

JJ loved being a cop. After becoming a detective, a dark-haired Amerasian beauty named Beth came into his life. She was born to an American White father and an American Japanese mother. Her face and body could grace the pages of *Sports Illustrated* swimsuit edition, but the most striking thing about Beth was her eyes.

She had beautiful, hypnotic hazel eyes. Looking into them was like looking into a kaleidoscope. Her eyes' green and brown specks cast off the illusion of being in constant motion as if the specks were swimming inside her eyes' irises.

Beth was the lead singer in a local rock and roll band. She grew up singing along with Karaokes. While in a Bay Area nightclub, while her band was on break, Beth walked to where JJ was sitting, "Handsome, I don't believe I've seen you in here before."

"I don't often go out to nightclubs. This is my first time here. By the way - I love the way you sing."

Beth spoke in the sexist voice he had ever heard. Her eyes seemed to place him in a trance. "Why, thank you. Do you mind if I join you while we're on break?"

JJ shook his head, "Not at all. I would love your company!"

JJ was a good-looking man, tall, with broad shoulders, freckles on his nose, and a thin waist. But he was somewhat shy around women. Beth wasn't shy at all, a woman's characteristic JJ found irresistible.

The band's break was way too short. As she lingered at JJ's table, Beth told him, "Handsome, you need to come here more often." JJ looked into

Beth's hypnotic hazel eyes and replied, "Yes, I most certainly need to do that."

While Beth was walking away from JJ's table and back to the stage, her right hand lagged behind, waving goodbye to JJ. She was wearing tight-fitting blue jeans that showed off her shapely hips and delicious derrière: *a blue jean baby, Mmm... Mmm... Good! Yes, JJ thought, I will definitely be coming back. Unfortunately, I need to head home and get a good night's sleep before going to work tomorrow morning.*

Beth's voice reminded JJ of Stevie Nicks, his favorite female rock vocalist. Beth could sing *Dreams* in a way that only Stevie could match. It was a song that took JJ into his dream world:

"Thunder only happens when it's raining

Players only love you when they're playing

Say women they will come and they will go

When the rain washes you clean, you'll know, you'll know..."

Six months after their initial meeting, JJ got down on one knee. He displayed a diamond ring and asked Beth, "Will you marry me?" And she replied, "Yes, Handsome, I'll marry you." He then placed the ring on her finger.

After four years of marriage, the ring came off; Beth filed for a divorce. Which was not a total surprise. To JJ's regret - they didn't have time for each other. They had no children because they were both too busy with their careers. They chose their careers over their marriage.

Beth left her band to become a big-time entertainment promoter. JJ got his MBA while working full-time on the force and putting time into the reserves. He liked telling people, "There is no rest for the weary or the wicked." During this time, Beth met a man who made time for her, around her busy schedule, something JJ failed to do.

When Beth handed JJ the divorce papers, she told him, "Handsome, there will always be a part of me who loves you, but this marriage is not working out. You never have time for me, and I've met a man who does." JJ seemed unable to get over Beth, leaving him for another man. Their priorities, as far as JJ was concerned, were totally fucked-up. Beth would continue to prey upon his mind, for many, many, years to come, no matter how hard he tried to forget her.

After the divorce, JJ became a dedicated bachelor. He had no interest in serious relationships. He wanted casual relationships with privileges. It turned out that in the San Francisco Bay Area, that wasn't difficult for a man to find.

However, there were times when JJ didn't want any strings attached at all, "Just the sex, ma'am." That was when he headed for Carson City, Nevada, for a weekend of "Wham-bam thank you, ma'am." He had no problems paying directly for sex when he wanted it and nothing else, as long as it was legal. In Carson City, it was.

After being in the Oakland Police Department for twenty-three years, and in the Marine Corps for thirty-one years, JJ decided *it was time that I retire.* He knew he would never become the Chief of the Oakland PD. He felt lucky that he had risen to the rank of Deputy Chief. Early in JJ's career, he had become friendly with several police officers who later became known as "the Riders."

The Riders were Oakland rogue police officers accused of planting evidence on Black suspects, acting as vigilantes. The arrest of the Riders made national news. JJ knew nothing of the Rider's illegal activities, but there were those in the department who said he should have. Some even believed he did know but chose to look the other way. But that wasn't the case. JJ hated corrupt police officers. He felt the worst type of criminals were the ones who hid behind a badge.

The new chief was pressuring him to retire. It wasn't a surprise that the new chief wanted to hire his own man to replace JJ, someone with no blemishes. The new chief never missed a chance to criticize him in front of others. Finally, JJ had enough, and one day he told the chief, "Go fuck yourself!" He was given the choice of being charged with insubordination or retiring. As much as JJ loved his job, he decided it was time to move on.

As a civilian, he found his life lacking. His job as a cop and Marine had been his whole life. Except for going to the gym every day, he didn't have any real hobbies. He was in his early fifties, in great shape, and bored to death. He craved the excitement he once had. JJ looked and acted much younger than his actual age; he appeared to be in his late thirties or early forties.

While dining at his favorite Thai restaurant in San Francisco, JJ ran into an old friend. A friend he knew in the reserves, a mixed martial arts fighter, who received Muay Thai training in Thailand. He had a lean, muscular fighter's physique, a tanned face with circles around his eyes from wearing sunglasses on sunny days, and short sun-bleached hair. In the reserves, JJ had been his First Sergeant.

They started talking about Thailand. JJ told him about his trip to Thailand as a young Marine. "At the end of that trip, I promised myself that one day I would return to Thailand. You know, I think it's time for me to keep that promise."

"Hey Top," Top is a nickname for a Master Sergeant or First Sergeant, "I know this dude." He always spoke like a California surfer and still did. He continued, "I know this dude, who trained me while I was in Thailand. His name is *Cowboy*. Not only is he a bitchin Muay Thai trainer, but he is also an English-speaking tour guide. I can give him a ring and let him know you are planning a trip to Thailand, and you want a good guide."

"That would be great. I would appreciate that. Give me his number, and

I'll call him after you make the introduction." His friend wrote down the number on a napkin and handed it to JJ.

"Top, I'll call him tonight."

"Thanks."

So, a year after retiring, JJ decided it was time to keep the promise he made to himself long ago. He started planning his trip back to Thailand. JJ called Cowboy. "A friend of mine recommended you to me. I'm coming to Thailand, and I would like a guide. You were highly recommended." They worked out the details, and Cowboy agreed to meet JJ at the Bangkok airport.

6

COWBOY

Like a lot of Thais, Phet went by the nickname, "Cowboy." It's a nickname he obtained due to his love of American Western movies and his Western wear. Cowboy stood out for more than one reason. He almost always wore faded blue denim jeans, a clean white t-shirt, cowboy boots, and an old beat-up straw cowboy hat. The day he met JJ was no different. His hat never left his head except when he slept, showered, or entered a ring to fight.

It had been years since Cowboy had fought in the ring. He had been a Muay Thai champion; a sport he no longer competed in. At the age of thirty-seven, he was too old to be competitive.

Cowboy's mother died when he was twelve years old from a heroin overdose. She was a Bangkok go-go bar dancer, and a prostitute, who came to Bangkok after growing tired of bending over in muddy fields planting rice. With no formal education and no marketable skills, she had trouble finding work. She finally sold the only thing that men were interested in paying her for.

The first time a farang, a slightly derogatory term reserved for White men, asked to place his dick into her mouth, she was startled and felt insulted. She had no idea this was a common farang sex practice. It nearly sent her running back home, back to the muddy rice paddies. It didn't take her long to learn when a farang asked, "Do you smoke?" They were not asking her if she smoked cigarettes.

She didn't leave the rice fields to become a prostitute. She hated being a prostitute. There were Bangkok prostitutes who enjoyed being in the Game. They enjoyed the thrill of the hunt for johns, some even enjoyed the sex, and of course, they all loved the money.

The only thing she liked about the Game, was the money. She didn't like selling her body. There were times when she regretted leaving her family. There were even times when she regretted leaving the muddy rice paddies. At least there was a sense of peace and serenity in the rice fields, but her life now held no peace or tranquility, just sex in exchange for money to feed her and her son.

She had given up hope of finding any comfort in her present life when she finally found some. It came out of the tip of a needle, 'China white,' 'the magical dragon,' and 'horse,' nicknames for heroin. The problem was it was a comfort she could only afford by repeatedly selling herself.

Cowboy didn't know who his father was; his mother never told him. She suspected his father might be her heroin supplier, or a corrupt Bangkok policeman named Chuen. However, she believed his father was Chuen, who didn't like wearing condoms.

She despised Chuen because he liked calling her, "My sweet little rice whore," while fucking her. But most of all, she hated the fact that he never paid her for her services. If she refused him, he would have sent her to jail. In turn, she called him "sewer-rat," which only made him laugh. Cowboy looked like the corrupt sewer rat, but it didn't matter who his father was. She didn't like these men, and she figured that Cowboy was better off not having either of these men in his life.

Cowboy never knew any of his mother's family. When she ran away to Bangkok she never looked back. Which meant that she also never spoke to her family again. She had mentioned to Cowboy that she had three sisters and two brothers, but she didn't want to talk about them and refused to do so.

His mother died without telling Cowboy where her family lived, or their names. Cowboy didn't even know his mother's last name. There were times when he thought about trying to find them, but just never got around to it. If he found them, he wasn't sure what he would tell them about his mother, the truth or a lie.

After his mother died, Cowboy was left on his own. He had no desire to be placed in a Bangkok orphanage. He fell in with a group of other homeless boys who roamed Bangkok's Khlong Toei District for anything they could use or eat. They stole, begged, and occasionally did odd jobs to survive.

Cowboy learned to defend himself the hard way. He got a reputation for being fearless. Even the older boys stopped picking on him after he nearly caved in the head of a boy nearly twice his size with a heavy rock. The other street kids learned sooner-or-later that Cowboy would seek revenge for any wrong committed against him; as the Jim Croce song goes, "You don't tug on Superman's cape / You don't spit into the wind / You don't pull the mask off that old lone ranger / And you didn't mess around with Jim...," but in this case - you didn't mess with Cowboy.

At the age of fifteen, Cowboy came to Bot's attention. Bot was a local criminal gang leader who was in his mid-thirties. Bot required obedience, loyalty, toughness, and a little common sense to be in his gang. He did not tolerate any of his gang members getting involved in drugs or excessive drinking. Bot incorporated self-discipline into the gang. He made them into professionals. When gang members couldn't cut Bot's high standards, he got rid of them; if the rejects knew too much, they would be killed.

Bot recognized that Cowboy had what it took to be a member of his gang and recruited him. New gang members were at first given minimal jobs, which steadily became more demanding over time. It usually took a recruit two years, or longer, to become a full-fledged member of Bot's gang.

After becoming a full-fledged member, the next step was to get a tattoo of a raging elephant that nearly covered their entire baack. Once tattooed "patched," you were a gang member for life; death was the only acceptable way to leave the gang. The gang became your family.

Before becoming patched, Cowboy took an interest in Muay Thai, which some Westerners mistakenly referred to as kickboxing. Kickboxing has rules. Muay Thai has a lot fewer.

In the UFC, you are not allowed to kick your opponent in the balls, but it has recently been allowed in Muay Thai. It's a lesson that Japanese martial artists have learned the hard way. Kickboxers are not allowed to use elbow and knee strikes; Muay Thai fighters can. In The Kingdom of Thailand, Muay Thai is the country's favorite sport.

When it appeared that Cowboy had lost interest in becoming patched, he received an ultimatum. "Cowboy, it's time for you to decide. You need to choose either Muay Thai or the gang." Bot said, hoping that Cowboy would come to his senses. To Bot's surprise and dismay, Cowboy chose Muay Thai over the gang. This deeply disappointed Bot, but Bot didn't order Cowboy's death. He knew Cowboy had the potential to be a valuable member of his gang. *He'll come back,* thought Bot. *Just give him some time.*

Cowboy used Muay Thai to channel his anger and frustration. In the ring Cowboy didn't just want to win, he wanted to destroy his opponent. His ring ferocity made him stand out. Regardless of his late start in Muay Thai, Cowboy eventually became a champion.

Too soon, Cowboy's fighting days ended. Muay Thai is a young man's sport. At the end of his Muay Thai fighting career, Cowboy became interested in Buddhism. He was tired of all the anger he had been carrying. Before entering the Sangha, monkhood, he had to learn to read and write, a requirement needed to become a monk.

At the age of thirty-three, he entered the Sangha, where he remained for three years. He wanted to obtain merit for his deceased mother and to improve his karma for all the violence he had committed. Upon entering the Sangha, his head and eyebrows were shaved, and he donned the white robe of a novice monk. Eventually, he was dressed in a robe in the color of a ripe mango, and his mind was elevated. In meditation, he found the inner peace he was seeking to find.

After finding the peace that he felt was missing in his life, he decided to leave the Sangha. With the peace and tranquility that his mother never had, Cowboy found a way to move on becoming a Muay Thai instructor and tour guide. He was all alone in his world, with no mother, father, or family, but as a Muay Thai instructor, he met people from all over the world who wanted to learn his form of art. He became friends with many of his students, a few of them were American.

One of his American students, who was already a competent Muay Thai fighter, wanted to improve his skills and asked Cowboy for help. In return for Muay Thai lessons, the American helped him improve his broken English. In addition, he referred Cowboy to Americans, such as JJ, who wanted an English-speaking travel guide.

Through the grapevine Cowboy heard rumors about Bot's gang and how they were becoming one of the largest street gangs in Bangkok. It was rumored that Bot joined forces with another criminal enterprise, the Network, which provided him with protection against police interference. They were growing filthy rich. But no matter how rich Bot and his gang grew, Cowboy had no desire to return to them. He wanted nothing to do with Bot or his gang.

7
THE NETWORK

The Network's origin began with Aroon Vaskik's grandfather who immigrated to Thailand from China. In Bangkok, his grandfather bought a small store and got into the jewelry business. Through hard work, he expanded his business. As his business grew, he became wealthy.

His grandfather made generous contributions to public officials he found useful. In return, these officials not only ignored his lucrative side business, fencing stolen jewelry, but they also protected it. When Aroon's grandfather died, his oldest son took over the family business, greatly expanding it, with many of the new enterprises being illegal.

Aroon's father used espionage to steal his competitor's secrets and would eliminate competitors when he felt he could get away with it. He had no qualms about using child labor to maximize his profits. Making money was all he was interested in, regardless of how it was made.

His father liked to portray himself as a great philanthropist, a real-life Robin Hood. He would often have truckloads of food delivered to Bangkok's poor. Whenever these handouts occurred, his father made sure there was plenty of media coverage. He had a favorite saying, "Who do the people love more: a man who says great things but does little or nothing to help them. Or a bad man who gives them food?"

At the early age of 59, his father died from a massive heart attack, brought on by rich fatty food and a stressful lifestyle. Keeping with the family tradition, Aroon, the eldest son, took over the family business.

Aroon had light golden-colored skin that seemed to shimmer in sunlight. He combed his freshly trimmed black hair straight back, with no part. He wore only the finest tailored suits. On his left wrist was a real Rolex, and on his right index finger was a 24-carat gold ring containing a Burmese pigeon blood ruby of the finest quality, his birthstone. He took pride in his appearance. On the streets of Bangkok, he often got lustful looks from the women he passed.

Aroon had two younger brothers, Chuen and Samak. Chuen was a member of the Royal Tai Police, while the youngest, Samak, was an officer in the Royal Thai Army. Both Aroon's brothers were completely loyal to Aroon and assisted in the family business whenever asked to do so.

Aroon, in some ways, was shrewder than his father. He started disassociating himself from businesses with unethical or criminal elements, but only if he deemed them too risky. Unlike his father, he kept a low profile and shied away from the limelight. But like his father, Aroon hungered for profit and power.

Some of the criminal enterprises are just too profitable to let go of. Aroon had tentacles extending into heroin & methamphetamine distribution, political extortion, and human trafficking, which Aroon referred to as the "Network." The Network was very profitable. From his high-rise penthouse in downtown Bangkok, Aroon orchestrated his Network like an invisible puppeteer, hidden from public view.

When Aroon took over the Network, he found that he was unhappy with some of the people working for his father. He viewed many of them as unprofessional, complacent, and sometimes just plain sloppy.

He was afraid their sloppiness would lead the wrong people back to him one day. This could not and would not happen during his reign. Following his father's death, with the help of his brothers, he started reorganizing the Network, separating the grain from the chaff.

This was a time of reorganization, and during this strategic time, Bot and his gang came to Aroon's attention. At first, he viewed them as pesky competitors. He had thoughts of eliminating them. However, Aroon decided to study them before making his final decision. He learned Bot and his gang were not amateurs. They made few mistakes and, even more importantly - they would go to jail or die before betraying their gang.

These were qualities that Aroon was looking for. The Network needed a Bangkok street gang. He quickly concluded he would make Bot an offer he could not refuse. Being reasonably intelligent, Bot accepted Aroon's offer to join his Network, which was a profitable decision for all parties involved.

At first, Bot was happy with the arrangement. Bot needed Aroon's police protection and his resources for his gang's expansion. His gang's territory grew from controlling just a few of Bangkok's districts to becoming one of the largest street gangs in Bangkok. Gangs that he used to fear, now feared his gang. Bot was able to use Aroon's connections with the police and the military to control his rivals, eliminating most of his competition.

Despite all the money Bot was making, as time went by, he grew greedier and began to resent the high price of Aroon's services. Unknown to Aroon, Bot started to work outside Aroon's Network. The profits made by these outside ventures were not shared with Aroon, something that would have likely gotten Bot killed if Aroon found out. Bot hoped the day would come when he didn't need Aroon's protection and wouldn't need to share any of his gang's profits with him. *For now*, Bot thought, *I need Aroon more than Aroon needs me.*

Bot would routinely send members of his gang to Burma and Laos to oversee the purchase of heroin and yaa baa. People came from all over the world to buy his drugs, to bring them back to their own countries for resale.

The use of yaa baa had become an epidemic in Thailand. Yaa baa is a mixture of caffeine and meth. It was originally given to horses to pull heavy carts uphill, but then it quickly spread to human workers. In Thailand, trafficking in yaa baa can result in the death penalty. Nevertheless, the profits his gang and the Network made from distributing yaa baa outweighed the risks. If someone from his gang got caught, he could count on Aroon to take care of it. The police and judges were well-paid to ignore his gang's illegal activities.

One of Bot's most profitable operations was human trafficking. His gang bought young women from Burma, Cambodia, Thailand, and other Southeast Asian countries and turned them into sex slaves. These girls were sold or traded to customers located all over the world, such as Malaysia, Russia, various Eastern European countries, Japan, Singapore, Macau, Hong Kong, the U.S., and to a very special customer in Saudi Arabia.

Newly acquired girls were made ready for the brothels and massage parlors by repeated rapes, beatings, threats, and sometimes by heroin addiction. The exception was the girls he sold to the *Saudi*. The only drugs given to these girls were mild sedatives to keep them calm, or make them sleep. The Saudi preferred to break in girls using his own methods.

The girls sold to the Saudi were never heard from or seen again. Bot suspected that when the Saudi grew tired of a girl, he simply killed her, or sold her to another man. These slaves were the Saudi's property; he could do with them whatever he pleased, including raping and killing them. For the past eleven years Bot had been doing business with the Saudi. During that time, he had sold the Saudi over a hundred girls.

Bot couldn't figure out how the Saudi could have kept all the girls he had sold to him. The Saudi's insatiable appetite for new girls had made Bot a rich man. The Saudi *always* paid Bot in *gold*. With all the gold the Saudi paid him, Bot could have cared less about what the Saudi did to the enslaved girls he sold to him. The gold the Saudi paid him was the only thing he cared about, and nothing else.

8

THE BEAUTIFUL FLOWER

Before the Khmer Rouge takeover, initiated by Pol Pot, death in Cambodia was at an all-time low. There happened to be a couple who were educators in Phnom Penh, the capital of Cambodia. After the Khmer Rouge takeover, they fled from Phnom Penh to the countryside, disguised as displaced rice farmers. They were forced to throw away their eyeglasses. Anyone wearing glasses was viewed as an intellectual and were killed. The ruse saved their lives.

The husband had been a professor at the Royal University of Agriculture, and his wife was a secondary school math and science teacher. The husband had learned to grow rice as a boy but was no longer used to the hard work it took to grow it. Nevertheless, he and his wife got acclimated to working long hours in knee-deep mud, planting rice seedlings, and the chores of harvesting rice. They seldom spoke in public and were very careful when they did.

They were afraid of saying something that would give them away. They didn't want to give someone the idea they were more than just uneducated peasant rice farmers. They didn't want to end up in the killing fields, with their hands tied behind their backs and suffocated by a plastic bag placed over their heads or clubbed to death. Pol Pot's

Khmer Rouge killed an estimated three million Cambodians. During Pol Pot's rule, over ninety percent of Cambodia's educators were executed.

After the fall of the Khmer Rouge, they returned to Phnom Penh and again became educators. The wife, at the age of forty-four, had given up on the idea of getting pregnant. When she learned she was pregnant with Bopha, she lit joss sticks giving thanks to Lord Buddha. Bopha Lee would be her and her husband's only child, whom they cherished. She would get their full attention and all their love. Bopha was more than they could have ever asked for.

In the Cambodian language, bopha means flower. Bopha was as radiant and as beautiful as any flower. Being physically attractive was not something Bopha particularly wanted, but she was.

Bopha at times resented her beauty. She wanted people to notice and respect her for her mind, not her looks. She never wore makeup, nor did she intentionally wear things that would enhance her looks. She deliberately tried to look as plain as possible, something she couldn't succeed at. It was like trying to turn a silk purse into a pig's ear; it couldn't be done.

Bopha's parents expected her to do well in school, and she exceeded their expectations. She was a straight "A" student in all her subjects. Following in her mother's footsteps, her favorite subjects in school were math and science.

In her last year of upper secondary school, Bopha was academically at the top of her class. She planned to become a famous theoretical physicist, just like her hero, Stephan Hawking, whose biography she had recently read. She loved his quote: "Remember to look up at the stars and not down at your feet. Try to make sense of what you see and wonder about what makes the universe exist. Be curious. And, however difficult life may seem, there is always something you can do and succeed at. It matters that you don't just give up." Bopha would never give up on her dreams, even when they changed. *Never!*

There was pandemonium in the house when her parents received a call from a person saying he represented a wealthy Cambodian, a philanthropist, who wanted to offer Bopha a sponsorship to attend Caltech, in the United States, all expenses paid! The representative said his client offered scholarships to only Cambodian's brightest students, and Bopha was one of them. The philanthropist's representative said he wanted to meet the young lady and her parents. He provided a date, time, and location for their meeting.

Bopha's parents belonged to the rare Cambodian middle class. They were neither rich nor poor. They could afford to send Bopha to a university in Phnom Penh, where she was highly likely to receive a full scholarship. They had no dreams of sending their daughter to the U.S. for her college education.

Bopha's mother did not want her daughter to leave. She advised her daughter to decline the offer and stay home. Bopha's father, on the other hand, saw his daughter's potential, which only a good education could bring to full fruition. He, too, did not want to see his daughter leave home, but he wanted what he thought was best for her. He convinced his wife this was an offer too good to be outright refused. "We need to meet with this man before we decide."

They settled on meeting the gentleman and establishing an excellent educational path for Bopha. The taxi dropped them off in front of an old downtown building, where they were to meet the rich philanthropist's representative. It was not what they had expected. The building was grim, with bits and pieces of its exterior crumbling to the sidewalk. The windows were dark and laced with cobwebs. It didn't feel right. They were getting ready to leave when a middle-aged man, in a nice, tailored grey-pin striped suit, came out to greet them. Wearing a smile, he opened the building's entrance door and waved them in, "I've been expecting you. Please, come inside." They should have followed their instincts and walked away, but instead, they headed for the open door.

9

THE CRAZY PSYCHOPATH

He found exactly what he had been looking for, and like her name, Bopha, she was a perfect flower. She was not only beautiful; he had learned she was also brilliant and well-educated. There was a market for such a girl. Bot came to his mind first, a Bangkok criminal street gang boss who was always on the lookout to buy beautiful girls. Bot was a longtime customer of his who paid well.

Bot had told him he had been looking to obtain a mistress for a high-end client in Bangkok. This client wanted a girl who was not only beautiful but someone with whom he could hold an intelligent conversation. Bot's client wanted a trophy mistress to show off to his Network friends. This client insisted that the girl had to be a virgin because he wanted her *first*. Bot would definitely pay Khen top dollar for such a girl. Khen always insisted on being paid in U.S. currency.

Khen had learned that Bopha, who had just turned seventeen years old, spoke four languages. Bopha spoke Cambodian, Thai, English, and Mandarin. Her parents started teaching her different languages while she was still a toddler. Bot's high-end client, of Chinese descent, spoke multiple languages as well.

Part of the hunt for girls required Khen to wiggle the right worm in front of his target's eyes. Khen knew the exact worm he would wiggle. He learned that Bopha yearned to attend an American college to major in physics, something she and her parents could never afford. He knew Bopha's parents had no external family; the Khmer Rouge had killed them all. They kept to themselves and had few friends. Their sole focus was on Bopha. No one would come looking for them if they went missing.

Khen sat up with his back straight, while holding the phone to his ear. He smiled while he told his imaginary story, "My boss wants to see Cambodia become great again. He plans to do this by offering the best education available to the brightest of Cambodia's youth and sending them to the best universities around the world. My boss recognized your daughter as being one of these youths. The only thing he's asking in return is your daughter's commitment to return to Cambodia upon the completion of her overseas education." It was almost too good to be true, but Khen was a professional at this and they accepted his offer to meet with him.

Khen planned to lure Bopha and her parents into a deserted building, a government building in the process of being renovated. Khen had worked out a deal with a corrupt city official, who happened to have a taste for young girls, girls much younger than the ones Khen normally acquired in the Hunt. After Khen gave the official what he wanted, the official gave Khen access to the building. He would need it for just one day. It would become his killing field.

An evil nature lurked in Khen, a creature searching for fresh blood. His sinister demeanor was well hidden by a disarming smile. He liked calling himself Uncle Khen, pretending he was someone's benevolent uncle, deserving of respect. However, he lived for violence, rape, and killing. Khen was a small man, even for an Asian. What he lacked in size, he made up with ruthless tenacity. He didn't think twice about poking an eye out or placing a bullet into someone's head.

As a child, he loved catching butterflies. Like a snake, he would slowly slither up on a butterfly. Then, quicker than a cobra's strike, his hand would snatch the butterfly off the flower it was feeding on. Once caught, instead of placing it into a jar to admire its beauty, he would pull its wings off and grind its body into the soil with his foot.

Khen's parents were former Khmer Rouge soldiers. His father had been a Khmer Rouge officer, and his mother a Khmer Rouge foot soldier. When the Vietnamese invaded Cambodia, his parents left the Khmer Rouge and fled to Phnom Penh. In Phnom Penh, Khen's father found he didn't fit into city life and routinely drank too much. His wife constantly berated him for not living up to her expectations. Then, one day, after seeing her husband finishing off a bottle of rice wine, unable to walk without stumbling, she threw her hands up in total exasperation. "What is wrong with you?" She asked. "You used to be someone I was proud of, but now you are just a lazy drunk!"

He answered in a slurred voice, "You know I hate it here; it's killing me. Let's move back to my family's farm, and I'll stop drinking."

"I can never feel any pride being married to a muddy rice farmer, knowing you are capable of doing so much more," she replied.

His voice progressively hardened, "I was a rice farmer before I met you, and so were my father and his father. We made a good and honest living. If that is how you feel, you should never have married me."

She shook her head and said, "You're smart, and you could find a good job here if only you tried. I was wrong thinking that I could change you. And you are right. I should have never married you."

The arguments between Khen's parents became more frequent and heated. Before he turned seven years old, his father abandoned him and his mother. Just before leaving, Khen's father caught him strangling a puppy. He never forgot the glare of disgust on his father's face. That was the last time Khen saw his father. The look of disgust on his father's face was a memory he would never forget. It amused and angered him at the same time.

Khen's disdain for his absent father and even his mother grew with time. He hated everyone and everything. He did not shed a single tear when his mother died after having a stroke, just before his seventeenth birthday. She was a loveless mother who could never be satisfied. She liked to tell him, "You are as lazy and worthless as your drunken father." After he turned fourteen years old, she didn't dare say a single harsh word to Khen; she became afraid of him. And she was right to fear him. If she hadn't died from a stroke, Khen likely would have killed her before she died of old age.

With no formal schooling, Khen learned to read and write on his own. He didn't drink or consume drugs. Killing was his drug of choice, which never failed to give him a beautiful natural high.

He would try to resist his urge to kill, for as long as he could. The urge was like water building up behind a dam; the weight of the water threatening to burst the dam. The time always came when he could no longer resist the urge, when the dam broke, when death came calling. For Khen, this was a time of pure euphoria and sexual gratification.

Khen made an exceptionally good living in human trafficking. He bought girls from families in desperate need of money, reselling them to the highest bidder. Obtaining virgins was his specialty.

He had a good customer in Phnom Penh, an old gentleman, who was willing to pay top dollar for young virgins. The old gentleman was a former commander in the Khmer Rouge and made a vast fortune selling ancient Khmer artifacts taken from Angor Wat.

When the old gentleman was finished with a girl, he would sell the deflowered girl back to Khen, at a discounted price. Khen would then resell the former virgin to a brothel, making himself a nice profit.

But Khen didn't always resell the girls he got back from the old gentleman. There were times when he couldn't control his killing urges. "Come here, Honey. Uncle Khen needs to talk to you." Suddenly, his hands found themselves wrapped around a thin neck. Watching the light go out of a girl's eyes made him feel so good while staring into her face. Just before the lights left the girl's eyes, he saw his mother looking back at him, begging for forgiveness.

Another way Khen obtained girls was through abduction, which he liked to refer to as the "the Hunt." He enjoyed the Hunt nearly as much as killing. The Hunt began when he was notified by one of the many informants he had in Cambodia's public and private schools, alerting him of a potential target. The targets were attractive girls, usually between the ages of twelve and twenty years old.

When made aware of a potential target, he would hire street orphans to follow her and study her routine. Phnom Penh and the rest of Cambodia had an overabundance of orphans. They could be found on every street corner.

The hired orphans and his school informants would find out everything he needed to know about his targets before he abducted them. He would learn things about his target's parents and extended family, and even how well they did in school. Khen was very meticulous. It's what made the Hunt so much fun.

The police never troubled Khen. People in Phnom Penh and its surrounding areas went missing all the time. In most cases, there were no police investigations. He only needed to be careful that his target's family did not have the political clout to force the police to do their job. If there was an investigation, and he became a prime suspect, he would pay the right people to be ignored. He was free to kill as he pleased, and he loved every moment of it.

Khen chose a grey-pin-striped tailored suit, a starched white shirt, and a red bow tie for this meeting. Under his jacket, he carried a 9mm G26 'Baby Glock' in a concealment express holster. He was waiting just inside the building's front door when the taxi arrived. He watched

Bopha and her parents exit the taxi. They looked nervous, and they started to walk away from the building when he stepped out to greet them.

Khen fixed his coat tail and shouted, "I've been expecting you. Please come in," as he waved them inside. "In case you are wondering, we are restoring and remodeling this building. My office is on the top floor." Khen walked to the elevator and pushed the top button. When the elevator's door opened, he said, "Please," and with his hand, he motioned for Bopha and her parents to enter the elevator.

Upon reaching the top floor, Khen led them to the office he had specially prepared for them. The floor of the office was covered in plastic sheets. Khen politely explained, "They are starting to remodel my office as well. Please sit down," he said as he pointed to three plastic chairs in front of a wooden desk.

The only furniture in the office was a desk, with a plastic chair behind it, and three plastic chairs in front of it. He told them it was temporary furniture, while the remodeling was going on. The office had bright, harsh, fluorescent lighting. Bopha and her parents had a feeling of uneasiness but sat as instructed.

Khen then walked over to Bopha's father, and in one quick-well practiced movement, he pulled out his concealed Glock and struck the top of Bopha's father's head with the butt of his gun. He fell unconscious from the chair to the plastic-covered floor. A small amount of blood pooled next to his head. Bopha and her mother screamed and stood up from their chairs.

Khen pointed his gun at them and said, "He's not dead; I wanted your full and undivided attention. You will be okay as long as you follow my orders. If you do not, I will kill you. Starting with you," he grinned, pointing his gun at Bopha. "Now sit back down and shut up! Do you understand?" They both nodded up and down and answered, "Yes," as they sat.

"Good." Khen walked to the desk while keeping his gun pointed at them. He reached into one of the desk's drawers. He took out three sets of handcuffs and one set of leg irons. He gave Bopha's mother one set of cuffs and ordered her to cuff her husband's hands. He then gave her another set to cuff Bopha's hands. Bopha's mother trembled while doing what she was ordered to do. She was then told to walk back to him. Khen got up from his chair, holstered his gun, and cuffed the mother. He then ordered her to sit back down.

Bopha's mother's voice quivered as she started to speak, "Why are you doing this? What do you want?"

Khen answered, "For now, I want you to stay quiet."

Khen walked over to where Bopha sat. To place the leg irons on her ankles, he had to kneel. While kneeling, he happened to look up under her skirt and saw a small portion of Bopha's white panties. He was tempted to run his hands up her smooth legs and pull her panties down for a glimpse of her pussy. He decided against it. He knew it would fuel his urge. He had to remain focused on the task at hand. He felt the water building up behind the dam; the dam was near its breaking point. Soon, very soon, he would need to kill. There was no stopping it!

When Bopha's father had regained consciousness, Khen helped him back into his chair. He then looked directly at Bopha and gave her his sweetest smile. It was a smile she would never forget. He again pulled his Glock from its holster and immediately shot Bopha's father in the forehead, and then shot her mother in the same fashion, killing them both instantly.

Bopha screamed and got up from her chair to run. In her panic to escape, she was tripped by the leg irons she wore and went crashing to the floor. While lying on the floor, Khen landed directly on top of her, knocking her breath away. He held his sewer-smelling mouth up next to her ear, "Don't ever try to run from Uncle Khen again." He imagined he could taste her fear as he licked the side of her face, before getting up and helping her to her feet.

Khen was instantly rewarded with a rush of dopamine, endogenous opioids, and adrenaline, which gave him a very satisfying high. For the rest of the time, Bopha was in his custody, he avoided physical contact with her. He decided to have someone else check her maidenhood to see if it was intact. A glimpse of her pussy would push him over the edge. He had to fight his urge to rape and kill her. She was far too valuable for that, or was she? It would take all his will to suppress his urge.

Bot was excited. He had received a call from Khen offering to sell him a Cambodian girl with exceptional looks and intelligence. She could be just what he had been looking for. Aroon was unsatisfied with the girls he had been providing for him. He wanted more than just a pretty package. He wanted a mistress with brains and looks to show off to the members of his Network.

Wanting a pretty mistress was something that Bot could understand, but why did Aroon want her to be intelligent as well? As far as Bot was concerned, women had three basic functions in their lives: One, to be fucked by men; two, to bear children; and three, to perform domestic work, and that's it. There was no need for them to be intelligent to fulfill their basic functions in life.

Bot figured there was no point in trying to converse intelligently with a woman since they were only interested in gossip. Despite this, it was in Bot's best interest to keep Aroon happy, so he would try to find what Aroon wanted: an intelligent "Trophy Mistress."

Aroon did not have his own street gang. He paid other people to do his dirty work; when he wanted a mistress, he contacted Bot. Bot was involved in human trafficking and had been providing Aroon with mistresses since joining his Network. None of these women had satisfied Aroon for any length of time. They soon bored him. Aroon called them, "mindless whores." He wanted someone special. He wanted a mistress who would invoke the envy of his associates with her looks and intelligence.

Aroon was in a loveless, arranged marriage of political convenience, which was just another family tradition. He and his wife hadn't shared a common bed for years. After Aroon's wife gave birth to their lazy playboy son and two daughters, he was no longer sexually interested in her. For that, *I want a young woman with a tight pussy.*

Aroon's wife could care less; his mistress could have him. She no longer wanted Aroon in her bed. She was still an attractive woman and now had a young lover to take care of her womanly needs, which surprisingly, Aroon did not object to. Aroon liked calling his wife, "My darling cougar."

Bot felt Aroon was making a serious mistake to ask for an intelligent mistress. Bot thought *the best mistresses were both dumb and beautiful. Aroon, be careful with what you wish for.* Aroon reassured Bot, that he would never talk business with his mistress, even his wife did not know about his illegal activities.

The girl Khen offered to sell Bot might be just what Aroon was looking for, that is, if Khen was not exaggerating. Bot arranged to meet Khen and the girl in Poipet. Poipet was a border town in Cambodia. Like many border towns, it's a town with a shady reputation.

After seeing and talking to Bopha, Bot concluded she was the very thing Aroon wanted. She was smart and stunning to look at. He thought, however, that Khen was asking way too much money for her.

"Khen, come on now! Just look at her. She's too skinny! Think of all the money I'll have to spend to fatten her up." Bot was right. Bopha was a little on the thin side, but she had the face of an angel.

"You've been looking for such a girl for months. You know it, and I

45

know it; you will not find another girl like her in a hundred years. She is unique."

And clearly, she was, and Bot knew it. Like two experienced used car salesmen, they haggled over her price before striking a deal. Ultimately, they were both satisfied, and Bopha was sold to Bot. Bopha was now Bot's property, to do with her whatever he pleased.

10

STICK OR CARROT

Bot would need to work with Bopha to get her ready for her first meeting with Aroon. Khen had terrified her. He had killed Bopha's parents, right in front of her. Luckily, she was in Khen's custody for only a few days. *That psycho Khen tends to permanently damage girls he keeps too long,* Bot thought. Bot didn't like Khen but continued to do business with him because he was able to deliver the products he was looking for.

Bot took Bopha to his compound just outside Bangkok. He would personally coach her to become Aroon's new mistress, but he was tempted to keep her for himself. There have been women, real or illusionary, throughout history, who have stood out because of their beauty: Helen of Troy, Rita Hayworth, Merlyn Monroe, Raquel Welsh, Holle Berry, and Jennifer Lopez, just to mention a few. Women who sparked the imagination of men.

Bopha was one of these women. Just as Khen had said, she was the perfect flower. Who could say which of these tens is the most beautiful in a room filled with perfect tens? It would come down to personal preferences. That is, as long as Bopha was not in that room of tens. Once Bopha entered, all eyes would be upon her.

Heroin addiction was commonly used as the first step in preparing a new girl for Bot's brothels. Bot had no intention of sticking a needle into Bopha's arm. She had to be controlled by other means. He decided to use the "Stick and Carrot" approach.

Bot told her, "If you ever try to escape, I'll find you no matter where you go. You are now my personal property; you belong to me. If you escape, and when I find you - and I will find you - you will then be placed into a Malaysian brothel. While there, you will be beaten and fucked by a thousand men."

He took her to a brothel in Malaysia to see firsthand what that was like. While in Malaysia, Bopha was forced to watch a recently captured escapee get beaten and ganged raped over and over again, causing tears to run down Bopha's face. This was the stick.

On the other hand, "If you are obedient and cooperative, you will be pampered and live a very comfortable life." Bot showed her how his high-end escorts were treated. They would eventually win their free-dom. This was the carrot. He told Bopha, "You can choose either the stick or the carrot. The choice is yours to make." What Bot didn't under-stand was that Bopha had no intention of escaping. *"Remember to look up at the stars and not down at your feet. Try to make sense of what you see and wonder..."* She thought to herself, reciting her favorite quote. Like a praying mantis, she would wait patiently for the right moment to strike.

With the help of his best escort girls, Bopha began her training. The training went well. She was taught how to satisfy a man, and how to fake an orgasm without making it too obvious. Bot's high-end escorts were true artists when it came to this.

Bot loved to stick his dick into Bopha's mouth and come inside her ass. Bopha gave Bot everything except her pussy. He could touch it, rub it, and kiss it, but he had to resist penetrating its hole, at least for now. Bopha would remain a virgin until her first meeting with Aroon.

The training included Bopha keeping up with current world events. She was given books and periodicals to read. She was even given a laptop computer and allowed to surf the internet. Bot and Bopha had long conversations. He found that she was far from being a mindless whore.

Each night, before going to bed, Bot invited Bopha to talk with him and share a goodnight drink. Bot drank only expensive single-malt Scotch whiskey, resulting in Bopha developing a taste for fine Scotch.

After a month of training, Bot had a serious discussion with Bopha. He told her that life had dealt her a rotten hand, but she would have to live with it; things could be far worse. Bopha appeared to have accepted her karma, but in her head, she heard, *"Don't just give up."* "

Near the end of Bopha's training, Bot began to regret his decision to make Bopha Aroon's mistress. But for now, keeping Aroon happy was more important than his own sexual desires. Bot was hoping that someday, Bopha would be able to provide him with useful secrets about Aroon and his Network. Aroon would have access to Bopha's body, but she would remain his property. When she wasn't with Aroon, he would still be able to enjoy her whenever he chose to do so.

Bopha no longer dreamed of becoming a famous theoretical physicist. However, she still dreamed. Bopha's mind had been fragmented like a fragile egg thrown hard upon a concrete floor when Khen had placed bullets into her parents' foreheads. Khen had transformed Bopha's brilliant mind into a cold, calculating intelligence bent on revenge. For now, she will do as she is told. She will cooperate. She will surpass Bot's expectations for her. She will bide her time, dreaming of the day when she would rock his world. No matter how long it took.

"Remember to look up at the stars and not down at your feet. Try to make sense of what you see and wonder about what makes the universe exist. Be curious. And however difficult life may seem, there is always something you can do and succeed at. It matters that you don't just give up."

11

FOR NOW

Bopha stood naked, posing, in front of a full-length mirror. The curves she viewed were enough to give an adolescent boy a week's worth of reoccurring wet dreams. She no longer resented her beauty. She stood tall, admiring her flat stomach, wide hips, and perky breasts. She turned around to look at the dark hair falling from the back of her head, ending just below her shoulder blades.

Just before she started to dress, she placed lubricants and a long-lasting moisturizer into her vagina. She was careful not to break her hymen. Sitting on her dresser was a bottle of Clive Christian Imperial Majesty, one of the most expensive perfumes in the world. She picked up the bottle of perfume and placed small dabs of it behind each ear, as well as other strategic locations on her body. She ran two perfumed fingers across the trimmed jet-black bush of pubic hair just above her legs.

After placing the bottle of perfume back on the dresser, she picked up a tube of red lipstick. Once she placed the lipstick on her lips, she lightly kissed the image on the mirror. She will use her beauty as a weapon, against her enemies to destroy them. It was the perfect plan, and for now, it was her only plan.

Bopha looked at the sleeveless black silk cheongsam dress with two long sender red dragons wrapped around it. There were slits on each side of the dress that would expose her legs. Black nylon stockings, a garter belt, a bra, and white laced panties were lying on her bed. Sitting on the floor was a pair of red Christian Louboutin high-heeled shoes.

Bopha was preparing for her first visit with Aroon, preparing to lose her virginity. She felt no joy in it; she thought, *what choice do I have?* As Bot told her, this was the hand dealt to her - *my karma. I will make the best of it. I will please my rapist and do everything in my power to make him happy... for now.*

12

A SOLID FOUNDATION

Bopha gave her name to the two guards at the building's entrance. They stepped aside, allowing her access into the building; she was expected. The guards' eyes followed Bopha as she walked to the elevator. Their eyes did not leave her until she was out of sight. Like Marilyn Monroe's walk, Bopha's walk demanded a man's full undivided attention.

The building contained Aroon's private office and penthouse. She boarded the elevator, and the bellhop pushed the top button, going to the sixth floor. She exited and walked down the Italian granite hallway.

Her high heel shoes striking the granite floor sent click-clack echoes down the corridor. The hallway ended at a massive teak door, with an elaborate carving of an ancient Thai war scene. She used the large brass knocker and softly "tap, tap, tap," as instructed; there was no doorbell.

Aroon answered his door as soon as he heard the light knocking. He anxiously awaited it; Bot promised that the girl he was sending would please him. When he saw Bopha standing at the door's entrance, her beauty momentarily stunned him, causing him to hesitate before letting her inside.

Bopha brought both her hands up to nose level, in a prayer-like gesture and bowed, a traditional Thai greeting called a wai. She then said, "Sawatdi Kha." Aroon returned her wai with a slighter bow, bringing his hands to just below his chin, and replied, "Sawatdi Khrap."

Aroon had never before returned a whore's wai; he had acknowledged all the other whores with just a nod of his head. He invited Bopha inside. As she passed him, he inhaled her perfumed scent, which filled his head with erotic thoughts.

Bopha made Aroon wonder, *how in the hell could the intelligence of this girl possibly match her beauty.* Bot told Aroon that Bopha spoke several languages including Mandarin. Aroon offered Bopha a place to sit and decided to test her language skills by asking in Mandarin, "Would you like something to drink?" She replied in English, "I would like a glass of Scotch on the rocks… please." With a smile on his face, he thought to himself, *this is no airhead like the other whores that Bot had provided him; she did speak multiple languages!* This greatly pleased Aroon. *Bot has not only delivered what I had been looking for but has far exceeded my expectations,* Aroon thought while looking at the splendid girl sitting in the over-stuffed leather chair.

Her shiny black hair was the perfect frame for her beautiful heart-shaped face, sitting with one of her legs crossed over the other - exposing a leg all the way up to its thigh. She was taller than the average Southeast Asian female, maybe 5'6", with a perfect hourglass body. Her ample breasts pushed up against the body-hugging cheongsam dress she wore. He couldn't help but imagine when that time came, what it would be like to see her completely naked and to run his hands over her perfectly formed body.

Bot felt himself growing hard. He admonished himself; *it is way too early to think like this!* Before leaving for his bedroom, he wanted to spend time talking to her. Their conversation would be his teaser, his foreplay to sex.

Aroon left his chair, went to the room's bar, poured her a glass of Johnnie Walker Blue over ice, and then poured himself a glass. He returned and handed Bopha her drink. With a slight grin on his face, he said to her, "It's very unusual for a woman to ask for Scotch; most women prefer a sweeter drink." Bopha swallowed the smooth whisky, giving her glass an approving look, and said, "I'm an unusual woman."

After returning to his chair, he replied, "Yes, you certainly are."

Aroon placed his drink on the table between them; he was no longer interested in it. He found Bopha utterly fascinating, and they talked for over an hour. He was thoroughly enjoying their conversation. Yet, the time came when he could no longer deny his sexual urges; butterflies were fluttering in his lower stomach. There was no resisting the raging fire down below; it felt like it would consume him if he didn't pacify it soon.

He took her hand and led her to his bedroom, where he watched her slowly undress, too slow for his liking. He found himself beginning to tremble with anticipation. She then helped him undress, and afterward took his erect penis into her soft hands; an involuntary moan of pleasure escaped his lips. She ran her hand up and down its shaft while licking and sucking his balls. Her tongue made light contact with his anus, circling it, before she placed his erection fully into her mouth, deep throating it, causing him to again moan with pleasure.

Even though Aroon had sex with over a hundred different women, he felt as if he were again a virgin. He knew Bopha was still a virgin, which excited him all the more. He was worried about his control; he didn't want to come too soon. Something he hadn't worried about since his youth.

He nearly came, after breaking through her hymen and inserting himself fully inside her. However, Bopha's training paid off. She managed to back him off, just in time, allowing him to stay hard inside her a little longer.

Then, the time came when there was no stopping it, and Bopha sensed it. She licked the inside of his ear and whispered, "Come, baby, come," and he did, longer and harder than he could ever remember. Very convincingly, she pretended to climax with him.

Waiting until he had finished ejaculating, using both her hands, Bopha cradled the sides of his face and fully kissed his open mouth, exploring it with her tongue. While looking straight into his eyes, she told him, "You made me feel so, so, good. As soon as I come back, I'm going to reward you."

"You are such a wonderful naughty girl," replied Aroon. Bopha smiled, "More than you can ever imagine," and then got up off the bed and went to the bathroom to clean herself.

The experience wasn't as painful as she thought it would be. There's some blood, but less than expected. Getting fucked for the first time wasn't as bad as she had anticipated. Aroon wasn't an ugly man. In fact, he was rather handsome. However, it was not what she would have called an enjoyable experience; no, it was a forced act. She had no choice in the matter.

Before leaving the bathroom, she opened her small purse and added new lubricant to her vagina. She returned to his bed with a warm damp washcloth and gently washed him, removing the blood and cum off his penis and pubic area. She then massaged, kissed, and sucked the head of his stiffing shaft. At the same time, she used one of her fingernails to gently scratch his scrotum.

In hardly any time at all, she had him again fully erected. While he was laying on his back, she mounted him cowgirl. At first, she rode him slowly, then harder and harder. She threw her head back and rolled her eyes back. She moaned in ecstasy. It was more than he could take, and he came for a second time.

Afterward, they lay down next to each other, side by side. While they were kissing, he ran his hands over her succulent body, becoming hard for the third time. This surprised him! He rolled Bopha over onto her hands and knees and entered her from behind, grabbing hold her long black hair, pulling her head slightly up. It didn't take long, just a short little ride, before he again shot his juices inside her.

This was the first time he had been able to fuck a woman three times in a row, but it would not be the last. When he fucked Bopha, he found himself wanting to fuck her again and again. She created a sexual thirst that he could not quench.

The sex had made Aroon sleepy, and he rested his head on Bopha's chest, and Bopha rubbed the back of his neck. She ran her fingers through his thick black hair and hummed him a lullaby. Soon, he was fast asleep.

As instructed, she quietly got out of his bed and dressed. A smile came to her face while walking out of Aroon's apartment. She had done well; *I've laid a solid foundation*, she thought. It wouldn't take long before she had Aroon right where she wanted him, *wrapped around my little finger*. People were wrong when they said, "The way to a man's heart is through his stomach." *No*, thought Bopha, *it was through his dick*.

13

THE ULTIMATE APHRODISIAC

Aroon had claimed exclusive rights to Bopha's body; he didn't want to share her with anyone. He told Bot, "No one is to touch her, but me!" Despite that, since Bopha was no longer a virgin, Bot allowed himself the pleasure of fucking her every now and then. Fucking Bopha was a pleasure he reserved for Aroon, and unbeknown to Aroon, for himself. And no one else.

Bot found that as much as he loved coming inside Bopha's mouth and ass, he loved coming inside her pussy even more. He liked to fuck her in the missionary position, so he could look directly into her eyes. When he climaxed inside Bopha, for a brief moment, Botha's eyes betrayed her. They showed the disdain she felt for what she was doing. And for Bot, this was the ultimate aphrodisiac.

Bot continued his evening chats with Bopha, something he had come to enjoy and looked forward to. They continued drinking his expensive Scotch whiskey during their evening talks. It didn't take long for Bopha to convince him she was more than just a pretty pleasure girl.

He soon realized that Bopha could be one of the smartest persons he had ever encountered, despite her gender. Before meeting Bopha, Bot had agreed with what the famous late revolutionist Che Guevara said about women, "A woman's place is on her back." For the most part, he still agreed with Che. However, he now believed Bopha was the exception to that rule; she had other talents that needed to be explored.

Bot grew up in a Bangkok slum. He never attended school, but he was not illiterate. Bot was a born leader, and at the early age of thirteen, he started to form his gang. His gang began by trafficking yaa baa & ganja and then branched into other illegal activities.

At first, there was no need to keep track of the gang's money and property or a need for bookkeeping. As the gang grew, Bot realized there was a need to track, analyze, and manage the gang's growing assets. He reluctantly took on the bookkeeping duties, something he found increasingly difficult to continue as his gang's assets grew. He didn't have the education nor the temperament to do it right.

Bot didn't trust anyone outside the gang, and no one in the gang he deemed capable of doing it. He had thought about asking for Aroon's help but decided that would be a bad idea. He didn't want Aroon to find out about the business he conducted outside his Network.

Bopha was a fast learner. Bot concluded that using her for the sole purpose of satisfying Aroon's and his own sexual needs was a waste of her talent - no matter how good she was at doing that.

And yet, he thought, *can I trust her with tracking the gang's assets?* That was his dilemma and a tough pill to swallow. Yet, he decided to give her a try. If she succeeded, he would make her the first female member of his gang, and she would no longer be an outsider. He would no longer view her as just his and Aroon's "beautiful fuck doll." Now, he saw Bopha as potentially a valuable member of his gang.

Like everything Bopha did, she exceeded the expectations he placed on her. He started giving her small assets to track and manage. It didn't take long for her to suggest ways to double and even triple the value of those assets. Soon, she took over the gang's bookkeeping; a job Bot hated.

As time passed, Bot steadily increased what he gave Bopha, allowing her direct control of certain gang assets. And he placed her in charge of laundering the gang's dirty money. That meant Bopha needed to give orders to some of the members of his gang. This caused problems since Bopha was a woman and not a full gang member. The latter problem could be remedied. Bot could do nothing about Bopha being a woman, nor did he want to - even if he could.

Bopha had found her niche; she loved managing the gang's assets. She became an expert at bookkeeping, accounting, and investing. She obtained subscriptions to financial publications such as *FinanceAsia* and took investing online courses to assist her in her endeavors.

She learned to launder the gang's money to avoid attention from Thailand's Anti-Money Laundering & Suppression Office (AMLO). She set up unanimous shell companies and invested the gang's illegal proceeds into high price real estate throughout the world, including the U.S. The gang now owned property in downtown New York City. She found the U.S. to be a great and easy place to launder the gang's money.

Bopha eventually became the gang's biggest earner. Bot was so happy with her that he bought her a red Mercedes Benz SLK class convertible, a new car stolen right out of the Mercedes' plant in Chakan, India. She had been insistently nagging him to get her a car. Since Bopha didn't know how to drive, he had to teach her. Bopha didn't change his opinion regarding women drivers. If he had his way, there would be no female drivers in Thailand.

As if he didn't have enough to worry about, now he had to worry about Bopha getting herself killed in a car accident. Thailand has the second-highest traffic-related death rate in the world. He now regretted giving her the car. He should have rewarded her by giving her a cute little dog. Something like a small Shih Tzu, which would have been so much safer.

14

PATCHED

Bot had never made a female a full member of his all-male gang; Bopha would be the first. Upon initiation into the gang, the new member received the gang's tattoo of a raging elephant that covered their entire back. Bopha would receive a much smaller version of the gang's patch on each cheek of her ass. This was Bot's idea and not Bopha's. Bot thought *only men should wear a full patch on their backs. Bopha will wear our patch where it belongs on a female, on her ass.*

As tradition dictated, and to the delight of the rest of the gang; they all witnessed her initiation into the gang. As Boha dropped her panties, she covered her bush with a well-placed hand. Even though the gang encouraged her to remove the offending hand, begging her for a glimpse of heaven, her hand remained in place until the tattoo was completed. But just before she pulled her panties up, Bopha relented. She removed her hand, bent completely over, spreading the cheeks of her ass, and gave the gang a full peak of the forbidden. Then she turned around, stuck her tongue out at them, causing the gang to howl and whistle. Bot, being the lone exception, just shook his head.

There were those in the gang who did not like Bopha; they resented her becoming a member of their previous all-male gang. Nevertheless, most of them welcomed her. They recognized her value. Whether they welcomed her or not, there was one thing they all had in common: they all desired her. They heard Bot's moans of pleasure on the nights Bopha joined him in his bedroom. On these nights, they envied Bot, wishing for a pleasure they would never get.

Aroon had no idea that Bot was taking Bopha to his bed. *She belongs to me not him,* thought Bot. However, Bot knew that if Aroon found out, he would demand that Bot give him full possession of Bopha. Aroon did not like the idea of Bopha's continued connection to Bot's gang. Bot overcame Aroon's objection by convincing him that Bopha was invaluable and needed to handle the gang's bookkeeping; that was only reason why he would not hand her over to him. It was a job she was perfectly suited for.

The new tattoo didn't go unnoticed by Aroon. Bopha explained to him, "I am now a full member of Bot's gang. But don't worry, Darling, I will always be loyal to you." And he stupidly assumed she was telling him the truth. Aroon no longer viewed Bopha as his whore; she had become his beautiful trophy mistress and a possible tool for the Network. Aroon suspected he had fallen in love with Bopha, at least as much as he could with any woman.

Now that she was a full member of Bot's gang, she would be able to provide him with even more important inside information about Bot's activities. She had told Aroon that Bot was working outside his Network, cheating him out of profits that Bot should have shared with him. Bot was unsuccessful in keeping this fact hidden from Bopha; it was something Aroon already suspected.

Bopha advised Aroon, "Darling, don't move against him. I have a plan. I'm going to take over his gang. Then you will never have to worry again about being cheated. But I need to be careful so that Bot doesn't find out what I'm up to. I'm working my way up his gang's chain of command. Hopefully, soon I'll have him right where I want him, and he won't even see it coming."

Aroon liked the idea and promised his support. However, he didn't like the kind of risk Bopha would be taking. If Bot found out, he would kill her. Then there would be an all-out war between him and Bot. The thought of losing Bopha scared him. "Be careful my dear!"

"Trust me Darling; I will," replied Bopha, wetting her lips.

If not for the fact that Aroon knew just how clever Bopha could be, he would have tried to stop her. He knew that Bopha would make a better gang leader than Bot. The rumors said that Bot had turned into a lazy drunk, and it was Bopha who was keeping the gang's profits up - as well as his Network's share of those profits.

15

NESTING VIPER

After being Aroon's mistress for eight years, Bot became worried about Bopha's loyalties. Bopha tried to ease Bot's doubts by giving him tidbits of information she obtained during her conjugal meetings with Aroon.

Unknown to Bot, she was very selective about the information she shared with him; it was just enough to satisfy him. She reminded Bot of all the money she was earning for the gang, millions of dollars per year. Bot's greed blinded him. Bopha told Bot, "I would be cutting my own throat if I betrayed you."

Until recently, Aroon, too, questioned Bopha's loyalties. He had wanted her to move to an apartment away from Bot's compound, but she resisted, telling him she had plans to take over Bot's gang. And she told him how she was going to do it. It was a plan that could work, and Bopha was the right person to pull it off. Now that Aroon knew of Bopha's intentions to take over Bot's gang, she needed to stay put. Besides that, when Aroon experienced any doubts about Bopha's loyalties, like in the story of Samson and Delilah, Bopha was able to wash away his doubts. She satisfied him as no other woman could.

Aroon tried not to talk business in front of Bopha, but he found himself doing it anyway. He had no idea just how much Bopha knew about the Network. He suspected he had given her more information than he should have.

At the beginning of their relationship, Bopha would leave soon after Aroon had finished having sex with her, a practice commonly referred to as a 'short timers'. It didn't take long for Aroon to find short-timers to be totally inadequate. After Bopha left, he found himself wanting her in the middle of the night and even the next morning. For the past six years, Bopha had slept the entire night with him before she left. Maybe he he had come to trust her, or perhaps he was just blinded by his lust for her.

During one of these overnight visits, Bopha placed Ambien into Aroon's drink. As usual, he fell fast asleep soon after Bopha gave Aroon his multiple happy endings. The Ambien ensured he wouldn't wake up until the following morning. He had a very restful night while she worked.

Aroon had a habit of leaving his laptop on his bedroom table, which was a careless mistake. While Aroon slept, Bopha copied the laptop's hard drive and hid a wireless keyghost to capture his keystrokes. This allowed her access to Aroon's password-protected files.

By hacking into Aroon's computer, Bopha was able to obtain confidential information, such as the names of Aroon's shell companies, information regarding payments to corrupt police, judges, and politicians, and most importantly, information on the Networks' hidden bank accounts, and the passwords to access them.

Of course, she didn't tell Bot about any of this. Whenever he questioned her about her visits with Aroon, she would tell him that Aroon seldom talked about his business; it was the furthest thing on his mind.

She told Bot that Aroon would occasionally let something slip, which is information she shared with him. For the most part, Aroon was only interested in bedding her, which wasn't hard for Bot to believe. Bot knew firsthand how enjoyable that could be. Unlike Aroon, Bot had other girls he enjoyed. The tactics Bopha used, a mixture of intelligence and sexuality, on Aroon, would not work on Bot. Seducing Bot would get her nowhere. That was not the way to his underbelly. It was his greed.

Both Bot and Aroon were oblivious to the fact they had invited a pit viper to nest in their homes. Bopha marveled at the ease with which she manipulated the two men. They were like putty in her hands. It was just a matter of time before each of them received a fatal bite. Until then, Bopha would continue to nest in their homes. She was loyal to no one but herself. In dealing with these men, she knew a single mistake would cost her life. She needed to be careful, very careful.

16
KAT

Khatchada, nicknamed Kat, came from a poor farming family. She was the oldest daughter. Her parents rented a plot of land where they grew rice and raised chickens and the occasional pig. Kat remembered wearing the same clothes day in and day out. Her mother would wash them after she went to bed so that Kat would have clean clothes to wear the next morning.

Kat did not attend school; she helped her mother with the house chores and took care of her younger siblings. She would have been uneducated if not for the landowner's kind and slightly nerdy daughter, who was home-schooled and didn't have many friends. She felt sorry for Kat, and since they were of the same age, a friendship blossomed between them.

For seven years, Kat would visit the landowner's home every evening to visit her friend after completing her chores. Her friend taught her to read, write, and do arithmetic. She even taught Kat how to read English. This friend always shared her American paperback romance novels with Kat. The girls liked fantasizing about what it would be like to be one of the characters in these books. Her eyes twinkled whenever her friend shared a new book with her. "Kat you are going to love this book!" she beamed. And almost always on the cover of the book -

was a handsome shirtless man, with long hair, embracing a beautiful woman. "The guy in this book is so… deliciously dreamy; he's sweeter than a bowl of jackfruit covered in whipped cream!" she said, licking her lips and pushing her Coke bottle glasses back up to the bridge of her nose.

Kat became addicted to romance novels. She was a daydreamer. She dreamed of marrying a rich and handsome man, her Mr. Right, raising a family, and living in a big house, just like the women in the novels that she and her friend enjoyed reading.

At the age of eighteen, Kat left her small family farm for Bangkok, where she hoped to earn enough money to help her family. She was an attractive girl with clear, light-brown skin and no blemishes. She stood about 5'5", a slender girl with an hourglass shape, and budding breasts. Her raven black hair fell just below her shoulder blades. Her nose was not a typical Asian nose; it was small and slightly pointed at its tip as if it had been shaped by someone pinching it often in infancy. Her oval face had high cheekbones, beautiful almond-shaped dark brown eyes, and long black lashes.

Kat's parents did not want her to leave. They were afraid she would be taken advantage of. They knew of families whose daughters had moved to Bangkok just to become prostitutes. Kat did not heed their warnings. She left with no money in her pockets; her parents had none to give her.

In Bangkok, Kat was identified as a country girl. Her clothes and naïve personality gave her immediately away. She had nowhere to sleep at night until the owner of a café allowed her to sleep on a bench under the café's back porch, as long as she was gone before the café opened. He allowed her to use an outside facet and bucket near the café's backdoor to wash.

At night, under the back porch light, when Kat believed the owner had left, she would undress and wash herself and her clothes. The owner would turn off all the lights inside the café, then turn on the porch light to make it look like he had gone home for the night.

The café's owner spied on Kat through a back window as she stood naked, washing. While he watched her bathe, he would pull down his pants and masturbate. After several nights of watching her, he decided it was time to make her an offer.

She had been searching for a job for over a week and still hadn't found one. Kat had no money to buy food. She found things to eat from various restaurants' trashcans. The owner of the café where she had been sleeping, would occasionally give her leftover food from patrons' meals.

On the night that changed her life forever, she felt desperate. She would need to go home if she didn't find work soon. She returned to the café's porch to sleep, feeling sick after eating something that didn't agree with her. The food wanted to come up, but Kat didn't want to lose the only food she had eaten that day. So, she fought to keep it down.

That evening, when she got to the café, she found the café's owner waiting for her. He asked Kat to come inside to talk and share some tea and almond cookies with him. She thought nothing of it. The café was already closed, with the employees and patrons gone. Kat accepted his invitation, hoping the warm tea would help settle her stomach.

After some small and meaningless talk, the owner made his offer. With misgivings, Kat accepted his money, and he took her virginity. He'd reluctantly agreed to her one condition: he wore a hat... a condom.

She woke up sore the next day. It hurt her to walk. Her memory lapsed to the previous night. Kat's first experience with sex was not a pleasant one; her panties were stained with blood. No lubricant had been used when the café's owner placed his dick inside her. The blood from her broken hymen was the only thing that fought the friction.

He somehow felt entitled to her and didn't like the fact that Kat demanded him to wear a hat. She remembered the twist of his face when he gave her the money and then ordered her to undress and get down on her hands and knees. The food she had eaten earlier that made her sick came up while he was mounting her. After finishing with her, he ordered Kat to clean up her mess. She refused, and he became angry.

It was a good thing Kat got her money before allowing him to take her, or she may have ended up with nothing. The money was only enough to last her for a couple of days. She would not return to the café. The owner told her she was no longer welcome. The one lesson that she learned during their exchange was to demand every one of her future customers to wear a hat… no exceptions.

While she was in a small neighborhood store, buying food, she noticed a group of boys watching her through the window. The boys were rough-looking and dirty. She had spotted them watching her before she entered the store. They had the look of a hungry cat stalking a bird. They frightened her. She stayed inside the store until she thought they were gone.

Shortly after exiting the store, she spotted the boys following her. She walked faster and changed directions, trying to lose them. They were getting closer. One of the boys yelled out at her, "Hey, slow down. We just want to talk to you." Kat yelled back, "Go away! I don't want to talk to you." and began to run through the pain that she was experiencing. With her long legs, she easily outran them and soon the boys gave up their chase.

After she stopped running, she found herself in a part of the city she had not been to before, the red-light district of Patpong. There were big flashing neon signs. It was getting dark and female touts, go-go dancers, in high heels, wearing booty shorts and halter tops, were shouting, "Come inside. We'll make you very happy," trying to lure customers, mostly farangs into their bars. Kat put her head down, looked at the ground, and walked as fast as she could. She hoped no one would pay any attention to her.

Staring at the ground, still shaking from being chased and the increasing pain between her legs, she ran into someone. It was a woman with heavy makeup, who gruffly stated, "Why don't you watch where you're going!" The woman had just exited one of the go-go bars. Kat responded meekly, "I'm sorry ma'am." She stared at the woman's face with tears in her eyes. She couldn't hold back how she felt but dared not say a word about it. The woman replied in a friendlier tone, "Baby, where are you going in such a rush?"

Kat didn't know why, but she broke down and cried, telling the woman everything. It just came out with her tears. The older woman took Kat's face into her hands and wiped her tears away. She told Kat, "It's okay Baby, everything is going to be all right." The woman said she had a house and Kat could stay with her for a while. Like a stray cat, she followed the strange lady to her home. The woman told her, "My name is Joy."

When they reached her place, Joy gave Kat some rice, vegetables, and fish to eat. She then had her take a shower and change her clothes. Kat's clothes were filthy, and her panties were even more stained with blood. Joy wondered if Kat had been raped; Kat told her she hadn't.

The older woman gave Kat clean clothes to wear and medicine to help fight off infection and alleviate her pain. Joy laid out a straw floor mat and blankets for Kat to sleep on. It didn't take long for Kat to fall asleep. Joy looked at Kat while she slept, and the memories of her youth came streaming back.

17

JOY'S STORY

When Kat bumped into Joy, Joy was forty-eight years old, and the head mama-san at Dizzy. She had been forced into prostitution at the tender age of fifteen when her father sold her to pay off his gambling debt. Joy came from a large family of three boys and four girls. She was the second youngest girl in the family and the prettiest, with long straight glossy black hair that fell to the middle of her back. With budding breasts, her body was starting to get its female curves. She had beautiful dark almond-shaped eyes with long natural eyelashes.

For her, being pretty wasn't a good thing. Her alcoholic father had a large gambling habit. He wagered too much on cock fighting, losing more than he ever won. The day came when her father lost a large bet and was unable to pay. He was given the choice of selling Joy to pay off his debt, or a bullet to his head.

Joy was sold to a Malaysian brothel located near the border with Thailand. The agreement was that she would work for the brothel for a year, to pay off her father's debt. She would then be released; not an uncommon agreement for Southeast Asian families who were heavily indebted.

The first time she was raped, she was given to a middle-aged man with reddish-black stains on his teeth from eating Betel nuts. She was displayed to several men and her virginity was auctioned off to the highest bidder. The man with the reddish-black stains on his teeth was the winner.

The winner had no wife, and he wanted to deflower at least one virgin during his lifetime. While lying on top of Joy, he covered her mouth with his. His sour-smelling breath made her gag. He raped her throughout the night, taking drugs to maintain his erections. She cried and begged him to stop, but he showed her no mercy. He wasn't about to stop; he had paid dearly for the privilege of being her first. He wasn't a rich man, and he was determined to get his money's worth; money he had worked long and hard for, for many years. The man would slap her whenever she refused to cooperate with his demands.

While living at the brothel, she was locked up in a room with five other girls. Twice a day, they received small servings of food, so they wouldn't get fat. Their meals usually consisted of rice, and soup containing vegetables and small amounts of fish, chicken, or pork; they were nutritious but inexpensive.

They had small portable potties to be used when needed. Twice a day, they were allowed outside to stretch their legs, exercise, bathe, and brush their teeth. The yard was surrounded by a large fence topped with razor wire.

They bathed by dipping water out of a fifty-five-gallon barrel, using a large tin can to pour water over their heads and a bar of soap. A guard stood watch, making sure they took their baths, brushed their teeth, and washed their clothes. The brothel's owner didn't want any of his patrons offended by one of his girls having bad body odor or rotting teeth.

Each new girl had their tubes tied, to avoid pregnancy. Most of the brothel's customers didn't like wearing hats, and they paid extra money to be allowed to fuck a girl without one. Birth control pills were too expensive and didn't always work, and the owner didn't want any unwanted pregnancies.

Following their surgery, the new girls were given time to heal. During this time, they were required to give the brothel's customers hand and blow jobs, but fucking was not allowed.

At various times, day and night, a brothel's customer would come into the room to choose one of them. The chosen one was escorted to a private room with a mattress covered with a fresh clean sheet. They did whatever the customer wanted, to avoid a beating.

One of Joy's regular customers enjoyed swatting her bare bottom, while he rode her doggy-style. The spankings left the cheeks of her ass bright red. This ill-treatment was permitted because the customer was a well-paying regular. Besides, the spanking didn't cause any real permanent physical damage to Joy; it only made her cry and after a few spankings, not even that.

Joy had been living at the brothel for over a year. Her father's debt was fully paid, and she should have been released. However, there was no way the brothel's owner wanted to release a girl who was making him so much money. Joy had become his biggest moneymaker. His customers were willing to pay him extra, to be with her. So, the brothel's owner came to an agreement with Joy's father to keep Joy for another year; as usual, Joy's father needed the money. His love of gambling was greater than his love of his daughter.

Since living at the brothel, Joy had unprotected sex with over a thousand men. She had become the brothel customers' favorite girl. She was fortunate not to have caught any diseases that couldn't be cured by antibiotics. It was a time before HIV manifested.

18

THE UGLY BOY

One day, Joy noticed the boy who had brought them their food and emptied their potties, smiling at her. She smiled back at the ugly hunchback youth, who happened to be the only son of the brothel's owner.

After returning his smile, Joy noticed she was getting larger food portions than the other girls. She began to flirt with the youth, and he started to bring her sweets to eat with her meals. The other girls teased Joy for flirting with such an ugly boy.

Then, one day, the seventeen-year-old came into her room. He stuttered, in a voice, she could barely hear, "W-w-i-ll you come with me-me?" She followed him to one of the private rooms, so they could talk without the other girls being around.

When they got to the room, the boy didn't say anything. He just stared at her. She asked the boy, "Do you think I'm pretty?" The boy just shook his head up and down but didn't say a word.

"What's the matter? Does a cat have your tongue? I thought you brought me here so we could talk. You do want to talk to me?"

. . .

The boy stuttered, "Y-y-es, but-but I'm-m-m v-v-very nervous."

Joy looked directly into his eyes, "You don't need to be nervous with me."

Joy kissed the ugly youth and gently pushed him down to lie on the mattress. She removed his shirt, and gently sucked and licked his nipples. Then she removed his shorts. He was hard and she encouraged him to take her, pretending to want him. She took hold of his erect penis and guided it inside her. He was a cherry boy and when the well-trained muscles inside Joy's vagina constricted on his dick, he was unable to control himself. To Joy's relief, it was over within sixty seconds.

When they had finished, Joy asked the ugly boy, "What is your name?"

He answered, "My-my name is Amir."

"Amir, I'm in love with you," Joy said, gazing deeply into his eyes. "Do you love me?"

"Y-Y-Yes."

"If you truly love me... then you will help me leave this place. I do not want anyone touching me but you. We can go to Bangkok to get married. Will you help me escape?"

. . .

"Y-Y-Yes," answered Amir, nodding like an obedient puppy.

Joy knew that if she stayed in the brothel, sooner than later, she would take her own life. She was willing to do whatever it took to escape.

19

FREE AT LAST

The next day, Joy and Amir crossed the border into Thailand and went to Bangkok. However, they didn't get married. Before leaving Amir, Joy took most of his money while he was sleeping. The last thing Amir said to her before falling asleep that night was, "I-I-I l-l-love you." She kissed his cheek, "Good night, Amir. Sleep well." She felt bad about taking his money. But she needed the money more than he did. Amir could always return to his father's brothel, but she had no home to return to.

It was early in the night as she wandered down the streets of Bangkok. She came to a street that looked like it belonged in another world. There were flashing bright neon lights on all the buildings and a bustling crowd walking up and down the long street. Girls dressed in skimpy outfits trying to lure men into their places of business. While walking down the street, one of the skimpy-dressed girls waved her over to her.

The girl said, "What are you doing? You look lost and out of place."

Joy replied, "I am not from here?

. . .

"I didn't think so," said the girl.

Joy examined her, "Why are you dressed like that?"

The girl replied, "You must be a naive providence girl! This is how I make my living."

"Doing what?" asked Joy.

"By attracting a farang willing to pay me to spend time with him," answered the girl as she waved to an old farang who was walking nearby. The old farang waved back but did not stop.

"I need money. Can you help me?" asked Joy.

The two girls became friends, and in no time at all, Joy was fully engaged in the Game and making money. She felt sorry for Amir, the ugly boy. She felt guilty for the way she left him, but there was no way she was going to marry him. The very thought of repeatedly making love to him, made Joy shiver. During her career as a prostitute, she would make love to men who were even uglier than Amir, but not by much. And they paid her dearly for that privilege.

She now made her living as a dancer at Dizzy. Dizzy was the go-go bar where her friend worked. Joy danced and striped on stage, while men cheered her on. When not dancing, she tried to find a customer willing to buy her a lady's drink. She was paid a small commission for each drink a customer purchased for her.

But most of her income came from providing services outside the bar. The customer would pay her mama-san a bar fine, allowing Joy to leave the bar with her customer. The customer would tell her what he wanted, and they would negotiate the price for those services. Joy's services didn't come cheap. Joy learned early on that you were worth only as much as you believed you were worth. She became a real professional.

Over time, Joy became very selective. She built a clientele who paid her well and did not abuse her. She was incredibly good at what she did. She gave her clients the illusion of love, unlike the amateurish American prostitutes who often wouldn't allow their johns to kiss them. She provided her customers with what is commonly referred to in the Game as a "Real Girlfriend Experience, or RGE for short."

Joy allowed her patrons to have their way with her petite shapely brown body. She gave them sexual pleasures they had never before experienced, fulfilling their every sexual fantasy. Fat, old, and ugly farangs were not used to having a beautiful woman, such as Joy, make passionate love to them. She gave them the illusion of wanting them as badly as they wanted her. In return, they paid her well, or she would never pleasure them again.

Many of her clients were convinced she was in love with them. They rewarded her with money and exotic vacations, and would buy her expensive clothing, gifts, and jewelry. Some of these men even proposed marriage. She was not interested in marriage. She was not interested in real love; Joy had become a grand counterfeiter of love. If the truth is told, she didn't care for men; she only wanted their money and she was very good at getting it.

As she aged, she started to lose her best customers. They wanted younger women. The go-go bar where she worked needed a new mama-san to help manage its dancers. The bar's owner recognized that

Joy would be an excellent choice, and he offered her the job, which she accepted. She eventually became Dizzy's top mama-san.

Occasionally, one of her old customers still wanted her personal services. Well past her prime, Joy thought, *if one of my well-paying farangs is still willing to pay for me, then who am I to turn them down?* She didn't like turning down money. *Allowing a man to fuck me,* she thought, *means little more than taking out the trash.*

Joy had saved enough money to buy a house and the land it was on. It's a nice house, fully paid for. She brought Kat to this house after the poor girl told her everything she was going through. After waking up, Kat would need to decide whether or not she would return home or stay in Bangkok.

Joy was not sure why she invited Kat to follow her home. Throughout her life, Joy had a habit of adopting strays. She was currently sharing her house with a three-legged dog, whom she adopted after he had followed her home; taking in strays was in her nature.

She would allow Kat to make up her own mind. The one thing Joy would not do – was become Kat's pimp; she hated pimps. It would be Kat's choice to go home or stay and become a go-go dancer. Joy was willing to mentor Kat.

Kat was very pretty, and with proper training, she could become very good at fleecing the farang. Joy thought it was too bad that Kat had sold her virginity so cheaply. She could have gotten Kat over one hundred times the amount of money the café owner had paid her, but Kat had no idea how valuable her virginity was when she sold it.

Joy would educate Kat. She would discourage Kat from entertaining the average Thai male, who she thought was nothing but trouble and could be dangerous. Kat was welcome to stay with her until she made up her mind. Joy and her young three-legged dog liked having Kat in their home.

20

SWEET LITTLE LIES

Kat decided to become a dancer at Dizzy. She didn't want to return home and was afraid to go out on her own. She decided to stay with Joy; Joy was kind to her, and she trusted her.

Joy taught Kat what to look for in a customer and whom to avoid. She taught her the art of using makeup, but at her age, Kat didn't need a lot. She used just the right amount to enhance her natural beauty. Joy liked to tell her, "Baby, don't use too much make-up. You don't need a lot of it until you reach my age."

Joy taught Kat how to dance, talk, and how to seduce and pleasure a man. She taught her the art of negotiation. She taught Kat whom to avoid. Most importantly, she taught Kat what her services were worth. Joy would tell Kat, "Baby, don't make the mistake of giving it away. You're far too pretty for that. If you sell it cheaply, then your customers will treat you cheaply." Over time, a strong bond formed between the two women, and Kat continued to live with Joy.

When not working, Kat continued reading the paperback romance novels she was addicted to; she dreamed of meeting her, Mr. Right. Yet, her Mr. Right always eluded her. The problem was that the only men she ever met were her customers, and Joy's first and most important rule was to never ever fall in love with a customer. They will only break your heart. Joy would tell Kat, "Baby, it's your job to give them the illusion of love, and for you to never forget it is just an illusion."

Like Joy, Kat became a grand counterfeiter of love. Again, and again, Joy reminded her that romantic love was only a childish illusion, just another sweet little lie; it was never real. Most of her customers were satisfied with the illusion, but she was not. Unlike Joy, Kat yearned for the real thing.

Over the years, Kat had had over a thousand penises inserted into her vagina, but in her mind, she was still a virgin. Every single one of those penises wore a hat. There had been men who had offered a substantial amount of money to have unprotected sex with her, but she always turned them down. She was saving herself for the man of her dreams, her "Mr. Right." *Only he will have the right to enter me hatless.*

During this time, Kat had been sending money back home. She missed her mother. Despite this, Kat didn't return home to visit, nor did she want her mother to come to Bangkok. She didn't want to disappoint her mother by telling or showing her how she made her living.

In her letters, she told her mother she was a waitress, working at night in a bar where she made exceptionally good tips. Recently, she told her mother she'd been promoted to the bar's manager. She didn't want to tell her mother the truth – she was a prostitute, something her mother already suspected. There was no way a waitress could afford to send them the amount of money Kat sent to them every month. Kat's parents now owned a house and land. In rural Thailand, they were well off. Their prosperity was a direct result of Kat's generosity; a fact Kat was proud of.

Once a month she received a letter from her mother, telling her how her family was doing. Then one day, she received a letter telling her that her teenage niece, Moon, wanted to go to Bangkok and move in with her. Kat wrote back, advising against it. Her mother replied saying, "Moon is a very strong-minded girl, just like you were. I can only trust that you will look after her. If you allow her to move in with you, please make sure she stays in school."

Kat didn't know what else to do. Could she protect Moon from her life-style? She would do her best to keep Moon out of her line of work and in school.

21

UNDER NEW MANAGEMENT

Dizzy was sold to a farang, named Mick. Mick was a middle-aged Brit, who liked wearing his favorite Newcastle United football shirt whenever it was clean. He had a slightly protruding belly and a Brumie accent. His favorite thing to do in all the world was to make his Thai wife May laugh, which she did often. It was music to his ears.

As a poor Isaan girl, May started working as a Bangkok go-go dancer when she was eighteen years old. She had dark skin, a beautiful body, and long silky black hair that hung all the way down to her well-shaped bottom. She had been in the Game for nearly sixteen years when she met Mick. She was getting too old to be a dancer. She was instantly attracted to him, loving his sense of humor. She decided to use all her womanly charms to make him hers. In no time at all, Mick fell deeply in love with her. Now, she would become Dizzy's manager and the top mama-san.

Joy was given a choice: take a demotion or retire. She decided, *it's time to retire; I have been in this Game long enough.* Joy had always been good at saving money and had invested it wisely. Over the years she had accumulated enough money to see her through her senior years. She no longer needed to work but was doing so because she enjoyed being the top mama-san at Dizzy and mentoring Kat.

Kat stayed at Dizzy as a dancer; she was too young to retire. May and Kat soon became close friends, and May offered Kat a job as one of the bar's mama-sans, and she accepted. In no time at all, Kat became May's best mama-san.

Three years after Mick purchased the bar, May was diagnosed with stage four pancreatic cancer with only months to live. Mick was good at bartending but couldn't control the girls or run the business. And now May could no longer manage the bar, or act as its top mama-san; she needed help. Kat came to mind, and May asked Kat for help, which she badly needed.

That was how Kat became Dizzy's top mama-san and manager. And just as May thought, Kat was an excellent choice. Kat was good at managing the bar and its girls; she was nearly as good as May before she got sick, and perhaps even better.

Mick's life was empty after May's death. She was the love of his life, and he'd purchased Dizzy to keep her happy. He met May while vacationing in Thailand. He didn't come to Thailand for the go-go bars, like many of the male sex-hungry tourists. However, he ended up being lured into one, while in Bangkok.

In that go-go bar, he met May, who was in her mid-thirties at the time. He was immediately attracted to her. She was so cheerful, beautiful, and caring that he fell in love with her. He had never met a woman like her. He wondered how a woman could avoid becoming jaded in her line of work. May was the freest spirit he had ever met. They had been married for four years before she died, and it was the happiest four years of his life.

He only bought the bar, because May did not want to live in London; she wanted to stay in Bangkok and own and run a go-go bar. Now that she was gone, he was no longer interested in keeping Dizzy. He wanted to sell it and move back to London where his brother, two sisters, and his son lived. Yet, Mick did not want to sell Dizzy to just anyone; he wanted the bar to continue succeeding after he left. After all, it was part of May's legacy.

Mick was relying more and more on Kat since May's death. He enjoyed bartending and talking with the bar's customers. What Mick didn't enjoy was managing Dizzy or its dancers. May not only managed the bar, but she also managed to make Dizzy profitable.

Kat took over all of May's previous duties and managed to keep Dizzy's finances in the black. This was something that Mick couldn't do on his own. She worked long hours but didn't mind.

Kat was hoping Mick would not sell the bar. She liked working for him and did not want to return to her former life as a go-go dancer. She wanted to remain Dizzy's manager and top mama-san. The last thing that she wanted was to have her niece, who was asking her and Joy to move in with them, to see her working as a prostitute.

She thought *if only I had enough money to buy the bar*, which she didn't. It was possible that she could have talked Joy into buying the bar. However, owning a go-go bar was a risky business. There were so many of them, like restaurants in San Francisco, only the best survived. If the bar failed, Joy would lose a considerable amount of her life savings. She couldn't bring herself to ask Joy to take on that kind of risk.

22

WHEN PIGS CAN FLY

When Kat's father needed help running the farm, because of his advancing age, Kat's oldest brother moved back to live with his parents. He brought with him his wife and their daughter "Moon." Moon was a lovely girl. Most newborns, to be truthful, are not attractive to anyone other than their immediate family. Moon had been lovely since the very start of her life.

Moon was named after her only blemish, a crescent moon-shaped birthmark, found on her right ankle. At the age of sixteen, she had a perfectly shaped face with big brown eyes that could melt the heart of any man. Her breast and hips were well on their way to full womanhood. She had straight glossy jet-black hair that fell to the middle of her back. In time, she will become possibly the most beautiful woman in all of Thailand, in a land filled with beautiful women.

Moon was not content living in rural Thailand. She was tired of sharing a crowded room with two younger female cousins. She was not interested in marrying any of the local boys, who were constantly coming to their house to court her. They annoyed her. When she had enough of them, she had her father shoo them away. She had no desire to become the wife of a farmer; she had other aspirations for her life.

Like her Aunt Kat, Moon was a bookworm. In upper secondary school, she was scholastically at the top of her class. She wanted to go to college to become an attorney. She wanted to get involved in politics and become Thailand's second female prime minister. Her dream was to follow in the footsteps of Yingluck Shinawatra, nicknamed "Pu", the first female prime minister of Thailand. It was unfortunate that Pu had to flee the country after a military coup.

Moon's dream of becoming Thailand's second female prime minister would never come true if she continued to live with her parents in rural Thailand. She wanted to move to Bangkok where she could get the type of education she so desperately desired. She hoped that her Aunt Kat and her aunt's friend Joy would allow her to move in with them.

After following Joy home, like Joy's three-legged dog, Kat never left. Joy had become something more than just her mentor. Kat viewed Joy as her second mother, and Joy viewed Kat as her adopted daughter. Kat was nervous about telling Joy that her teenage niece, Moon, had asked to move in with them. The house had only two small bedrooms. Finally, Kat built up enough nerve.

"Joy, my teenage niece has asked if she can move in with us."

"Baby, I don't like it. I'm too old to tolerate teenage shenanigans, and most teenage girls are boy-crazy."

"She's a good girl and will give us no trouble. She is a very serious student and doesn't have time for boys."

. . .

With an inquisitive look on her face, Joy thought to herself, *Next, she'll be trying to convince me that pigs can fly*. After much pleading, Joy gave in and agreed to give Moon a chance.

"As long as she behaves, she can stay with us." Joy warned Kat, "But Baby, the moment she gets out of control she will have to leave. And you are the one who's going to tell her to 'Go.'"

Moon was told if she misbehaved, she would be asked to leave. Moon was enrolled in a private upper secondary school for her final year, a good school that Kat could afford.

Moon did not regret her decision to leave her rural home. She did miss her parents and siblings, but she was enjoying her life in Bangkok, except for a small group of schoolboys who persisted in hitting on her; like her Aunt Kat told Joy, Moon was too busy to entertain boys. She liked her school, her new friends, and living with her Aunt Kat and Nay Joy. Moon started calling Joy "Nay," meaning grandmother. At first, Joy didn't like Moon calling her "Nay"; it made her feel old, but now she didn't mind.

Kat and Joy had reservations about Moon moving in with them. Those reservations have evaporated. Both Kat and Joy had come to love Moon. She had become the granddaughter Joy had never had. Even Joy's three-legged dog loved her and had taken to following her. Moon was always game for giving the pup a good belly rub and a pat on his head; besides that, she always made sure he had plenty of water and food in his bowls. And he liked sleeping on her new bed.

Joy started feeling her age, yet she refused to slow down. She could afford to hire someone to help her but didn't. Joy did most of the house-work and the cooking, with Moon's help. Her motherly instincts made sure that Moon had a freshly pressed school uniform to wear each morning. Kat worked long hours at Dizzy and didn't come home until early morning, but Joy always had a meal waiting for her.

Joy never expected to find love during her current lifetime. She believed she would have to wait until she was reborn, *my karma*. Joy had not found romantic love; however, she had found love. In a life that had been hard and cruel to her, Joy, at last, found some measurement of happiness and contentment. She loved both Kat and Moon, and they loved her. They made her life worth living. If anything ever happened to them, she didn't know what she would do.

23

DILEMMA

JJ was enjoying his visit to Thailand. He and Cowboy traveled extensively, taking in all the sights. JJ found Cowboy to be an excellent guide and someone he enjoyed hanging around with. During the evenings, he and Cowboy often returned to Dizzy for entertainment, a cool drink, and the welcome company of Dizzy's women. JJ had even gotten to know Dizzy's owner Mick. They would talk while JJ sipped bourbon, and Mick gin and tonic.

"JJ, I don't feel at home here now that May is gone. I want to go back to London," explained Mick, while taking a sip of his drink. He continued, "If I can find the right person to sell the club to, I'll sell it. When I'm here, all I can think about is May and how much I miss her."

JJ slowly nodded his head, listening to Mick and wondering what it must feel like to be him. Every now and again he felt lonely, still missing his former wife. He thought about her more than he wanted to admit. He also realized how bored he had become since he retired. He continued to listen to Mick until they were both finished with their drinks.

When it was time to leave Thailand, JJ realized he didn't want to. He did not want to go back to his ho-hum retired life in California. He thought about what Mick had told him, thinking he might enjoy owning a Thai go-go bar. It might bring back the excitement in his life that he'd been missing so much. Yet, he had no experience in this type of business and was afraid he would lose his shirt. He had a moral dilemma to resolve as well.

Before making his decision, JJ had to make up his mind if he felt okay with buying a business that patronized prostitution. Prostitution in Thailand was illegal, but it's a law the government had no intention to ever enforce. The infusion of cash prostitution brought to Thailand was too great to stop.

Many Thai women liked the economic freedom it gave them. If they had drunken husbands who cheated on them, prostitution gave them the economic means to leave. Prostitution was one of the few decent-paying jobs available to them.

In America, online porn is a multibillion-dollar business; it's a land of masturbation and sexual hypocrisy. The Bible belt is online porn's biggest consumer. In Thailand, the acceptance of prostitution allowed men to follow their true nature, whether that's a good thing or not.

JJ wasn't naïve enough to believe the sex industry was victimless, especially in Southeast Asia where human sex trafficking was rampant. Despite this, he had been told that only a small portion of the women in Thailand were forced into sex slavery.

He thought long and hard about it. JJ believed that prostitution was not a dirty or nasty profession, as long as the women participating in it were not forced into the profession against their will. The women working at Dizzy were independent contractors; they had no pimps. They could quit anytime they wanted to.

What he didn't like was that many of the women at Dizzy became dancers because they had no viable alternative to making a living wage; however, there was nothing he could do about that. He concluded that if he were the owner of Dizzy, he could make a difference. JJ would make sure the girls were treated as fairly as possible. He would try to establish a symbiotic rather than a predatory relationship with these women. With his mind made up, JJ set out to find Mick.

JJ found Mick nursing his usual gin and tonic with a slice of lime. Mick had a small private upstairs balcony where he liked to watch the action down below when he was not bartending.

"Hi, Mick. I'm interested in buying your bar, but I need to ask you some questions first." As a cop, JJ often relied on his gut instincts. His instincts told him he could trust Mick.

"What would you like to know?"

"I have absolutely no experience in running a bar, much less a Thai go-go bar. If I buy this place, how do I keep it profitable?"

"It's all about hiring the right people. After May died, my manager, Kat, saved this place from going belly-up. If you decide to buy my bar, then she needs to be your first hire." Mick lifted his glass to his lips, and took a gulp of his gin and tonic.

JJ nodded, processing the information that was given to him. "Do you think she'll work for me?"

"Ask her," said Mick, before turning around to look over the balcony. He hesitated just enough for JJ to notice. "And JJ there is another thing you need to know. As a foreigner, you are not allowed to own Thai property.

Fortunately, I know a Thai attorney who can help you get over that hurdle."

"Mick, would you mind letting me look at Dizzy's financial books? I need to know if I can financially make it work for me."

"Yes, that is something I would expect from a potential buyer."

After looking over the books, JJ said, "Your bar looks like it's doing well. It's making a very nice profit. How much are you asking for it?" After getting his answer, JJ decided that buying the bar would be a costly investment. It would be a huge gamble, but one he could afford to lose, which he had no intention of doing.

JJ decided to return to Bangkok in two months to talk with the attorney Mick recommended. If their talk went well, he would make Mick an offer. Before leaving, he approached Kat.

"Kat, my name is JJ Sullivan. I am thinking of buying this place. If I do, Mick said I should hire you to manage the bar. Would you like to work for me?"

This caught Kat by surprise. She stood there dumbfounded and just stared at him before replying.

JJ's offer is too good to believe, thought Kat. She knew Mick was going to sell the bar, and she didn't want to lose her job. "Sir," began Kat.

JJ interrupted her, "Please call me JJ."

"Ok, JJ, I need this job and if you hire me, I can make you a promise."

. . .

"And what is that?" asked JJ.

"You'll never regret hiring me."

JJ's offered her a salary that nearly doubled her old one. Kat accepted, "I'm looking forward to working for you." JJ also offered a job to Cowboy. Cowboy would oversee the bar's bouncers and would be his and Kat's personal assistant. *This could work,* JJ thought to himself. *I think this is just what I have been looking for.*

After JJ's return to California, his first call went to Clyde. "Clyde, you won't believe what I'm planning to do."

"Well, then tell me."

"I'm going to buy a Bangkok go-go bar."

"You are going to buy a Thai go-go bar?... Are you out of your mind? You got to be kidding. JJ, as your friend, I'm advising you don't - do - it!"

"I've got to. I can't take this boredom any longer. I love living in Thailand, but I need a job to keep me busy. I think this is what I've been looking for."

"Find something else to do. Any American who would buy a Thai go-go bar is insane!"

. . .

"I've made my mind up. I can't take the boredom any longer! And I think this will be more than just fun. I think I'm going to love it."

"Then if you are going through with this, I want a job. In a few months, I'll be retiring from the Corp. Hire me as one of your bartenders. Buddy, someone needs to keep an eye on you."

In what seemed to be no time at all, JJ was back in Thailand, and things were going well. He was now the proud owner of Dizzy, and Kat and Cowboy were working for him. When Clyde arrived at the Bangkok airport, he was introduced to Cowboy. Clyde and Cowboy hit it off immediately. It was early in the morning and JJ took Clyde directly to Dizzy, where he met the bar's manager Kat. And, of course, Clyde found Kat enticing.

Kat is easy on the eyes, thought Clyde, *a beautiful middle-aged woman.* She was still slender, she had gorgeous brown eyes, and ebony black hair that fell to the middle of her back. Clyde wondered if anything was going on between her and JJ. He found out later there wasn't. JJ believed in the adage - *you shouldn't fish off your own dock*. JJ was old school in this regard and would never consider having a romantic relationship with a woman he worked with.

Clyde didn't think JJ would like for him to be hitting on his bar's manager. In the meantime, Clyde was content with just being her friend. That could change later. He couldn't help sneaking looks at Kat whenever he got the chance. *She might not be the most beautiful woman I have ever seen, but "Wow, she is wonderful!"*

There's something special about Kat, he thought, but he just couldn't quite put his finger on it. It was like there was a little voice in his head, telling him. "You need to get to know that girl." The voice sounded familiar; it sounded a lot like his grandmother's.

Clyde was then introduced to Mick. Mick was willing to stay on until he taught Clyde how to bartend. Mick was one of the best in the business. Before Mick left for London, Clyde was able to make just about any cocktail a customer could ask for, from a Long Island Iced Tea to a Mint Julep. And like Mick, Clyde loved talking to the customers and flirting with the dancers.

There was one thing Clyde didn't like. Away from the bar, he found many Thais to be racists. In Thailand, dark-skinned people are looked down upon. But this discrimination wasn't built on a history of slavery. No, this discrimination was the result of hyper-social-class consciousness and intellectual snobbishness. There are Thais who view dark-skinned people as being lower class. To them, dark skin suggested that you were a laborer and that you worked outdoors. If you were light-skinned, it meant you worked indoors and were well-educated.

Clyde even had to be careful when he bought skin lotions. He had to closely read the ingredients listed on the labels. Many of the Thai lotions contained skin whiteners.

However, Clyde learned not all Thais are racist. There were Thais he had gotten to know who discarded all the nonsense they had learned about Black Americans - like his friends Cowboy and Kat. The go-go dancers didn't care about the color of his skin; they cared only about the color of his money.

There was another thing Clyde didn't like about living in Thailand. He didn't like paying for sex. He wasn't used to paying a woman to go to bed with him. In the U.S., women freely gave him what he wanted, but not in Thailand. Go-go dancers did not like to give freebies. As time passed, Clyde learned how to score outside the go-go bar scene and get his fixes without paying for it. It wasn't always easy, but it was doable and quite enjoyable.

~

With Mick's help, Clyde picked up bartending in no time, and with his athletic build, he was able to serve much faster than Mick. He relished his work. He loved being around and flirting with all the lovely-sexy-Thai dancers; he felt as if he had died and gone to heaven. *What a life,* Clyde thought to himself. *This beats the shit out of sitting in front of a boring TV, watching reruns. Just maybe, JJ wasn't as crazy as I thought he was. I can get used to this.*

Kat became JJ's right-hand man, or should I say his right-hand woman. If not for her, his inexperience would have gotten him into serious trouble. In all likelihood, he would have lost the bar. He gave Kat another pay raise, this time nearly tripling the amount of money Mick had been paying her. She was worth every penny of it.

Kat liked working for JJ, even though JJ at first didn't have a clue on how to run a go-go bar. Like Clyde, JJ, too, was a quick study and had some understanding of how to run a business. After all, he did have an MBA. JJ was paying her well, and money was no longer a big concern for her.

She also discovered she was physically attracted to JJ but wouldn't allow this to interfere with her job. For now, she would keep her romantic desire for JJ to herself. She wondered if JJ could be the man she dreamed about, a man right out of one of her paperback romance novels, her Mr. Right. She sometimes caught herself drifting into daydreams but always snapped back to reality. She wondered if JJ could be that dreamy man that her childhood friend talked about, "Sweeter than a bowl of jackfruit covered in whipped cream."

Every now and then, she allowed Moon to visit the bar with some of her school friends on the weekends. Moon was such a well-behaved niece that she figured a little time outside wouldn't hurt her. Kat didn't like it initially but later realized it was a safe environment for Moon and her friends to have a little fun. They had an isolated area, roped off, in the corner of the bar, away from the bar's customers and dancers.

Moon and her friends would dance together, drink sodas, listen to music, and keep to themselves. In the U.S., they wouldn't consider allowing school kids into a bar filled with seminude women, but it wasn't a big deal in Thailand. Thais aren't so uptight about nudity and JJ didn't seem to mind as long as they behaved, which they always did.

Dizzy became a great place to escape Bangkok's heat, have a cold one, and admire the female form at its finest. What more could a man ask for? The remodeling included a new center stage, with fog-making machines that would shroud the dancers in mist that cascaded down the stage's sides. The new lighting came with all the colors of the rainbow. Sideshows, such as women blowing smoke rings or darts out of their vaginas, were discontinued. Dizzy became the first Bangkok go-go bar with a no-smoking policy, a policy most said would doom Dizzy, but it didn't. There were plenty of smoking bars in Bangkok, but Dizzy was one of only a few that didn't allow smoking.

Under JJ's and Kat's tutelage, the bar attracted a richer clientele, making the bar and the working girls more money. When JJ took over the bar, it was unusual to see a single Thai customer in the bar. The bar now had a well-mixed crowd of Thais and foreigners.

The women were encouraged to use safe sex practices with their customers and were routinely tested for venereal diseases. Violence against them was not acceptable. Cowboy made sure that Dizzy's dancers were not treated roughly. When it came to his girls, Cowboy reminded JJ of an old mother hen, who would do anything to protect Dizzy's dancers.

Cowboy posted pictures of abusive patrons on a bulletin board. Patrons who committed violent acts against any of Dizzy's women would never be welcomed back into the bar. In some cases, Cowboy gave these men a dose of their own medicine. The men who abused Dizzy's dancers brought out the rage that he felt when he was fighting in the ring. His police connections allowed him to get away with whatever he did.

When Cowboy used violence, the next day, he would visit a local Buddhist temple to pray and meditate in an effort to wash away the bad karma. He used violence only as a last resort but didn't hesitate to use it when he felt it was justified. Word on the street was to "not mess with Cowboy's girls, and that wild-ass Cowboy won't mess with you."

Finding attractive dancers who wanted to work at Dizzy was not difficult. Among the go-go dancers in Bangkok, Dizzy had developed a reputation as one of the best places to work. The women knew they would be treated fairly at Dizzy, and it was a place filled with good-paying customers. Dizzy was a place where they could feel safe and protected, which was particularly important in their line of work.

This allowed Kat to pick and choose the dancers who worked at Dizzy. She hired only the finest, and Kat didn't hesitate to get rid of a dancer who hindered Dizzy's reputation. There were house rules that the dancers were expected to follow, and Kat made sure they did.

24

PICKLE IN YOUR POCKET

Bot's men liked going to Dizzy. Dizzy had become one of Bangkok's most popular go-go bars; it had the hottest dancers in town. Bot's men were always on good behavior at Dizzy. They did not want to get on Cowboy's bad side.

Now that Bopha was a full member of the gang, Bot's men decided to invite her to accompany them to Dizzy, their favorite go-go bar. Bot's men secretly believed that Bopha was a closet lesbian, who might like being in a bar full of foxy-looking women. She gave no indications of liking men. She only allowed Aroon and Bot to touch her because she had no choice in the matter. They wrongly thought she would appreciate Dizzy's beautiful female dancers.

Bopha, being somewhat bored that night, accepted their invitation. She thought she might enjoy the music in the bar. All the men in the gang raved about Dizzy, and she was curious to know why. After arriving, it didn't take her long to find the music too loud, and she wasn't particularly enjoying herself. She wondered, *How in the hell did I allow myself to be talked into coming here?*

Bopha could see her effect on him, and her old confidence returned. In a typical Thai greeting, she brought both of her hands up, palm to palm, just below her chin, wai-ed, and said, "I'm glad to meet you JJ. My name is *Bopha*."

JJ returned her wai, and to JJ's relief, they sat down. JJ asked Bopha if she would like something to drink. She requested Scotch on ice, and he ordered her a glass of his bar's finest Scotch, Chivas Regal 18, on the rocks. For himself, he ordered a tall glass of Wild Turkey on ice.

Curiosity trailed his thoughts as to why this beauty was with Bot's men. Cowboy had told him that these men were gangsters, frequent guests of the bar, but he didn't feel comfortable enough to ask her why she was with them.

Bopha began the conversation. She stared deeply into his eyes, "I would like to know how you came to own this bar. It's very nice."

"I came to Thailand on vacation, with no intentions of staying, but I fell in love with the country and its people." JJ paused for a moment, chewing on a piece of ice, a nervous habit he wanted to break.

"Please go on," Bopha insisted.

"Well, one day, I went into this bar and sat down. The bar's owner, Mick, approached my table and we started talking. Mick had bought Dizzy for his Thai wife. After she died from cancer, he decided to sell it." He matched her gaze while waiting for her next question.

"So, you decided to buy it?"

"No, it was two days later. I was packing my luggage, getting ready to leave, and I found myself not wanting to go."

. . .

"Did you ever own a bar before?"

"No."

"Why would you go into a business you know nothing about? I don't want to sound rude, but that sounds rather rash." For some reason, Bopha felt comfortable enough with JJ to make such a comment. It was very odd for her to be so direct with a stranger.

"I was scared, but I did it anyway. Mick told me he had someone he completely trusted working for him. She knew the business inside out and could help me if I hired her."

"I take it that you hired her?"

"Yes, I did."

"I can see that the bar is remarkably successful. If she played such a major part in its success, this is someone I would like to meet."

JJ pointed down to an attractive middle-aged woman standing behind the bar next to a tall farang dam, a Black man. "That's her standing next to an old friend of mine. Would you like for me to invite her to join us?" Bopha wondered if Kat and JJ were romantically involved. For some odd reason, she hoped that wasn't the case and found herself wanting to know more about their relationship.

. . .

"Please."

Kat joined them on the balcony, and introductions were made. While they were making small talk, Kat told Bopha about her niece, Moon, who wanted to become an attorney. Kat loved talking about Moon and did so whenever she was given the chance.

Bopha asked Kat if she had a picture of her niece. Kat took out her cell phone. Before showing Bopha the photo of Moon, Kat took a long and hard look at Bopha and said, "In some ways, she looks a lot like you," then showed her Moon's photo.

For a few seconds, there was a look of confusion on Bopha's face. If Bopha had a younger sister, this girl could be her. Twice this night she had been surprised: first by her strong attraction to JJ; and then by the photo of this girl, Moon, who did resemble her. She decided *it was time to leave, to regain balance.* She thanked JJ for his hospitality, and said goodbye to Kat, then to JJ's regret, she left.

On her way out, Bopha noticed that the men she had been with were gone. They had paid the bar fines for the dancers, whom they had been sitting with, and had gone into the night to enjoy themselves. She headed back to Bot's compound to sleep the night alone. Until now, that was exactly what she desired – sleeping alone. However, tonight was different; she didn't want to spend the night by herself. After falling asleep, she dreamed of JJ, which was a very sweet dream.

JJ too had difficulty falling asleep that night. All he could think about was Bopha. He had never met a woman as beautiful as Bopha, not even Beth. Her satin sexy voice, her perfect figure, jet black hair, the softness of her hands, and her beautiful dark eyes. He loved her eyes, maybe even more than he loved Beth's eyes. When he finally did go to sleep, like Bopha, he had a very nice dream.

The next morning, just after waking up, Bopha discovered silvery dust in her hair. Unknown to Bopah, it was the enchanted dust that resided in Dizzy; unknowingly its magic would amplify her attraction to JJ and her feelings for him. *Where did this dust come from*, she thought? It took repeated shampoos to remove it. But the very next morning, she found that the silvery stuff was back. It was as if someone was intentionally putting it in her hair. Bot noticed and asked her, "Why are you putting glitter in your hair?"

"I'm not! I have no idea where it's coming from."

There were only two people in Bopha's life she had ever had sex with, Aroon and Bot. She went to Aroon's penthouse once a week and visited Bot's bedroom twice a month. She didn't particularly enjoy these visits, even though she found Aroon to be somewhat physically attractive. Under other circumstances, she might have found having sex with Aroon enjoyable, but she resented the fact that she had been forced into a sexual relationship with him. In her eyes, both Bot and Aroon were rapists; before joining them in their beds, she made sure to lubricate.

She fantasized about an attractive older boy she knew in Cambodia when she was with them. It was her fantasy boy, not Aroon or Bot, whom she was making love to. Bopha tried to forget JJ - but couldn't. A week after meeting JJ, he replaced her fantasy boy. It's now JJ's face she sees whenever Aroon and Bot have their way with her.

She faked orgasms with Aroon, something that was not necessary with Bot. Bot couldn't care less if she climaxed or not. It was all about his pleasure and not hers. Besides that, Bot knew she took no pleasure in being in his bed. While with Aroon, something unusual happened. She became so enthralled with her new fantasy she climaxed for real. It felt so good that the fantasy would no longer suffice. She needed the real thing; she needed to see JJ again, to have his lips pressed up against hers and his arms wrapped around her.

Bopha was also having a hard time forgetting Moon. The younger version of herself kept haunting her. Like honey to a bee, Moon had become an irresistible beacon. She felt an unexplainable need to get close to her. She wanted to mentor her. She wanted Moon to be her little sister, a sister she did not have. It was a feeling she didn't understand or could suppress. She needed to meet Moon in person.

So, a month after her initial visit, Bopha decided it was time to return to Dizzy. She would need to be careful. She didn't want Aroon or Bot to find out how attracted she was to JJ. She was also worried about Moon. If Bot ever saw her, because of her exceptional looks, Bot would be tempted to abduct her and sell her as a sex slave. She could not allow that.

It was early evening when she arrived at Dizzy, an hour before the bar opened. She wanted to keep a low profile. Her Mercedes-Benz was parked at an expensive clothing boutique she had recently purchased in downtown Bangkok. She took a taxi from there, not wanting anyone to see her car parked anywhere near Dizzy. Bopha was happily surprised when she found the front door unlocked. She opened the door and walked in, seeing JJ helping Kat arrange tables.

Just seeing JJ sent shivers up and down her spine. She wasn't used to these strange feelings, but she liked them. She tried to keep her new feelings under control. She told herself; *I'll make this JJ my 'man toy.' When I have grown tired of him, I will simply discard him.*

Bopha walked over to JJ, and very un-Thai-like, she offered him her hand instead of giving him a wai; she spoke slow and steady, making sure to give him complete eye contact, "Hello JJ, it's nice to see you again." JJ took her hand and looked directly into her ebony eyes. He found it difficult to look away from them. Again, he was reluctant to release her hand, but did so; he didn't want to embarrass himself again.

Bopha didn't mind JJ holding onto her hand; she liked the feel of her hand in his. That was why she didn't wai but instead extended her hand to JJ. Like the feelings she so often gave to men, she felt a stirring down below. JJ was making her juices flow. She was becoming wet; with him, there would be no need for artificial lubrication. She longed to have his hands caress her body, his naked skin pressed up against her. As in Peggy Lee's song, he gave her fever, a sexual yearning that she didn't think was possible. Like JJ's ex-wife, Beth, Bopha was not afraid to go after something she wanted.

A sudden feeling of shyness came over JJ; it was like he was back in high school. During his high school prom, he was too shy to give his date a good night kiss, no matter how badly he wanted to. He had thought that he had rid himself of that stifling shyness, *but perhaps not.* JJ took in a deep breath, trying to relax, before saying, "It's good to see you as well. Would you like something to drink?"

"A glass of iced tea would be nice," Bopha replied. JJ walked to the bar and returned with two glasses of Thai iced tea. Bopha was wearing a white sleeveless dress and red heels. And when she smiled at him, it caused his heart to beat faster than a drummer playing "Wipe Out."

Still smiling, Bopha asked, "Do you have time to talk?" JJ looked at her for a moment before saying, "With you, always," gesturing with an outstretched hand to the stairway leading to his balcony. With a grin on her face, she started walking up the stairway.

When they reached the balcony table, JJ pulled out a chair for Bopha to sit on, and he then sat in the chair next to her. "What brings you here today?"

"You," replied Bopha.

JJ blinked uncontrollably before clearing his throat, "Me?"

· · ·

109

"Yes. I am attracted to you."

JJ's right hand was nervously tapping the top of the table. Bopha reached for the hand, and took hold of it, stopping the tapping. While looking into his eyes, Bopha said, "When I want something, I go after it. And JJ...I want you. Am I embarrassing you?"

I am embarrassed, JJ thought, his face as red as a blushing girl's. Not even in his wildest dreams could he see this happening.

He answered, "Maybe a little. But don't worry. I think I can get over it." Bopha gave JJ's hand a reassuring squeeze and replied, "Yes, I think you can."

With her free hand, Bopha brought her glass of iced tea to her mouth, tilted her head back, and took a deep swallow of the cool sweet drink. Licking her lips, she said, "How refreshing." She then sat the glass back down on the table before focusing her eyes on JJ.

A cheery thought entered Bopha's mind, *in no time at all, like all the men in my life, I'll have this one wrapped around my little finger. And he'll do whatever I want him to do.* Bopha's manipulations often came with an unpleasant price. *JJ will be different. This seduction is going to be quite enjoyable.*

After Bopha left his bar, like Rick in the movie "Casablanca," after Ilsa departed Rick's bar, JJ lamented about Bopha's visit. And like Rick, he thought, "*Of all the gin joints in all the towns in all the world, she walks into mine.*" JJ knew he had fallen for Bopha, head over heels.

Over the next couple of months, Bopha became a regular visitor of Dizzy. She liked coming to the bar early before it became busy. As soon as she arrived, she got JJ's full attention. She always got the full attention of men, unless they were gay.

She easily seduced JJ. As intended, JJ was under her spell, but she didn't realize until later that she was also under his; something that was not meant to happen. Bopha knew nothing about the silvery magiclly enchanted dust that resided in Dizzy, and Bopha was not immune to its manipulation nor to JJ's charm and good looks.

When they made love, JJ made her feel like she was the most valuable thing in his world. His mouth, fingers, and tongue, were magical, touching the most sensitive parts of her body. He was more concerned with her pleasure than his own. For the first time in her life, she felt the freedom to explore her own desires. She liked the feel of his cock inside her, and the way his tongue explored her mouth. What she loved most was the feeling of security he gave her when he wrapped his arms around her. It made her feel like nothing bad could ever touch her, a feeling she hadn't had since the death of her parents. During their love-making, she didn't climax once, or even twice, but multiple times. They say you can become addicted to crystal meth after using it for the very first time. Bopha discovered something even more addictive than meth.

And JJ discovered something as well. He was finally over Beth, and this time for good. Bopha was now the only female on his mind and there was no room for Beth.

Kat had not expressed any attraction for JJ, and JJ had not expressed any romantic feelings toward her. Regardless, Kat was not happy when it became apparent that JJ had fallen for Bopha. It wasn't that she particularly disliked Bopha; she was jealous of her. Kat was attractive, but she couldn't compete with Bopha's beauty.

Unlike Joy, who never enjoyed having sex with any of her customers, male or female, Kat had customers she enjoyed having sex with. Unexpectedly, now that she was out of the Game, she found she missed it.

She had been hoping for the day when JJ would sweep her off her feet. A man she would welcome inside her, hatless. Before Bopha showed up, she felt JJ could possibly be her long-awaited Mr. Right. Bopha had ruined that possibility. Just when she thought she had a chance for love, she found out that Joy was right all along; love was only an illusion. Bopha had shattered her illusions of love; now, she needed to pick up the pieces and move on.

~

After questioning JJ about Moon, Bopha learned Moon routinely came to the bar on Saturday nights with a group of friends. Saturday nights were the busiest nights of the week, a time when Bopha normally avoided being in Dizzy. Despite this, she needed to meet Moon, so on a busy Saturday night, she showed up at the bar.

As usual, as soon as JJ saw her, he invited her to his balcony. As badly as she wanted to accept his invitation, she didn't. Instead, she asked JJ to introduce her to Moon. He blinked blankly at her several times before asking, "Why do you want to meet Moon?"

"She reminds me of myself when I was her age. Do you think we look alike?"

JJ looked at Moon and then at Bopha. He instantly saw the resemblance. He wondered, *why didn't I notice this before.* "Yes." Until now, he had never realized just how pretty Moon was. *I still don't understand why she wants to talk to Moon.* He then made the introductions and left. He was content that he would later see Bopha. *At least, I hope.*

Bopha sat next to Moon, and they started to talk. Moon did not disappoint her. The photo she saw on Kat's phone didn't do Moon justice. Moon looked even more radiant in person, and to her delight, she also found Moon to be a very bright girl!

Moon was initially startled by Bopha. Bopha looked so much like her, just an older version of herself. It didn't take long for them to start talking to each other. They act as if they had known each other for years. They were completely at ease with one other.

Moon told Bopha about her plans to become an attorney. She hoped to receive a full scholastic scholarship offer to attend Chulalongkorn University, one of Bangkok's most prestigious universities. Bopha remembered her dreams of becoming a theoretical physicist. She hoped Moon's dreams would become a reality, unlike her original dream.

Bopha and Moon began meeting twice a week at a café to drink Thai coffee or tea, and to talk. They no longer met at Dizzy. Moon loved talking to Bopha. She found Bopha intriguing. Moon found she could talk to Bopha in ways she could not with other people; they are intellectual equals. She began to think of Bopha as her big sister, and referred to her as, "Big Sister."

Bopha enjoyed her conversations with Moon. They were long and reminded her of the ones she used to have with her parents. Moon helped fill the void left by their death. A day didn't go by when she didn't miss her parents.

Bopha could not help talking about Moon to JJ, and the developing relationship between them. She told JJ she was now calling Moon, "Little Sister," and had come to love Moon as if she were her little sister.

During a physical examination, a doctor told Bopha there was no need for her to continue to take precautions to avoid pregnancies; she was sterile. She had no living relatives; they were all dead, except for one. Bopha now saw Moon as her only living relative, and she clung to the thought of protecting her with everything she had and to help her achiever her ambitions.

25

AN EMPTY PROMISE

It had been a while since Bot had gone out drinking and womanizing with his men. He decided to go to Dizzy. It was a Saturday night, and like most Bangkok nights, it was hot and muggy.

Entering the bar was a cool relief. The beads of perspiration on Bot's forehead quickly evaporated. His men found a table near the raised platform. The women dancing on the platform were some of Bangkok's most attractive go-go dancers. Dizzy had come a long way since he was last there.

Bot was enjoying himself. He had two hot-looking young ladies sitting on each side of him. Each of the girls had placed a hand on his lap and took turns gently messaging his crotch. He was getting ready to ask the girls to call their mama-san, so he could pay their bar fines when he saw one of the girls waving to a group of teenagers located in the back corner of the bar. Except for a few males in the group, the group of teenagers showed no interest in the go-go dancers.

The teenagers were not mingling with the bar's customers. And they were not being entertained by any of the dancers. Occasionally, a couple of the girls got up and danced together, staying in their roped-off area.

On one of those occasions, a girl caught his attention, a girl with exceptional looks. Few women in Bangkok, or all of Thailand, could rival Bopha's beauty, but this girl was every bit as attractive as Bopha!

His immediate thoughts went to the Saudi. He thought of all the gold the Saudi would be willing to pay for such a beauty. *I need to find out who this girl is and where she is living.* He had several of his men follow her home.

The next day Bot found out the girl's name was Moon, the niece of the manager and top mama-san for Dizzy. However, there was a problem. This was the girl Bopha had asked him to leave alone, and he promised her he would. It was a promise he would not keep.

Bot was irritated with Bopha. She had tricked him into making a promise to leave Moon alone. Bopha should have known how much the Saudi would pay for such a lovely girl. Since he had not seen the girl, he made the promise. But the instant he laid eyes on Moon; his greed took over. The Saudi's gold was irresistible. Bot's love of gold could only be matched by an Irish leprechaun's appetite for the yellowish metal.

Bopha had begun to make Bot nervous. Lately, she had been overstepping herself. She acted as if she was the gang's boss, and some of his men appeared to be more loyal to her than to him. He didn't like that.

He was also worried that Bopha could be giving away gang secrets to Aroon, something extremely dangerous to the gang and himself. He would have to do something about it. He was tempted to take the gang's asset management duties away from her, but she was so...so... good at finding ways to increase the gang's profits. She had made him extraordinarily rich, a multimillionaire, creeping ever closer to becoming a billionaire.

If he took away her duties, it would indicate he no longer trusted her. He would then have to kill her. She knew too much to remain alive. But killing her would put him in a war against Aroon. *I bet Aroon loves her. He has to love her by now,* he thought. Bot was just beginning to see how manipulative Bopha could be. He suspected she was playing him and

Aroon as fools, for her own game's end. *And Aroon, blind by his lust, couldn't see it. Why did he have to have a smart one like Bopha? Just plain stupid!*

Bot was forced to make a difficult decision. In the near future, he would order Bopha's death. He had to make sure he gave those orders to members of his gang he could still trust. Her death needed to look like an accident, maybe a car accident, something that even Aroon could believe. Bopha was still a terrible driver, after all. Aroon had asked Bot to take away her Mercedes, or at least hire her a chauffeur. For now, Bot decided he would keep a watchful eye on Bopha. *Fuck that promise. I'm going to get Moon and the Saudi's gold that he will pay me for her.*

It didn't take long for Bot to make his move once he had Moon's routine down. She was very predictable. Monday through Friday, Moon left her aunt's house every morning at the same time to go to school. When she returned home, she never deviated from her normal route. On her way home, she always stopped for a glass of Thai tea, with a few of her school friends, at a sidewalk café.

It was no problem convincing the waiter to slip an Ambien cocktail into Moon's tea. The waiter was given an old Mexican proposition – "You can choose either lead or silver."

After leaving the café, Moon was walking alone down an alleyway, when she started feeling lightheaded and very sleepy. The people in the alleyway saw a police van pulling up next to what looked like a drunken teenage schoolgirl. Two officers got out of the van. They led the seemingly drunken, beautiful girl to their police van and gently pushed her inside. She felt the sting of a needle before everything went black.

Moon's abduction went down as planned, with no complications. Bot used only his most trusted gang members to carry out the plan, warning them not to talk to other gang members about the abduction. But his warning did not specifically mention Bopha's name, a big mistake.

116

Moon was taken to one of the gang's safe houses, located just outside of Bangkok. The police van pulled up to the house. Moon was still unconscious and carried inside. They took her to a windowless room and placed her on a mattress. Her hymen was examined, and she was found to be a virgin. The Saudi will pay extra for this, *a lot extra*. Bot's eyebrow started twitching as he thought about all the gold the Saudi would pay him.

Bot witnessed the examination. Moon's beauty dazzled him, a sleeping angel. *She's perhaps even more beautiful than Bopha, if that was possible*. He was tempted to take her, but his greed for the Saudi's gold tempered his lust. She needed to remain a virgin if he was going to get all the gold, he wanted for her. The examiner rolled Moon over onto her stomach. He plunged a needle into the bare cheek of her ass, ensuring she would not wake up until the next day.

Regretfully, Bot left Moon and went to another room, where he slept until the morning sunlight filtered through the window's curtains to wake him. A sixty-year-old Burmese woman, of Rohingya origin, who was abducted in her youth, and sold into the sex trade, knocked, and then entered his room. She was now too old and worn out to attract male customers and now she was Bot's personal servant. She brought Bot a cup of coffee. He sipped the hot sweet drink until there was another knock on his door. The two expected guests were allowed into the room.

One of the guests was a large heavyset Black man, named Abdul, who worked for the Saudi. Abdul had a clean-shaven head and face, and a queer high-pitched voice that did not match his size. Abdul's voice reminded Bot of the voice of the former American heavyweight champion Mike Tyson.

A Thai doctor accompanied Abdul. Abdul hired the Thai doctor to examine Moon; he wanted to make sure he was getting the virgin that the Saudi was paying for and that she was healthy.

. . .

"Where is she?" Abdul asked Bot.

Bot grinned, "Follow me." *Yes, you can have her after you pay,* he thought.

Bot led Abdul and the doctor to where Moon lay unconscious. The doctor removed Moon's restraints, her school uniform, and then her panties. He examined Moon to see if her hymen was intact; it was. He also gave her a quick physical examination, listening to her heart and breathing, making sure she was fit. The doctor gave an approving nod to Abdul, and then redressed and placed the restraints back on Moon. An ammonia capsule was broken under Moon's nose. Everyone left the room, leaving Abdul and Moon alone.

Moon woke up in a small smoke-filled room, with a noisy ceiling fan. A single naked incandescent 60-watt light bulb sent its light across the fan's unbalanced blades, tossing dancing shadows across the room. There were no windows, and no pictures hanging on the walls. Her arms and legs were bound, and she could not move. She lay on a mattress covered with freshly laundered white cotton sheets. The mattress was resting on wooden pallets on a concrete floor.

A huge Black man was sitting in a wooden rocking chair near the room's only door; the chair creaked as the heavyset man slowly rocked himself back and forth. He was intensely staring at her, while smoking an unfiltered Turkish cigarette, filling the room with a smoky haze.

Her voice was shaky, but she managed to ask, "Who are you? Why am I here?"

"I'm here to take you to your Master," Abdul answered in broken Thai. "Soon you will be part of his harem, his newest Flower. You will be treated well, as long as you are obedient. If you are a good girl and please your Master, then one day you'll get to go home; if not, you will die painfully."

Moon was too groggy to reply. Abdul called for the doctor, and he reentered the room carrying a syringe. Moon again felt the prick of a needle and fell to the too-familiar blackness that surrounded her. Bot was not disappointed; Abdul gave him more gold than he had expected, and departed with Moon in his possession.

26

THE BRIEFEST OF MOMENTS

The Saudi was an ugly man, with a huge belly that hung over his belt. His oversized hawk-shaped nose dominated his acme scarred face. He preferred short Asian women over tall Caucasians. Standing 5' 7", he didn't like women that were taller than him.

Moon was flown from Bangkok to Saudi Arabia in the Saudi's private Cessna Citation X jet. She didn't fully wake up until she was in the Saudi's desert compound. Moon had her own room, as did all of the Saudi's Flowers. Moon was now the Saudi's newest flower. The room she was in once belonged to another Flower, a wilted one.

Moon was laid out on a queen-size bed, on white satin sheets, on her back, naked, and spread-eagled. Her arms and legs were bound to the bed's carved wooden posts with silk scarves. She was bathed with unscented soap; her hair, face, and nails were expertly prepared by one of the Saudi's female servants. Abdul and a female servant were preparing her for her first conjugal visit by her master.

Her head rested on a white silk-covered pillow filled with goose down. A smaller version of this pillow had been placed beneath her hips, angling them to give the Saudi an unobstructed entry into her vagina when it was time to mount her. Her vagina was lubricated with care not to break her hymen. Such an accident would bring death to the servant.

As part of the preparation, Moon was injected with a small mixture of Fentanyl, Demerol, and Diazepam prepared by a pharmacist. The drugs did not put her asleep, but they did place her into a dreamy state of mind. Moon was conscious, but she didn't seem to care what they were doing to her. She did not resist.

When the Saudi entered Moon's room, he was wearing a yellow and maroon-colored terry cloth robe, made from the finest Egyptian cotton. The smell of cigar smoke emanated from him. The Saudi smoked only special cigars that were hand-rolled on brown Cuban thighs. A braided, thick Italian gold chain hung around his pudgy neck; the chain had never left his neck since he received it from his father, at the age of thirteen.

He waved Abdul and the servant out of the room. He saw his reflection on one of the two-way mirrors that covered all the walls and ceiling. He disrobed and rubbed his protruding naked belly with his right hand before walking slowly over to Moon's bed, admiring her beauty. In his left hand was a bottle of fragrant oil, bearing the scents of frankincense and jasmine.

Each of his Flowers had their own unique scent, perfumes he personally prepared for them. He loved the earthy woody smell of the frankincense and the sweetness of the jasmine; it was a good mixture of smells. This will be the scent for this new special Flower.

He started rubbing the fragrant oil over Moon's body. His fingers raked through the freshly trimmed bush of raven-black pubic hair; it had been trimmed to his liking. His hand slid down below the bush until he found the opening to her hole. He spread its lips to touch her pink clitoris with his forefinger, before bringing his hand to his mouth to spit in. He then brought his fingers back to her hole, adding his own moisture to the lubrication placed there earlier by his servant.

He slowly brought his hands back to her bare breasts. They were a perfect size, neither too small nor too large, and flawlessly shaped. They appeared to be supported by an invisible bra. The nipples standing above the auras were just too alluring to ignore. The Saudi cupped each breast with his hands, and like a gentle lover, he lightly nibbled and sucked each nipple, resisting his urge to bite. He looked down at what he liked to refer to as his "Golden Rod." It was fully erected, ready to enter her.

Laying on top of her, he placed his throbbing rock-hard, circumcised Golden Rod up against the entrance of her pussy and then briefly paused before he began his penetration. She was tight, but her muscles were relaxed due to the drugs. He stopped when he felt the slight resistance of the hymen. Then with a sudden hard thrust, he broke through and buried himself all the way into Moon.

He momentarily stayed all the way in, reveling in the fact that he was the first and only one to have penetrated and explored this glorious hole. Moon let out a nearly silent sob. The Saudi licked the salty tears rolling down the sides of Moon's angelic face, savoring each tear as if he were dining on fine caviar before he began to fully enjoy her.

It didn't take long for his first ejaculation to erupt. At the peak of his rapture … for the briefest of moments … he entered a place where the believers of all major religions pray to go … a place every cell in his body craved to return to. He was so excited he didn't go soft. He stayed hard and fucked her again, ejaculating a second time. This time, he was unable to maintain his erection, but he wasn't ready to quit.

He returned to his robe and removed a small syringe loaded with Trimix to give life back to his Golden Rod. The Saudi hated needles, but he disregarded his aversion as he plunged the thin needle into the most sensitive part of his body. He knew he'd be well compensated. It would give him precious additional time inside Moon's sweet pussy.

After fucking her for nearly an hour, and coming for the fourth time, regretfully, he pulled his Golden Rod out of Moon; it was exhausted.

While looking at the combination of blood and cum smears on Moon's private parts, and on his own Golden Rod, a warm feeling of satisfaction suddenly radiated through him, starting with a tingling sensation at the top of his scalp that traveled down his spine to the very tips of his toes.

He had the urge to lay back down on her and kiss her inviting mouth, but he knew better. He's learned the hard way not to kiss a Flower on his first visit. This lesson had left its mark on him, a small scar on his lower lip. He'll be patient with Moon and wait until she was properly trained. Then he'll kiss her lips and place his Golden Rod into her beckoning mouth.

He sighed in anticipation, thinking, *this Thai beauty was worth every gram of gold I paid Bot, and then some. It will take a very long time before I grow tired of my new flower. She will not wilt soon.*

It was eight in the morning, the day after Bot and his crew spent the night drinking at Dizzy's. JJ, Clyde, and Cowboy were already hard at work stocking the bar when Kat and Joy entered. There was something wrong. They appeared disheveled and nervous. Neither of them were wearing makeup; something JJ had never seen before.

JJ glanced at Kat from her head to her feet and back up, "What's wrong?"

"Moon didn't come home last night," Kat managed to say.

JJ knew Moon wasn't the type of girl who would stay out all night without first letting her Aunt Kat or Nay Joy know. "Do you have any idea where she is?" JJ asked.

Kat shook her head and said, "No, and neither do her friends. We went to her friends' houses early this morning before they left for school. The last time any of them saw Moon was yesterday at a sidewalk café, a café where they go for tea after school."

"What did they tell you?"

"After finishing their tea, Moon said she was feeling very tired and was going home to take a nap," said Kat. One of her friends offered her a ride home but she refused it."

"How far is the café from your house," asked JJ.

"About two kilometers," answered Kat.

Cowboy stopped what he was doing, looking first at Kat and then at JJ. He said to JJ, "I have a bad feeling about this."

"Why," asked JJ.

"Bot and his men were in the bar the other night, and so were Moon and her friends. I saw Bot looking at Moon, and then overheard him commenting how pretty she was."

"Did you tell Kat that you saw Bot staring at Moon," questioned JJ.

. . .

"No, at the time I didn't think much of it," admitted Cowboy.

JJ had a bad feeling. Members of Bot's gang were frequent customers of Dizzy. They often came into the bar to drink and for the companionship of Dizzy's dancers, but this was the first time in a long time that Bot came with them. They always behaved themselves and were never abusive.

Kat knew Cowboy, in his youth, was part of Bot's gang. Cowboy looked at Kat and told her, "Bot prefers getting his girls from the Thai countryside and Thailand's neighboring countries. Bot believed they were easier to control than Bangkok girls; he used to say he didn't like fouling one's own nest. This did not comfort JJ. He had a gut feeling that told him that Bot had taken Moon, as a cop he had learned to trust his gut.

JJ, Kat, Joy, Cowboy, and Clyde went to the café where Moon was last seen and questioned the employees. JJ suspected that one of the café's employees may have slipped something into Moon's tea. They found out that the waiter, Johnnie, who had served Moon and her friends, had just quit his job. Johnnie had come to work that morning to collect his last paycheck. He bragged about winning an exceptionally large amount of money on a cockfight the previous night.

Betting on cockfighting was Johnnie's favorite pastime. Johnnie told his coworkers he was going to start raising fighting cocks as a full-time occupation. This information wasn't free, and after providing some additional monetary persuasion, Johnnies' coworkers told them where Johnnie lived. It was time to visit Johnnie.

Johnnie was your average Joe. Staying unnoticed suited him fine, because all he wanted out of life was to be left alone to raise fighting roosters without interference. Johnnie's house sat next to a small canal. His shack was made of coconut wood with a rusty corrugated metal

2 7

AYE HEEAH

They concluded that Bot was responsible for Moon's kidnapping. Likely, the police couldn't or wouldn't help get Moon back; they couldn't be trusted. If they went directly after Bot, there would be, without question, bloodshed. Would they be willing to kill to get Moon back? Would they be willing to risk their own lives? Their answer was a resounding "Yes."

JJ, Kat, Joy, Cowboy, and Clyde agreed they would be willing to do whatever it took to get Moon back. Time was not on their side. They needed help from someone inside Bot's inner circle. They needed to decide – could Bopha be trusted?

They all knew Bopha had a real affection for Moon. Bopha had told JJ she thought of Moon as her younger sister. *Would Bopha approve of Bot kidnapping Moon, and selling her as a sex slave? Hell no, she loves Moon*, JJ thought. *Bopha has my complete trust.*

After the rest of the group decided that Bopha could be trusted, JJ called her. "Can you come to the bar? I need to see you right away. It's important, and something I cannot talk to you about over the phone. Please don't ask why."

Bopha thought, *what could be so important? And why couldn't he talk about it over the phone?* Bopha accepted his invitation without demanding an explanation, and told JJ, "I'll see you shortly."

As soon as she arrived, Bopha joined JJ on his private balcony. JJ had never asked Bopha about her ties to Bot. JJ instinctively knew it was a forbidden subject, but on this day that would change.

After ordering Bopha a drink, JJ began, "As you well know I want to be near you all the time, but unfortunately, that is not why I invited you here today."

Before she could reply, Bopha's Scotch on ice arrived. While sipping her drink, she shyly looked at JJ. With a wide smile on her face, she said, "Oh, really..., and here I thought you invited me here to take advantage of me. How disappointing," she said, giving JJ a pouting look. "Then why am I here?"

JJ stared directly into Bopha's ebony eyes and said, "Moon has gone missing, and we believe she has been kidnapped by Bot." Bopha's smile was replaced by a look that made the hairs on the back of JJ's head stand up. It was like witnessing an angel being transformed into a demonic figure; the transformation of the little possessed girl in *The Exorcist* came to mind.

Bopha's voice was stern and deep, "When did this happen?"

"Yesterday," JJ replied. "I've never asked you about your relationship with Bot, but now I must. Do you know anything about Moon's abduction?"

With an icy look, she replied, "No...but why do you think Bot kidnapped her?"

. . .

JJ then told Bopha what they had found out after Moon's disappearance. Bopha was clearly upset. She was angry with Bot. He had promised her to leave Moon alone. She was also angry with herself. Bot was able to abduct Moon without her knowledge. She had come to believe Bot couldn't even wipe his ass without her knowing it. She had underestimated him; it was a mistake she was bent on never to repeat.

There were members of the gang who were now more loyal to her than to Bot; in fact, nearly all of them. Bot was no longer the leader he used to be, and she took advantage of it. In the early days, Bot placed the needs of his gang before his own, but no longer. Now his greed came first, and everyone in his gang knew it.

She needed to be careful with what she told JJ. JJ was under the impression she and Bot were close business partners. JJ didn't know she was a full member of his gang. JJ wasn't stupid though. He knew that whatever business Bot and Bopha were involved in was illegal. His infatuation with her made him overlook certain things. When it came to Bopha, like Clyde often did when it came to women, JJ let the head between his legs cloud his judgment. He just couldn't help it. JJ thought, *what man could?*

Bopha knew she had to get her little sister back. She loved Moon and had plans for her, and the thought of Moon being turned into a sex slave turned her stomach. Bopha told JJ, "Give me a few hours, and I will find out what happened to her. I promise I'll do whatever I can to get her back." She took hold of JJ's hand. "I need to go." She looked again like the angel JJ knew and loved. Before walking out, she brushed her lips against his and whispered in his ear, "I'll call you as soon as I find something out."

Bopha had gone to Dizzy expecting to spend the night with JJ. It was something she really wanted, and strangely, something she now needed. Nevertheless, her desire to stay was no longer important. She was furious with Bot and with herself. She got into her dinged-up Mercedes-Benz and drove off to confront Bot. Her anger did not improve her driving, but she managed to make it back to Bot's compound in one piece.

~

When Bopha arrived at the gang's compound, she spotted Jong, a long-time member of Bot's gang, sitting outside enjoying a cigarette. Jong was someone that Bot completely trusted, even though he wasn't very bright. She knew Bot would have used him in Moon's abduction. She walked up to Jong and asked, "Do you know what Bot plans to do with the girl you abducted the other night? I hear she is young and very pretty. Are you going to have any fun with her tonight before she is sold?"

Jong mistakenly thought Bopha knew about Moon's abduction, and replied, "I wish, but Bot ordered us to leave her alone. With a frown on his face, Jong went on, "And now it's too late; she's gone. This morning she was sold to that Black man."

They all knew the Black man, Abdul, who worked for the Saudi. Jong confirmed her deepest fear; Moon had been sold to the Saudi. Bot usually reserved his best-looking girls for the Saudi because he was Bot's highest-paying customer. For a girl as pretty as Moon, Bot could expect a lot of gold from the Saudi.

Bopha left Jong to finish his cigarette, and walked inside to confront Bot. She was shaking with anger. She knew the Saudi would rape her little sister, and there wasn't a thing she could do about it. Bopha had been repeatedly raped, and she knew firsthand what that experience was like.

Bopha still remembered the first time Bot stuck his filthy dick into her mouth, and commanded her, "Suck it like it's covered with honey," trying to force it all the way to the back of her throat. She pretended to gag on his little dick to keep from laughing. She remembered Aroon taking her virginity and having to pretend to enjoy it. She was still allowing Aroon and Bot to fuck her, to repeatedly rape her. But she felt she had no choice, that is, if she was going to continue down her chosen path. *"And however difficult life may seem, there is always something you can do and succeed at. It matters that you don't just give up."* She was willing to do whatever it took to follow her new dream.

When she found Bot in his office, she shouted at him, "Aye heeah," meaning asshole. "I hear that you sold to the Saudi the girl you promised to leave alone!" She didn't realize until it was too late that she had cursed Bot; he would never tolerate such insubordination. She had let her anger get the best of her. She didn't know how she was going to get Moon back, but she had to! But first, she needed to calm down if she was going to get her little sister back alive.

Bot got up from his chair, "What did you call me? Whom do you think you are, barging in here and talking to me like that?"

"I'm sorry. I didn't mean that. It's just that I'm upset. You promised me you would leave that girl alone. I had plans for her. She would have made a great asset to our gang."

"What girl?"

"You know, the one you just kidnapped and sold to the Saudi."

He nodded, rubbing his hands together, "That was before I saw her. You failed to tell me how pretty she was. The Saudi paid more gold for her than any previous girl that we've ever sold him. I don't know why you are making such a big fuss. You've personally sold women to the Saudi in the past year."

What Bot said was true, something Bopha regretted. She had been willing to do anything to ingratiate herself with Bot and his gang, even to sell women into sex slavery. She told herself it was necessary. Selling women to the Saudi was very profitable and made Bot happy. She had to gain Bot's complete trust to become his second-in-command. Bopha justified her behavior by telling herself, *only after gaining power can I hope to change things.*

Bopha realized it would do her no good to argue with Bot. All he cared about was making a profit in the present; he couldn't care less about Moon's potential value. "I'm sorry. It was just that I had plans for her. She was highly intelligent, and I was going to train her to become my personal assistant. She could have made our gang a lot of money. But you are right. I apologize for cursing you. Please forgive me," she said with fake sincerity and gave Bot a low wai.

She then turned around and started stalking out of Bot's office. As she was walking away, Bot sat back down, "By the way, who told you that I had sold her to the Saudi?"

"Jong," she answered as she exited his office.

Bot was not happy with Jong. He thought *Bopha must have tricked him.* For many years, Jong had been a faithful member of his gang. Jong couldn't help not being smart. Therefore, he wouldn't kill Jong, but he'd make sure that Jong wouldn't repeat this kind of mistake in the future.

I was foolish to confront Bot, Bopha thought. *It wasn't necessary. Jong had already told me all I needed to know; he had confirmed that Bot had abducted Moon and sold her to the Saudi. I let my anger get the best of me. I need to be smarter than that if I'm going to get my little sister back alive.*

Lately, she noticed Bot had been treating her differently. It had been a while since he had invited her for a goodnight drink. *He's not even fucking me as often as he used to.* She had recently learned, from another gang member, that she no longer had Bot's complete trust. *That means my life is in danger. If I don't act soon, he will.*

Bopha went to her room. She needed to cool off before deciding what to do next. Her anger was causing her to make stupid mistakes, something she could not afford at this time. She needed a cool head before making her next move; she concluded it was time to rock Bot's world. She had been steadily eroding Bot's influence and authority with the gang. Now was the time - to act. *Whom can I trust, and who will resist my takeover?* She had a good idea.

In addition, Bopha needed to let Aroon know it was time to activate her plan. He was beginning to wonder why it was taking her so long and was getting impatient. Aroon asked her, "Do you need my help?" He was tired of letting Bot cheat him. He felt as if he was allowing Bot to thumb his nose at him, something Aroon hated. Bopha told him, "Not yet darling, I'll take care of him. Be patient - just a little longer."

The old members of the gang remembered how Bot used to run the gang before he got greedy, and lazy - before he became a drunk. They resented Bot's new management style; they longed for the old days when Bot was fair.

In the old days, Bot freely shared the gang's profits equally, but no longer. Nowadays, Bot was a big believer in the trickle-down theory. He kept the lion's share of the profits and let the small remaining profits trickle down to the rest of his gang.

Things had gotten so bad that several gang members started conducting business on their own; Bopha didn't blame them. In the old days, Bot would have caught the cheaters and would have had them killed. But that was before Bot became a careless drunk.

Currently, most of the gang was taking their orders directly from Bopha. She ran the gang's everyday business, while Bot was foolishly content to stay inside the compound drinking his expensive Scotch and counting his money. If it came down to a choice between Bot and Bopha, most of the gang would choose Bopha.

There were old members of the gang who resented having a female member in their gang, especially one who gave them orders. But only a few. Most of the gang members recognized her as the most capable member of their gang and the biggest moneymaker. Bopha had become the de facto second-in-charge.

Now was the time to make her move. She could no longer wait, and Bot had to be killed before attempting to rescue Moon. The Saudi was Bot's favorite customer, and he would resist any attempt to eliminate him. Bopha meant to do just that; there was no way she would allow the Saudi to live, not after raping her little sister.

On the night of the takeover, just before going to bed, Bot and Bopha shared their last goodnight drink. It had been a while since he had invited Bopha to drink with him. Bot broke out his favorite whiskey, 18-year-old Yamazaki. Yamazaki is made in the traditional Scotch whiskey style, but technically, it cannot be called Scotch because it's distilled in Japan and not in Scotland.

Bot planned to enjoy Bopha one last time; he would call it *"Bopha's farewell fuck."* He had decided the next day would be a good day for her to die in an unfortunate car accident. He would miss having her in his bed, but most of all he would miss all that money she generated. Unfortunately for Bot, his decision to kill Bopha came too late.

After finishing their drinks, they went to Bot's bedroom. He started to undress and motioned Bopha to join him in his bed. She told him, "I'll be right back. I have a surprise for you," as she rubbed her hands over her body, and licked her lips, "something you'll find very sexy." When she walked out of his room, Bot found himself smiling – anticipating what he thought would soon come. Then a frown came to his face thinking, *I'm going to miss her.*

When she returned, Bopha was still fully dressed, and Bot was fast asleep lying naked on his bed. She had placed a roofie into his Yamazaki. In her hand was her Sig, loaded with SXT Remington Golden Saber rounds. When a Golden Saber bullet hits flesh it mushrooms out to what looks like a flower with petals, and cuts the flesh like a thousand razor blades, as it rips through it.

While Bot slept, and with her men positioned just outside Bot's bedroom door, Bopha emptied ten rounds of Golden Saber into his body and one to his head. She didn't make Bot suffer. But Khen, *oh Khen you will suffer... greatly*. Eventually, she would get around to killing Aroon, his brothers, and the men who helped Bot kidnap Moon. Bot was just the first to suffer her fatal bite.

After killing Bot, she called JJ. She told him that she had killed Bot. Now she will need to find a way to get her little sister back before the Saudi could kill her. It would not be easy. Her next call was to Aroon with the happy news her coup was successful. "Darling, I've done it. I'm now the gang's new leader! Bot is dead."

2 8

DUTY BOUND

Zareb looked every bit like the Nubian warrior he was, dark-skinned, lean, and muscular. He was a serious man, who never wore a smile. The old servant had been watching over the Saudi since he was a baby. Zareb came from the Sudan; the Saudi's father hired him when he was a young man. His Sudanese name "Zareb," meant the protector from enemies. He was first employed as one of the Saudi's father's body-guards. After the Saudi's birth, Zareb's duties changed. He was charged with protecting the young Saudi. Wherever the Saudi went, Zareb could always be found nearby.

The Saudi's parents did not allow Zareb to show the Saudi any affection, something Zareb would have found unpleasant. Zareb thought the Saudi was a spoiled brat. Zareb felt no affection for the Saudi, but he was willing to give his life to protect him. It was his duty, and he was duty-bound.

The Saudi had an arranged marriage made by his parents before they died. His wife was a minor member of the House of Saud, the Royal Family of Saudi Arabia. As a dutiful husband, he had given his attractive wife three children. He did not see his family very often.

He always told them that he was on business trips. The Saudi's family didn't care if he was home or not; everything was fine as long as they were financially taken care of, and he made sure they were. The Saudi spent most of his time living with his secret harem. It was now Zareb's responsibility to take care of the Saudi's harem and to protect it with his life.

When Bot was alive, he never knew the Saudi's name; he had never met him face-to-face. But he knew he was from Saudi Arabia, so he called him "the Saudi." He had always done business with the Saudi's intermediates, first with an old man named Zareb, and then with a man named Abdul.

Abdul was a tall heavyset Black man. Abdul came to Thailand to purchase women for the Saudi. The big African made Bot nervous. There was something odd about Abdul that he couldn't quite figure out. The big African made Bot nervous. Abdul came to Thailand to purchase women for the Saudi. There was something odd about Abdul that he couldn't quite figure out.

What Bot hadn't known was that Abdul was a eunuch. Abdul was sold to the Saudi at the age of eight. He had been born to an educated family in Uganda. His father had been a medical doctor. Uganda's military dictator had Abdul's parents killed after his father made the mistake of speaking out against him.

The Saudi had been looking for a young intelligent boy to train, to assist his aging trusted servant, Zareb. Abdul was obtained to help Zareb with the Saudi's harem. Like in the old days of his great-grandfather, he had Abdul castrated before he reached the age of puberty. He trusted Zareb not to touch any of his Flowers, and he wanted to make sure that Abdul wouldn't either.

Abdul was trained to find, manage, and guard the women in the Saudi's secret harem. He was home-schooled, and Zareb took him everywhere he went. Since Zareb never married and had no children, he thought of Abdul as his adopted son. Soon after Abdul reached adulthood, Zareb had become an old man.

Zareb knew there would be no rest home for him when he grew too old to perform his job. The Saudi viewed him as an asset, and once he became a useless asset, the Saudi would get rid of him. He suspected he would be treated as one of the Saudi's wilted Flowers when that day came.

When he felt his time was near its end, Zareb went to his room and shot himself in the head. He didn't want the Saudi to order Abdul to strangle him; he wasn't sure if Abdul would obey such an order. The Saudi ordered Abdul to cremate Zareb's body and toss his ashes into the sand just outside the compound's walls.

The order infuriated Abdul. *The Saudi has no honor.* Zareb had been a faithful servant; he should have been treated with respect. He disobeyed the Saudi's orders. Abdul secretly washed and shrouded Zareb's body before burying him next to a palm tree inside the walls.

Afterward, Abdul decided he would get even with the Saudi for the disrespect he had shown Zareb, and for his own castration. He would have never considered conspiring against the Saudi while Zareb was alive. Now that Zareb was dead, things had changed.

The Saudi's harem was located in a walled complex, built in the middle of the Rub al Khali desert, and surrounded by miles of shifting sand dunes. High whitewashed walls topped with electrically charged razor wire and cameras encircled the compound. The compound had once been a former Turkish fort that the Turks had deserted long ago.

The compound's tall walls enclosed a small oasis with towering palm trees, two buildings, and a garage. The smaller of the two buildings are the quarters for the guards. The largest building contains the Saudi's harem.

The building, housing the Saudi's harem, had only one entrance with a seemingly impregnable stainless-steel door. The inside was like a modern high-security prison fashioned by a highly skilled interior decorator. Apart from occasional privileged guests, the Saudi and Abdul were the only males who resided in this building.

The Saudi referred to the women in his harem as his "Flowers." The Flowers were kept in locked individual rooms containing digital video and audio cameras. A refrigerated room containing the servers recorded everything in his harem. When a Flower became wilted, the Saudi invited a special guest, usually someone of importance, to enjoy them. It would be the final time the Flower was enjoyed by anyone. The guest was never allowed to see any of the Saudi's fresh Flowers.

The Saudi was addicted to fresh Flowers. When the Saudi grew tired of a Flower, one who was no longer appealing to him, he deemed them *"wilted."* Abdul took care of the wilted Flowers. Wilted Flowers were strangled and cremated, and their ashes were scattered in the desert wind. The Saudi was always on the lookout for fresh Flowers. He kept only fourteen Flowers at any one time. And like real flowers, all his Flowers would eventually wilt, to be replaced.

When a Flower arrived, she was introduced to a point system. For pleasing her Master, the Saudi, she was told she would earn points. For displeasing him, she would lose points. The Flower was told that when she reached a thousand points, she would be released with a substantial amount of money. If her total points became negative, she was warned, she would be tortured to death. For a serious rule infraction, regardless of their point total, she would be tortured and killed. In reality - there was no point system. It was all a sham. It was a way for the Saudi to give his Flowers false hope, that one day they would get to leave his harem alive.

Each Flower wore an electric collar locked around their neck to ensure their obedience. This collar could deliver enough voltage to render a Flower unconscious. Early on, each Flower received an electric shock just to demonstrate what would happen to a disobedient Flower.

Newly arrived Flowers were shown videos of disobedient Flowers being tortured to death by Abdul, showing him performing unspeakable acts of cruelty. One of the videos showed Abdul taking a blow torch to a Flower's face. The collars and videos fully inspired the Flowers to please their Master and to perform any sexual act he commanded.

If a Flower committed a minor indiscretion, such as disrespect, she would be punished, but not killed. All Flowers were required to address the Saudi as "Rayiysay" meaning "Master" in Arabic. If they failed to address the Saudi as Rayiysay, the Saudi personally spanked them.

The Saudi loved to spank his naughty Flowers, using a wooden paddle that resembled a sturdy pizza peel. He liked the way it made him feel when he placed the wood on their naked bottoms.

Most Flowers wilted within a year. A wilted Flower was required to perform one final act of obedience. For the first time, since arriving at the harem, she would be required to have a sexual encounter with a man other than the Saudi. She was told she needed to satisfy this other man's every sexual fantasy. "If you fail to do so," the Saudi warned, "If you embarrass me, by not fully satisfying my guest, you will lose your thousand points. Abdul will then torture you to death." They did whatever the Saudi's guest commanded, to make the guest happy, very happy.

After entertaining the special guest, the wilted Flower was given a farewell party. The Saudi had constructed a special occasion room for training, dinners, and farewell parties. A center room was encircled by fourteen individual cells with glass walls. During the farewell party, thirteen of the cells were occupied by a Flower. One at a time, the Flowers were allowed into the center room to congratulate the departing Flower. These were joyous occasions; the remaining Flowers wished the wilted Flower a good farewell and gave her goodbye kisses, not knowing her true fate.

At the end of the going away party, the wilted Flower's collar is removed, and she is escorted out by Abdul. Once out of sight, she is strangled. No Flower had ever left the Saudi's harem alive. The ashes of over a hundred wilted Flowers reside in the sand just outside the white-washed walls.

Until recently, the Saudi had never allowed a Flower into his room. He always enjoyed his Flowers in their rooms. But he never had a Flower as lovely as Moon, and he made an exception for her. Twice a week, he wanted her next to him when he woke up in the morning.

Moon had restored morning wood to his Golden Rod. She gave him the sexual drive of a teenager. He spent hours viewing her on his 110-inch Ultra HDTV when she was not with him. While watching her, he often held a pair of her unwashed panties up to his nose, inhaling her fragrance as if he were smelling a rose.

He decided to make Moon his second wife; she would no longer be a Flower. She would not wilt. Unlike his first wife, Moon would be a wife he felt he could genuinely love. He wanted Moon to bear him a son. A son with whom he'll share everything, including his haram, unlike his other son.

He instructed Abdul to stop giving Moon contraceptives. If the child was, unfortunately, a girl, the aborted baby's ashes would join those of his wilted flowers. They would try again for a boy.

The Saudi's wealth came from oil, black gold, and a high-rise construction business. His father was an Arabian sheik from a prominent Saudi family. The Saudi gave the appearance of a practicing

Muslim, but he believed in no god; he was an infidel. He lived for the moment, believing only in his own gratification.

He had wanted a harem, like the one his great-grandfather had since he was a teenager. Having his own harem soon became an obsession that he dreamed about nightly. His very first ejaculation occurred during one of these dreams.

He developed a taste for Asian women when his father took him on a trip to Thailand to celebrate his fourteenth birthday. It was a father-and-son trip; his mother was not invited. On this trip his father bought him a great gift, a night with a beautiful Thai woman; she was his first.

The next morning his father told him, "You are now a man; you have tasted a woman. Once a man gets the taste of a woman, he will crave it for the rest of his life." The Saudi craved women, especially Asian women, ever since.

His parents died in a plane accident over the Mediterranean. They had given the Saudi a good education; he could speak five languages including Thai. He had the IQ of a genius, and soon, he learned every aspect of the oil and construction business he had inherited. It took him only twelve years to become a multibillionaire, and now he was content.

With his money well invested, he now spent most of his time living with his secret harem, and with the woman, he believed he had fallen in love with. The electronic collar around Moon's neck was replaced by a band of gold on her left index finger. From the start, the first day he tasted her, the Saudi knew she was special.

29

DEATH CALLING

Following Bopha's coup, a few members of Bot's gang decided they didn't want Bopha to be their new leader. They left to form their own gang. These former members knew all about the Saudi's insatiable appetite for acquiring new women and decided they wanted his lucrative business. And they had a girl they thought the Saudi might be interested in.

They contacted Abdul and told him that Bopha was upset with the Saudi. She had killed Bot after finding out that Bot had sold a girl to the Saudi. They didn't know why Bopha was so angry over this, but she was. "It's not safe for you to come to Thailand right now. She might try to kill you if you return to Thailand. But you can continue to buy Asian girls from us in Myanmar. We have a girl we think your boss will like. We'll send you, her photos."

After receiving the photos, Abdul agreed to meet the renegade gang members in Myanmar, but it was an agreement he had no intention of keeping. This was the opportunity that Abdul had been waiting for. As soon as the call ended, Abdul immediately called Bopha's cell number. For the past year, he had been buying girls directly from her and not Bot; Moon had been the lone exception.

It didn't take long for Abdul and Bopha to make a deal. Abdul agreed to help her rescue Moon, for a price. Abdul also identified the former gang member who had called him. He gave Bopha the date, time, and place, where he agreed to meet with the renegade gang members.

These renegades were dead wrong in thinking that Bopha would allow them to live. Death was still the only acceptable way to leave the gang. And she would make sure death came calling for them.

There's nothing sweeter than seeing your enemy fall. Especially, when it was someone, you have hated from the very start. *Yes, she was beautiful, but so arrogant. And you my dear Bopha will soon fall*, he thought. Phat, called Pinky by fellow gang members, wanted people to know who he was, a Thai gangster. He wore spit-polished black leather shoes, with pointed toes, starched ironed white slacks, and pleated Hawaiian shirts. On each pinky finger, he wore gold rings with 1-karat solidarity diamonds, hence his nickname "Pinky." His glossy black hair was combed straight back and reached his shirt's collar.

Pinky was recruited off the streets of Bangkok. He was one of the original members of Bot's gang. With his temper in check, Pinky was resourceful and clever. However, Bot had to keep Pinky on a short leash, because of his wicked temper. Pinky had once beaten a man to death for accidentally spitting on one of his shoes. If left on his own Pinky would have ended up in a Thai prison, or dead. Bot saved Pinky from that fate, and Pinky knew it. Despite not being happy with the way Bot had been running the gang before his death, Pinky remained loyal to Bot.

He never liked Bopha. She was too pretty and too intelligent. He saw Bopha's steady rise in the gang's hierarchy from a lowly prostitute, obtained for the sole purpose of Aroon's pleasure, to take over his spot as the gang's second-in-command.

Pinky wasn't sure if Bot was blinded by Bopha's beauty, or the amount of money she was making for the gang. It could have been the combination of the two, but likely, Pinky thought, it was the money; something Bot had become excessively too fond of.

Pinky tried repeatedly to warn Bot that Bopha was dangerous, but his warning fell on deaf ears. When it finally appeared that Bot had taken his warning seriously, it was too late. Pinky wanted to avenge Bot's death, and he needed to kill Bopha to save his own life. While she was alive, he would never be safe.

On the night Bopha executed Bot, Pinky had just left for the Golden Triangle to buy opium and yaa baa. While in the Golden Triangle, he was contacted and warned by another gang member who had escaped Bopha's attempt to kill him. He said that Bopha was killing everyone she thought was disloyal to her, and Pinky was at the top of her hit list. Those who had escaped were forming their own gang. Pinky was invited to join them. Pinky said he would consider the invitation, but first, he had a debt that needed to be taken care of.

30
HUNGRY PIRANHAS

Bopha, JJ, Clyde, and Abdul came up with a plan to rescue Moon. They arranged to use one of Aroon's cargo ships, flying a Taiwanese flag. The ship would dock in Dubai, isolated from the other docked ships, during the holy month of the Hajj.

Hidden in one of the ship's special cargo containers would be a UH-1 Huey helicopter. In the middle of the night, the roof of the cargo container would be removed, and its sides folded down, then the Huey would be launched. The Huey was unmarked and painted black. It would contain an assault team consisting of six members: JJ, Clyde, two members of Bopha's gang, a pilot, and his gunner.

Aroon had arranged for the pilot, gunner, and chopper to be borrowed from the Royal Thailand's Army, through his brother Samak. With radar-jamming equipment, the Huey would fly in at a low altitude to avoid radar detection.

It would head southwest and travel two hundred and fifty miles to the Saudi compound, hidden in the middle of nowhere, in the vast Saudi Arabian desert. Five miles before reaching the compound, the Huey would land and refuel. Abdul had prepared a refueling site for the helicopter. He gave Bopha the GPS coordinates for the refueling site and the Saudi's compound.

Inside the walled compound were two buildings, a garage, two guard towers, and a helipad with a Bell 505 Jet Ranger helicopter sitting on its tarmac. The smaller of the two buildings housed the guards. Inside the garage were two four-wheel-drive Land Rovers. The larger building housed the Saudi's harem.

Once the Huey reached the compound, it would immediately launch rockets into the guards' shack, the guard towers, and the garage, destroying them. Then the rest of the compound's yard, including the Bell helicopter, would be sprayed by an M134 GAU-17 Vulcan Cannon. Its six barrels could deliver 6,000 rounds per minute. It was unlikely that any of the six compound's guards would survive this onslaught.

The Huey would then land next to the bullet-ridden Bell. The pilot and his gunner would stay with the helicopter, to protect it, just in case any of the guards had survived. The rest of the team would head for the larger building, where the Saudi's harem was located.

Abdul would be waiting for the attack. As soon as it started, he would disable all of the building's generators and batteries by remotely detonating the Semtex he planted next to them and unlocking the building's entrance door. Abdul had planted Semtex in the refrigerated room where the surveillance servers were kept. Abdul wanted to make sure there were no incriminating digital recordings of him torturing and killing the Saudi's Flowers.

After destroying the generators and batteries, all the electrical power in the building would go out. Abdul was instructed to wait for members of the assault team at the vault, to receive his promised reward. Secretly, Abdul had rigged the entire building with Semtex, which he planned to set off if doubled-crossed.

The team had diagrams of the building, provided by Abdul. After entering the building, the team would split up into two teams. One team would go after the Saudi and force him to open the vault; then kill him. JJ and Clyde would go after Moon.

Abdul had told them the vault contained diamonds worth over fifty million US dollars; it also contained external hard drives with incriminating video recordings of visiting dignitaries, ten million in gold bars, and a fortune in cash. He knew this because he had personally helped the Saudi place each of the items into the vault, but only the Saudi knew its combination. In addition, the Saudi's private room was filled with stolen artwork and antiquities worth a fortune.

For his help, Abdul had been promised three hundred diamonds, forty boxes of one-hundred-gram bars of gold, and a suitcase filled with currency. Each diamond was worth approximately $20,000, and the box contained twenty-five one-hundred-gram bars worth over $90,000. His reward would amount to over $10,000,000 U.S. dollars.

Abdul had hidden one of the Land Rovers outside the walls of the compound to prevent it from being destroyed during the attack. When the attack was finished, Abdul would leave for Omen in the Land Rover, as a wealthy man. He felt no regret for betraying the Saudi; he deserved what was coming to him.

JJ's and Clyde's sole mission was to rescue Moon. The promise of diamonds, gold, currency, and artwork perked Aroon's interest and got him and his brother's help. Bopha had promised Aroon half of everything.

Aroon was told of Abdul's willingness to betray the Saudi and the chance for them to make millions. Bopha told him she also wanted to rescue a Thai girl who had recently been sold to the Saudi. Bot had sold the girl to the Saudi against her wishes. Bopha had special plans for this girl. She didn't tell Aroon what those plans were, and he didn't care to ask. She didn't even tell Aroon the girl's name. Aroon wasn't interested in the girl, not at all. He was only interested in acquiring the Saudi's valuables.

After Moon's rescue, an anonymous message would be sent to the Saudi Arabian authorities, giving them the GPS coordinates of the Saudi's compound. They would be instructed to rescue the remaining Flowers, who were to be treated well and to be monetarily compensated before being released to a country of their choice. If not, X-rated videos of dignitaries, which included members of the House of Saud, and a certain prince, enjoying the Saudi's wilted flowers would be released for the world to see. It would be an embarrassment the Saudi authorities would not want, especially during the holy period of Hajj.

Murphy, as in Murphy's Law, loves to throw monkey wrenches into plans, even good ones. Any planner worth his salt expects this and adapts when the unexpected happens. The assault on the Saudi's compound started as planned.

All but one of the guards were killed within the first thirty seconds of the attack. The lone survivor came down from his tower just before the attack. He decided to take a cigarette break under one of the palm trees growing next to the compound's koi fishpond. The guards added ice to the pond to keep it cool on hot days.

The guard was taking drags off his cigarette when he heard the thumping sound of a helicopter, then bullets and explosions erupted all around him. The smell of smoke hung in the air. The guard saved himself by diving behind a tree. He remained unnoticed as he watched the copter land. Four men exited the copter and headed straight for the main building's entrance door. Not knowing what to do, the guard decided to wait and see what would come next.

Abdul took out the generators as promised, and the team entered the building through the unlocked entrance door. The team came ready for a midnight entry, wearing night-vision goggles. They were dressed in tactical gear and armed with MP5 assault rifles with sound suppressors.

In addition, they carried explosives to open safes and any locked door they encountered.

Soon after entering the building, the team saw what looked like ghosts wandering the hallway. Beautiful ghosts in glowing nightgowns. The ghosts turned out to be Flowers. When the electricity went out, the Flowers were set free. The locks on their doors were controlled magnetically and opened when the electricity went off.

Moon had been expecting the attack. Just before it occurred, Abdul came and told her about the rescue plan. She wanted to spit in his face but refrained from doing so. She wondered why he betrayed his master, but she didn't ask. Abdul instructed her to stay put in her room; her friends would be coming for her. When he left, she pulled out a hidden seven-inch stiletto knife she had stolen from the Saudi's room.

Stealing and concealing a knife had been risky. The Saudi had a large collection of knives in his room, and Moon hoped he wouldn't miss this one. The Flower's rooms were constantly searched for weapons. However, the Saudi had become careless when he came to her.

When the door of her room unlocked, she took the knife and immediately exited, disobeying Abdul's instructions to stay put. She was on a mission. She needed to get to the Saudi before anyone else did. The Saudi was hers and hers alone.

Moon easily made her way to the Saudi's room; it was only a short distance away. She didn't need any light. She had been there often enough and could find it even in the dark. However, she was added by the skylights that allowed moon light to filter into the hallway. As she reached his room, she saw a shape emerging from it. It was the Saudi.

She called out to him, "Sweetheart please wait for me. I'm scared." As he turned around to face her, she buried the stiletto, nearly all seven inches of its cold steel, into the side of his chubby neck, just behind the clavicle. He howled in pain and disbelief and dropped the gun he was holding in his right hand.

After she pulled the knife out, the Saudi gave her a bewildered look. He placed a hand over his bleeding neck, finding it hard to believe he had been stabbed in the neck by the woman he loved. He asked her, "Why?" Just a few days ago he learned she was carrying his child; the son he had hoped for.

Moon didn't bother answering his question. She stabbed him again, this time just below his sternum, pushing the blade upward, piercing his heart. The Saudi fell to the ground, dead. As Moon stood over him, she reached down and grabbed and ripped the gold chain from his neck. She then kicked his corpse, before picking up his fallen gun.

She will keep the Saudi's gold chain and the wedding band. They will serve as reminders that she'll never allow anyone to sexually abuse her again. She would rather die first. She hoped to see Abdul again to place a bullet into his evil heart.

Abdul was making his way to the vault when he was hit on the head by hard object and fell to the ground. The little black box he had been carrying rolled out of his hand and clattered to the floor. With his head bleeding, Abdul looked up and saw a Flower. She had hit him with a metal object that she still held in her hand. Before he could stop her, the Flower picked up the fallen black box and pushed the silver-colored toggle switch to the "on" position. Only four ounces of downward pressure on the boxes' red button was needed to detonate the Semtex and send the whole building crashing down upon them. Abdul got up on his knees, holding his hands out in front of him, "Don't push that button. If you do, you'll kill all of us, including yourself."

"Why do I care? Death is preferable to living like this."

Just before she pushed the button, she heard a voice from behind her. A female voice. "You don't have to die here. We are being rescued. The Rayiysay is dead, and the one in front of you will soon be dead."

Pointing the gun at Abdul's chest, Moon pulled the trigger. Abdul fell to the floor, face down. However, he was not dead. The bullet missed his heart, but not his spinal cord; Abdul lay paralyzed and unable to move.

A group of wandering Flowers rounded the corner to see Abdul lying on the floor. They fell upon him, punching, clubbing, clawing, and biting off bits of Abul's flesh. It's as if Abdul had fallen into a lake of hungry piranha. Before dying, he felt fingernails digging into his eyes ripping out of their sockets. Pieces of his nose, ears, and fingers were bitten off. His death screams could be heard throughout the building. Abdul will get neither diamonds nor gold for his betrayal, only a painful death; a death like the ones he had given to so many others. The Flower handed the black box to Moon, who turned the toggle switch back to the "off" position.

The Saudi could no longer be used to open the vault. The team found him dead, lying in a pool of blood. He had been stabbed twice, once on the side of his neck and again in the chest. On their way to the vault, they found Abdul; the team had heard his screams. He was missing chunks of flesh and both his eyes. And like the Saudi, he too lay dead in a pool of blood.

After removing the valuable artwork and artifacts from the Saudi's room, including a painting entitled "*Poppy Flowers*," by Vincent van Gogh, stolen years before from Cairo's Mohamed Mahmood Khalil Museum, the team proceeded to the vault with caution.

They gained entrance to the Saudi's vault using the explosives they carried. It was opened with minimal damage to its contents. Within minutes, all of the vault's contents were bagged and placed onto a cart. They no longer needed to provide Abdul with his share. They then made their way back to the helicopter.

JJ and Clyde found Moon right where Abul told them they would find her. Moon went back to her cell room after shooting Abdul. Moon told JJ, "I'm not leaving until I know that all the women in here are going to be safe." There was enough water and food stored in the building to last them a year. However, Moon was worried about the daytime heat since there was no electricity to power the air conditioners. Fortunately, the building was well insulated, and they would be okay for a couple of days even with the cooling system off. After assuring Moon that the remaining women would be okay, they headed back to the helicopter.

The lone surviving guard should have stayed hidden behind the tree, but he decided to move in closer. He was angry with himself for leaving his AK-47 up in the tower when he came down for his cigarette break. His only weapon was a hand grenade attached to his belt. He crept closer to the helicopter. *Just a little closer, that's all I need.*

No one saw him; they were too busy loading the chopper. When he felt close enough, he pulled the grenade off his belt and pulled its pin. Just as the guard threw back his arm to toss the grenade, JJ caught sight of the movement through the corner of his eye. He swung his MP5 around and with deadly accuracy, fired a burst of three rounds, killing the guard. The grenade fell well short of its target before exploding. The explosion sent dust and sharp metal shrapnel in all directions. Just before the explosion, JJ pushed Moon to the ground, covering her body with his. Shrapnel hit the back of his flak jacket. JJ was lucky; none of it hit his unprotected areas. A few pieces hit the helicopter but did little damage.

Moon had mixed emotions about her rescue. She had been ready to activate her escape plan. The Saudi had given her way too many liberties, liberties he had not given to the other Flowers. Her escape plan included killing the Saudi and Abdul. On the one hand, she was grateful for not having to spend another moment as the Saudi's fake wife. On the other hand, she would never know whether or not her own escape plan would have succeeded.

Defeating the Saudi on her terms would have greatly decreased the humiliation and self-loathing she felt for the things she had done; the things she had been willing to do, to convince the Saudi she loved and cared for him. She had been very convincing. The thought sickened her, *never again.*

But Moon wasn't completely void of satisfaction. A warm feeling of satisfaction came from remembering the bewildering look the Saudi gave her after stabbing his chubby neck, and the way Abdul died. Her biggest concern now was getting rid of the parasite the Saudi had planted inside her womb. She would ask for her big sister's help; she didn't want anyone else to know that she was pregnant.

As soon as Moon disembarked from the ship, Kat and Joy ran up to her, wrapping their arms around her, and cried unabashedly. Moon didn't want to talk about the Saudi, or her time spent in his captivity. When they got home, she asked to be left alone in her small bedroom. "Maybe when I'm feeling better, when I'm up to it, I can talk to you about what happened. But not now."

She had missed her small room and was happy to have her old life back. Her nightmare was finally over. Joy's three-legged dog joined Moon, on her bed, as she turned off the lights. He rolled over on his back, and Moon rewarded him with a good belly scratch before falling asleep.

Kat and Joy immediately noticed the change in Moon. She was a different person. Regardless, they were happy to have her home again. They wouldn't press her to find out what happened to her. They knew it was terrible.

Joy too had suffered from sexual abuse, and so had Kat to a lesser extent. It was one of the downsides of being a working girl; if you were willing to go to bed with strangers for money, soon-or-later bad things happened. If Moon ever wanted to talk to them about her experience, they would wait until she was ready. Moon had planned never to talk to anyone about the Saudi, except to one person, her big sister. However, she wouldn't tell Bopha everything.

Upon their return to Bangkok, the Saudi's diamonds, videos, money, artwork & artifacts, and gold were taken directly to Bopha. Afterward, Aroon's share was delivered to him. Without Aroon's help, she would not have been able to rescue Moon, and for that, she was grateful. She did not cheat Aroon out of any of his share, with two exceptions. Her lone exceptions were the incriminating camera coverage of the Saudi's visiting dignitaries and his little black book that recorded the names of the people he bought his Flowers from. These she would keep and make good use of.

Van Gogh's painting, *Poppy Flowers*, is now hung in Aroon's private office. She lied when she told him she was giving him the painting for being such a great lover, and he foolishly believed it. Bopha had given him the painting as a reward for his help in rescuing her little sister, and besides that, she didn't want a stolen piece of art, of such notoriety, in her possession. One day, the authorities might get an anonymous tip where they could recover *Poppy Flowers*.

Aroon was ecstatic with the mission's success; it had made the Network a lot of money. The stolen painting, *Poppy Flowers*, alone had an estimated value of over fifty million U.S. dollars, that is, if it could have been sold on the open market which it couldn't. He invited Bopha to his penthouse to celebrate and to spend the night with him.

Bopha had wanted to spend that night with JJ, but grudgingly, she accepted Aroon's invitation. She didn't want him to become suspicious as to why she turned down his offer on such a happy occasion. Before going to Aroon's suite, she had to first see Moon. Moon agreed to meet Bopha at their favorite meeting spot, the Bangkok Coffee Café.

Moon had been the Saudi's captive for only four months, but she was no longer the happy-go-lucky teenager that Bopha remembered. Moon was now even more like her, not just in her looks but in her psyche. Moon had metamorphosed into something much darker than her older self. Regardless, Bopha was happy to have her little sister back.

When it came time to leave, Bopha said goodbye to her adopted little sister, hugged her tight against her chest and kissed both her cheeks. They departed with tears in their eyes. They would meet again in the following days. Moon told Bopha, and only Bopha, that she was carrying the Saudi's child. Bopha discreetly arranged to have it aborted before anyone noticed that Moon was pregnant.

Moon had missed her school graduation. Before her disappearance, she had been at the top of her class. With the help of Bopha's new political connections, she got Moon her upper secondary school diploma, with honors, and a full scholarship to attend Chulalongkorn University.

Since taking over Bot's gang, Bopha made several substantial political connections. Connections that were hidden from Aroon and his two younger brothers. From the information she obtained from Aroon's computer, she knew whom she could bribe. Being able to help Moon was one of the benefits of her new connections. *"However difficult life may seem, there is always something you can do."*

31

VOLCANIC HOT

Upon his return to Bangkok, Pinky kept a low profile. He avoided areas where he might run into any of Bopha's gang. One of the first things Pinky obtained was a Chinese-made Dragunov sniper rifle and a box of 7.62x54mm rounds. The Chinese-made Dragunov was a far cry from being the world's best sniper rifle. However, Pinky thought, *it will be good enough*. He would use this rifle to kill Bopha. Pinky was a decent shot, but he was no sniper. He would need to get within one hundred and fifty meters of his target to ensure a fatal hit. He went into the countryside to practice and to sight his rifle.

Before the coup, Bopha had started to invest the gangs' money into legitimate businesses; one of the methods she used to launder the gang's money. She had purchased a high-end boutique clothing store in downtown Bangkok that she was particularly fond of. He would stake it out; he needed to get her routine down before making his hit.

Pinky knew if he surveyed the store long enough, sooner than later Bopha would show up, and sure enough, she did. Pinky spotted her red Mercedes approaching the store. It appeared she had recently taken the car to a body shop to repair all the dents and dings from minor accidents. Bopha parked her car at the back of the store. A short time later,

Bopha exited the front of the store and hailed a taxi. He wondered, *what is she up to?*

He followed the taxi in his rental car. The taxi stopped in front of Dizzy, and Bopha got out and walked in. It was early morning, and nothing was going on at the bar. He was curious why she was there, at this time of the day. *Why hadn't she driven her car to the bar?*

Pinky had heard from other gang members that she was interested in purchasing the bar and had approached the owner to buy it. Maybe she had purchased the bar and was keeping it a secret. It would be the perfect place to launder the gang's money. He wouldn't put it past Bopha to keep that information secret from the rest of the gang. Maybe, she feared her gang would expect freebies from the dancers if they knew the bar belonged to Bopha, which in all likelihood they would.

Bopha was secretive, and it was hard to determine her motive. Pinky had no clue she was there to meet her lover. She had shown no interest in romance. She used her body as a tool; both Bot and Aroon were just too stupid to see it. He thought *it was just a matter of time before Aroon became another one of her victims. That is if I don't kill her first; a favor I doubt Aroon will appreciate.*

This could be the chance he had been waiting for. There was a hotel just across the street from Dizzy. Pinky quickly walked into the hotel and rented a room, on the third floor, with a view of Dizzy's front door.

Once Pinky was in the room, he took the Dragunov out of its case and reassembled it. He cracked open the window facing Dizzy's front entrance and then set up a platform to rest his rifle on. He was approximately ninety meters from Dizzy's front door. At this distance, he wouldn't miss. He only needed to wait until Bopha came out, hoping it would be sooner than later. It was a hot day, but he had to open the window, not wanting to shoot through glass, allowing the outside heat to enter the room.

Just before Pinky walked into the hotel, Cowboy was coming to work. He saw Pinky entering the hotel just across the street from Dizzy. He knew Pinky. Pinky had been part of Bot's old gang but disappeared immediately after Bopha's takeover. He knew that Pinky and Bopha were now mortal enemies. Cowboy waited several minutes outside before following Pinky into the hotel. He wanted to find out what Pinky was up to.

It was common for Dizzy's customers to rent rooms at this hotel and bring their ladies after paying their bar fines. Kat had arranged with the hotel's owner to give Dizzy's patrons discounts. In return, the dancers would recommend the hotel to their customers.

Cowboy knew the hotel's owner, who was at the front desk talking to the hotel's desk agent. The owner was a regular customer at Dizzy. The owner told Cowboy that the person he had described to him had just checked in, using the name Plaek Pibum. "He requested a room facing Dizzy on the third floor. He's in Room #315." He tipped his hat to the owner, thanking him, and left.

Cowboy interrupted JJ and Bopha, while they were conversing. Cowboy told JJ that he saw Pinky, a senior member of Bot's old gang, enter the hotel across the street. He shook his head while explaining, "He's obtained a room, under an assumed name, facing Dizzy's front entrance, on the third floor. His only luggage was a small case."

JJ exited Dizzy out the back door. He followed Dizzy's pathway until he found a walking space between two buildings. After returning to the street in front of Dizzy and the hotel, he took out a pair of binoculars. He surveyed the windows on the hotel's third floor until he found one that was about a third of the way open. No one would intentionally open a window in this heat. He saw a man hidden in the room's shadows. He wouldn't have spotted him if he had not been looking for him. The man had a rifle trained on the front door of Dizzy.

JJ returned to the bar and advised everyone what he had seen. Bopha told JJ that she would handle Pinky. JJ wasn't comfortable with Bopha's decision. Before leaving the bar, Bopha made a phone call and then left. She used the same narrow walkway that JJ had used. She entered the hotel unobserved by Pinky. She went to the back of the hotel's bar, where she waited for her gang members to arrive. Like always, she was carrying her Sig.

In the meantime, just after Bopha left, JJ went to Dizzy's rooftop, where he hid behind an air-conditioning vent. He had brought with him his M40, a Marine Corps Vietnam-era sniper's rifle. It was a rifle he had disassembled in the U.S. and hid its parts in various packages; the packages were mailed to him by a friend.

He had held an M40 in his arms longer than any woman in his life. He even thought of his rifle as being a lady and treated her like one. He looked through the M40's scoop at the man waiting to kill Bopha. *I can't stand the thought of someone trying to kill her.* He decided he couldn't risk losing her.

Before taking aim, he took a deep relaxing breath, slowing his heartbeat. With the rifle's strap tightened around his right upper arm with her butt up tight against his shoulder, he placed the scope's crosshairs on his target. He then gently squeezed the rifle's trigger until a round went off, seemingly of its own volition. The bullet flew true to its target. It was an easy shot for a former Marine sniper. Every Marine, from a private up to the Commandant, is a rifleman, and Marines are the best overall riflemen in the world.

Bopha heard the shot and thought maybe Pinky wasn't there to kill her after all. She wondered whom Pinky had shot. It didn't even enter her mind that JJ had taken the shot. No one else seemed to have taken notice of the gunshot; it sounded like a car's, or motorbike's backfire, an everyday occurrence on the streets of Bangkok.

When the members of Bopha's gang arrived, they went to Room #315. They silently picked the lock on the door of Pinky's room and entered. Their guns were equipped with sound suppressors. They found Pinky shot in the head, but who shot him? No one from her gang had killed him.

Because Cowboy had questioned the hotel's owner about Pinky, Bopha had Pinky's body secretly removed, and the room thoroughly cleaned. The glass in the window was replaced. None of the hotel staff would be the wiser that someone had been killed in the room.

~

The next morning, Bopha returned to Dizzy. She found JJ sitting on his balcony, drinking iced tea. She asked JJ if he knew what had happened to Pinky. Like he often did, he placed his hands on top of hers and lightly squeezed them.

In a soft voice, barely above a whisper, he replied, "I took him out."

With anger in her voice, and anger in her eyes, Bopha asked, "You did what? Why? I told you that I would take care of him. I don't want your hands dirtied in my business!"

"I couldn't stand the thought of someone trying to kill you, and I couldn't stand the thought of losing you." Bopha could see the emotions stirring in JJ's face when he said, "As if you don't already know... I love you." It was the first time he had said those words to her. It was the first time he had uttered those three words to any woman, since Beth.

Bopha hesitated and then found herself saying, "And I love you," and she knew it to be true. She couldn't imagine living her life without him in it. He had become her anchor in the crazy world she now lived in.

A feeling of happiness came over Bopha that she hadn't felt since before her abduction and the death of her parents. They got up from their chairs, JJ embraced her, and they kissed. She never felt so good. On that day, a small portion of Bopha's mind, which had been so completely shattered by Khen, became mended.

A particular type of love had developed between JJ and Bopha. It was not a mature love, the love that came after living with the same person over an extended period of time. It was more like young love that is volcanic hot. The type of love that will burn inside you until the last days of your life.

3 2

UNCLE KHEN

Word reached Khen that Bot had been killed. Bopha had thoroughly surprised him. Not even in his wildest dream could he envision Bopha killing Bot and taking over his gang. *She truly is exceptional!* He knew it was only a matter of time before she came after him to get revenge for her parent's deaths. He would need to be careful, but Phnom Penh was his territory. She would have to come to his playground, that is if she wanted him. *I should have fucked and killed her when I had the chance. I should have never sold her,* Khen thought.

Bopha had been secretly keeping track of Khen, even while Bot was still alive. Khen had been Bot's main supplier of Cambodian women. That beautiful girl who Khen had kidnapped so long ago was now in a position to dry up Khen's market in Thailand. But she continued their trade.

Bohpa was hoping Khen would think everything was okay. In addition, trade with Khen had been very profitable and certain members of her gang, whom she would deal with later, would be upset if she abruptly ended it. Very soon, she planned to do just that. She would end her gang's involvement in human trafficking and punish those involved in it; she was willing to do anything to fulfill her new dream.

Khen thought it was strange that Bopha's gang had remained to be one of his main customers. He figured Bopha would have immediately stopped her gang from buying his product. He was happily surprised when she didn't.

Of course, he had other customers. His product was always in demand, such as the old gentleman in Phnom Penh, who needed his steady supply of virgins. The old gentleman believed virgins were his fountain of youth, and he needed to fuck one every week to keep his vitality up. Khen was more than happy to assist the old gentleman in maintaining his youth.

Yet, Khen didn't want to lose his main Thailand buyer of Cambodian women. The constant stream of girls he had been selling to Bot, allowed him to live in a way he had grown accustomed to. Bopha's takeover, so far, had not placed a dent into that lifestyle. *Maybe she is more interested in making money than revenge. At least I hope so.* What Khen didn't know was that all the girls he had recently sold to Bopha's gang would be released - unmolested.

However, Khen wasn't going to take any chances. He had several layers of defense. His first layer was the street rats; parentless kids, he hired to help him in the Hunt. There were hundreds of them. In Phnom Penh, they were his eyes and ears. He would tell them to keep an eye out for an attractive woman asking questions about him. If someone asked questions about him, the street orphans would let him know.

His second layer was the corrupt police and politicians of the city. He had paid them a small fortune in bribes over the years, while he conducted human trafficking under their noses. He had made a number of them quite wealthy. They would arrest and kill anyone trying to remove his deep pockets. If Bopha was spotted in Phnom Penh, she would be in for a nasty surprise.

His third and most important layer of defense was - himself. He knew he was ultimately responsible for his protection since he didn't have a gang or belonged to one. He didn't believe in bodyguards. They were expensive, and he didn't trust them. No one could look after him the way he could. He always had a contingency plan and was keenly aware of his surroundings. He was good at counter-surveillance; it was as if he had a second pair of eyes on the back of his head. *It will be difficult for Bopha to sneak up on me.*

$$\sim$$

Bopha returned to Phnom Penh, wearing no makeup, trying to look as plain as possible, wearing a wig and sunglasses. She tried her best not to bring attention to herself or the people she brought with her. This was her first return to Phnom Penh since Khen had abducted her, and she wanted to visit her old home where she had lived with her parents, but she didn't. Khen could have someone watching the house, waiting for her to make such a mistake. Instead, she went to the building where Khen had killed her parents. They had finished restoring the building years ago.

She looked at it from across the street. However, she didn't go in. As if it were yesterday, she could see Khen smiling at her just before he shot her parents in the forehead. She could still feel Khen's tongue licking the side of her face after whispering in her ear, "Don't ever try to run away from Uncle Khen again." She stood across the street staring at the building, rekindling all the hatred she felt for Khen. Justice was slow to come, but like a bull pawing the earth, it was coming.

Khen had done well for himself. Trafficking young women was very profitable. He owned a large house in one of the more fashionable parts of Phnom Penh. A twelve-foot cinderblock wall, topped with rod iron spikes, surrounded its yard. The driveway had a large metal security gate. Surveillance cameras had been placed in strategic locations throughout the property. His house and yard were protected by a sophisticated alarm system, hidden cameras, and hostile dogs. It would not be easy for an intruder to sneak inside Khen's fortress undetected.

Bopha had no desire to sneak inside Khen's fortress. She knew Khen's routine inside and out, and there was no need to ask any questions about him. One of her associates had arranged to purchase a girl from Khen.

The girl was a sixteen-year-old secondary school student that Khen had just recently abducted. She was pretty and Khen was expecting a handsome profit from selling her. Khen arranged a meeting at a small house outside the city that he often used to sell his girls. He had made the mistake of becoming complacent and predictable, fatal mistakes.

As usual, Khen arrived at the house an hour early. He wanted to check out the house before anyone else arrived. Nothing was out of place. The girl was scared shitless and would do whatever she was told to do; he knew all the right buttons to push. Khen took her to a windowless room and told the girl, "Sit down, and keep quiet," pointing to a rattan chair. "You don't want to make Uncle Khen mad at you. Do you?" She didn't answer. She just stared back at him with terror on her face. Feeling stratified and smiling, he left the room locking the door.

The house had a long dirt road leading to it. When he saw a cloud of dust, he knew a car was approaching. He had a contingency plan if he didn't like what he saw coming out of the car. In the back of the house was a narrow path, too narrow for a car to use but a motorbike had no problem traveling down it. Khen parked a motorbike next to the trail just in case there was a need for a quick exit. Nevertheless, he wasn't expecting any trouble today. He had done business with this buyer many times before.

He took the motorbike out of the house, and onto the path. Before hiding the bike behind a large bush, he wanted to make sure it would start. Its engine started on the very first kick. Satisfied, he turned the engine off and walked back to the house. He sat in the house's living room, looking out its front window, with a fan blowing on him, smoking an American Marlboro and drinking a bottle of Coke-a-Cola, waiting for the girl's buyer to show up. After an hour of waiting, he spotted in the distance a small cloud of dust kicked up from an approaching car.

Bopha knew about the house Khen had chosen to meet her associate. It was a house he often used. She and several members of her gang arrived at the house before Khen. They came on motorbikes, now hidden from view. They watched Khen take a motorbike out of the house, and test-start it. After Khen returned to the house, the sparkplug wires on Khen's motorbike were pulled.

Only three people were expected to attend this meeting: Khen, the girl, and the buyer. When Khen saw four men getting out of the car, he knew something was wrong. He ran out the back door for his motorbike. He tried several times to kickstart it, but the engine wouldn't turn over. Khen was so intent on getting the motorbike started that he didn't see the man who came up from behind. The man tased Khen, stunning him. Khen and his motorbike fell to the ground.

He was quickly handcuffed, his hands behind his back, and leg irons placed on his ankles. After taking his gun away, he was rolled onto his back. Bopha stood over him, looking down at him. She had one of her men sit on Khen's chest, then watched her other men take turns pissing on Khen's face.

Bopha instructed one of her men, "Go get the girl from the house." She told the girl to squat down just inches above Khen's face and to pull down her panties; "Sweetie, I want you to piss on his face." The girl did as she was told. Bopha then told Khen, "That is the last pussy you will ever see. Before I am finished with you, you'll wish you were never born."

They drove the sixteen-year-old girl to her parent's house and released her. Her parents were given a cover story, to tell the police. They would say their daughter had run away with her boyfriend, and after a few days, she decided to return. The parents did as they were told, grateful to have their daughter back. The police never questioned the story.

Khen was tortured until he revealed to them where he had buried Bopha's parents. Bopha had the site checked before she finished torturing Khen; she wanted to make sure he was telling her the truth. He did not lie.

Afterward, Khen was necklaced with a strip of rubber taken from the front tire of his motorbike. The strip of rubber, soaked in gasoline, was wrapped around his neck. Then baling wire was wrapped around the rubber to keep it in place.

Khen was duct-taped to a post, standing up, with his forehead taped tight up against the post. Bopha took out a box of wooden matches. After striking a match, she watched the look on Khen's battered face. She wasn't sure if it was a look of horror or relief. Just before lighting the rubber, she licked the side of his face, and whispered in his ear, "Uncle Khen, you have no idea how much I'm going to enjoy this." She then lit the rubber.

Closing her eyes slowly, she listened to Khen's screams. It was music to her ears. She would dream of his dying screams for many years to come. The memories of his screams were an evil pleasure she felt that one day she might pay for, if not in her present life, then perhaps the next.

At the site where Khen had buried her parents, she found two deteriorated bodies wrapped in plastic sheets. Although the bodies were badly decomposed, she instantly knew who they were. They were wearing remnants of the clothing they were killed in. She noticed the ring fingers on both her parents' hands were missing. Khen must have cut them off to remove their wedding bands.

Bopha's parents' remains were cremated, and their ashes were scattered in the famous Royal Park Rajapruek Garden. As a girl, she had visited the garden often with her parents; it was one of their favorite places.

She lit joss sticks and prayed her parents would be reborn into a better life; they were good people. She hoped the Buddha would reward her for killing Khen, such an evil man, and hopefully overlook how she killed him.

She needed to do only one more thing before leaving Phnom Penh. There was someone she needed to visit. While he was being tortured, Khen had told her all about the old gentleman and the way he kept his vitality.

Bopha picked up a rod of rebar and held it in her hand. Looking at it, she had a brief flashback. She remembered the way Bot enjoyed ramming his cock into her ass. Then Bopha's frown was replaced with a smile; *I'm going to relish sticking this piece of iron up the old gentleman's virgin asshole.*

After finishing her visit with the old gentleman, it was time to go home. It was time to see JJ. She had come to see her visits with JJ as rewards for accomplishing a job done well. Regretfully, this would be her last visit with JJ, until she could deal with Aroon. She needed to kill Aroon before he found out about her true love.

3 3

PAY ATTENTION

Clyde was finding it harder and harder to suppress his romantic desire for Kat. He admired the way she managed the bar and its dancers, and she was so...so damn attractive. If it were possible for him to be content with just one woman, he believed that woman would be Kat.

He could not help seeing the looks Kat gave JJ; they were looks of longing. He wondered how JJ didn't seem to notice. *Is he blind?* But, of course, he was. JJ was blind as a bat to all women except Bopha. He felt sorry for Kat. As long as Bopha was in JJ's life, Kat didn't stand a chance. He hadn't said anything to JJ about Kat because he knew it would embarrass her if she found out.

He had become close friends with Kat. At first, Kat had the same biases most Thais had regarding Black Americans: biases based on ignorance. Once they got to know each other, her biases disappeared.

After work, he and Kat often went out for a meal together. At their favorite restaurant, they often ate Yam nunsen kun, a spicy salad with glass noodles and prawns. On their days off, they would go to Muay Thai matches with Cowboy, which featured his students. They found that they enjoyed each other's company.

Kat had no problem conversing with Clyde in English. Yet, Clyde wanted to talk to Kat in Thai. At least twice a week, she invited Clyde to the house she shared with Joy and their three-legged dog. They went to Kat's bedroom, where she gave him private Thai language lessons. There were times when he found it difficult to concentrate. During one of these times, Kat asked, "Clyde, are you paying attention to what I'm saying?"

All he could think about was how much he wanted to make love to Kat on her bed. He replied, "It's the best I can do under these circumstances. I'm sorry. I'll try harder."

Kat suspected why he was distracted but pretended she was clueless. She gave him a sturdy look and shook her head, "Please do."

Recently, Clyde noticed a change in his behavior. He no longer wanted every pretty woman that came his way. His womanizing had come to an abrupt halt. He could not get Kat out of his head. She was the one he wanted, and no one else would do.

Clyde wanted to tell Kat how he felt about her but was afraid to. He feared it would ruin their friendship if she didn't feel the same way. Nevertheless, he knew he would need to tell her. If she rejected him, he would go back home to the States. He wouldn't be able to stand working so close to a woman he desired so much if she didn't share the same feelings for him.

Kat realized her infatuation with JJ wasn't healthy. She could see he was totally in love with Bopha, and she could do nothing about it. Maybe, if she had expressed herself to JJ before Bopha came into his life, things could have been different. But that's water under the bridge. She was beginning to doubt she would ever find her Mr. Right. She thought, *maybe I'm being punished for misdeeds committed in a previous life, my karma.*

Recently, she found herself attracted to another man. He's a man a few months ago she would have never considered as her "Mr. Right." He had a problem, though; he seemed unable to keep his dick in his pants. She didn't want a relationship with a man who went from one woman to another. She didn't want to fully give herself to a man who was not fully committed to her.

Lately, she had noticed a change in his behavior. He was no longer acting like a butterfly, going from flower to flower. She could tell he was attracted to her. Kat decided to give him a chance, but until she could be absolutely sure he was her Mr. Right, he would need to wear a hat. It's been a long time since she's had sex, and she's found herself longing for it.

≈

Cowboy was troubled about the relationship between the boss and Bopha. They tried to hide their ever-growing romantic relationship but couldn't from the people who knew them. Bopha was bad news. She seemed every bit as bad as Bot and a lot smarter. She took over Bot's drug and human trafficking operations without missing a beat. Maybe JJ was hoping to change Bopha, or he just accepted her faults. Cowboy thought *it's strange how love or lust can twist a person's morality.*

Before working at Dizzy, Cowboy had no family. Now he felt that JJ, Clyde, and Kat were more than just his friends and coworkers. He also had a special relationship with Dizzy's go-go dancers. He felt as if he was their guardian angel. At Dizzy, he no longer felt like an orphan. It was a place where he had a family, a home, a place where he belonged.

≈

Bopha was concerned for JJ's safety. There was little doubt, about what would happen if Aroon found out about their affair; Aroon would order JJ killed. She wasn't ready to go to war with Aroon. There was also the problem with Aroon's brothers; if she went after Aroon, she would need to deal with them as well. She had secretly gained access to several of Aroon's hidden bank accounts and other assets, worth over two billion U.S. dollars. She would rock Aroon's world, just not yet.

She didn't want to take any chances with JJ's safety. In her mind, her affair with Aroon was not cheating. She didn't love Aroon. In fact, she had come to despise him. Copulating with Aroon was just a means to an end and nothing else. JJ was her true love. She wondered if JJ would be sympathetic to this fact. She doubted that and was afraid to tell him. She feared she might lose his love if he ever found out. Until she can figure out what to do, she'll play it safe and stop seeing him.

JJ didn't know why Bopha had stopped coming to Dizzy. He felt an emptiness that he had never felt in his life. Even when Beth left him, he didn't feel like this. He saw that coming, but not this. He tried calling Bopha, but she wouldn't answer his calls. *What would a woman like Bopha see in me anyway? Maybe like Beth, Bopha has grown tired of me and has found someone else.* Like water leaking through the cracks in a dam, threatening to burst it, some of his old insecurities came seeping back.

Then as suddenly as these insecurities came, they vanished - as if washed away by a tsunami. Deep in his heart, he knew that Bopha loved him and no one else. *There's no doubt about it. She must have a good reason for avoiding me, but what? I need to find out!*

Moon had learned that it was Bopha who had orchestrated her escape, after taking over Bot's gang. She was startled when she found out that her big sister was now the leader of a gang involved in human trafficking. Human sex trafficking was the very thing that Moon detested more than anything else.

Moon had learned that her big sister was a victim of human trafficking. She had been sold for the purpose of becoming the mistress of a major

174

crime lord, a man named Aroon. She was still acting as Aroon's mistress. At first, she could not understand how Bopha could be involved in human trafficking. Now she did.

Bopha had revealed her plans to her; her trust in her big sister was complete. Like the time when Moon was one of the Saudi's Flowers, she did things that turned her stomach. Bopha had done and would continue to do things she hated, but that would soon change. For now, her big sister wanted her to continue her education to become an attorney, and she will. Moon was still an ambitious young woman, and like her big sister she would never give up on her dream.

Unbeknown to all but Moon and herself, Bopha had plans for the future. She will have the full support of her intelligent little sister. Bopha will be required to do ugly things in her fight against human sex trafficking. At times she wondered, *do the ends justify the means?* She concluded it did.

What Bopha failed to understand was that when you violate a core value – a part of your soul dies. She knew killing was wrong. But Bopha was willing to do anything and pay any price to stop sex trafficking, including risking her life and those she loved. It was a dream she was willing to live for or die for.

She felt that the people she had killed and would kill so richly deserved it. In that way, she had become like the person she despised more than anyone else in the world, Khen. Like Khen, there were times when killing brought her unbelievable joy.

Psychopaths are born psychopaths. Sociopaths are made. What they had in common was a lack of empathy. They were like vampires, creatures with no souls. Some may wonder if Bopha is a sociopath. She has no empathy for the proprietors and patrons of sex trafficking, but she has unending compassion for its victims.

Bopha's cell phone was ringing. It was JJ. She had been ignoring his calls. She didn't know what to tell him, but this time she had the courage to answer his call. They needed to talk. She needed to tell him the truth, regardless of the consequences.

34

THE FORSAKEN SON

Aroon was not the brightest or the most ruthless of the three brothers, just the oldest and most ambitious. The most ruthless was Chuen and Samak the brightest.

Like all of the Vaskik brothers, Chuen was naturally good looking. He wore a high and tight military style haircut. A spotless and ironed police uniform. He didn't really like women, but he loved to fuck them. He wanted to see either fear or hate in the eyes of the women he forced into his bed.

He joined the Royal Thai Police, and his younger brother Samak joined the Royal Thai Army. The three brothers had no scruples and were willing to do just about anything for a profit. The Network's total net worth was over eight billion U.S. dollars.

Chuen, with the help of Aroon, rose quickly in the Royal Thai Police ranks. He obtained rank in the Royal Thai Police in the usual way, through bribes and not merit. Chuen was eventually able to bribe his way to the rank of colonel and had become the Royal Thai Police commander of Bangkok's District Twelve.

As a Royal Thai Police commander, he had removed all the competition to the Network in his district. He had no qualms about using extreme prejudice to accomplish this. He provided Aroon classified police Intel that helped the Network in the other forty-nine districts of Bangkok. Aroon's investment in his brother's career had paid off nicely.

It was early in Chuen's career when he started banging his little rice whore. Chuen was stupid back then, having unprotected sex with dozens of whores. He finally learned the hard way to use a hat. He came down with syphilis and then gave it to his wife.

Soon afterward, his wife divorced him. Her butterfly husband didn't have enough common sense to use a hat when he was out whoring. Chuen was lucky she didn't chop off his dick, a common practice among Thai wives when they caught their husbands placing their dicks where they didn't belong.

His wife and son moved out of Bangkok to live with her wealthy land-owning parents. He wanted to take his son back from his ex-wife, but his fear of her parent's political connections prevented him from doing so. It was for the best; he would have made a terrible single father. Besides that, he didn't want the responsibility. He didn't want any responsibility that would interfere with his philandering lifestyle.

Chuen never remarried. Marriage was out of the question. He enjoyed being single and being with as many women as he wanted. Because of his Royal Thai Police position, he got free pussy. He had the power to close any go-go bar in his district. If a prostitute refused him, he could have her arrested on a trumped-up charge. What he didn't want was an interfering wife who placed restrictions on his favorite pastime. Neither did he want, to have to worry about having his dick chopped off.

The first time he saw Cowboy, he knew he was his son; their resemblance was undeniable. Despite that, Cowboy was not his responsibility. He was his little rice whore mother's responsibility. She was the one who should have taken the proper precautions to keep herself from getting pregnant. The little rice whore's son was not part of his family and never would be - at least, these were Chuen's initial thoughts.

Chuen was now fifty-eight years old, and his son, by his ex-wife, was thirty-seven years old. A son who didn't want to have anything to do with him. His only family now was his two brothers. He never lost total interest in his youngest son. Despite this interest, he did not attempt to contact Cowboy. He didn't offer any help to Cowboy, even after his mother's death.

When Cowboy became a Muay Thai champion, Chuen developed a certain amount of pride in knowing that Cowboy was his son. He loved the way Cowboy utterly destroyed his opponents. Cowboy's rage fascinated him. He would drag his two brothers to watch Cowboy's matches. They had no idea when they went to watch Cowboy, they were watching Chuen's son. They thought Cowboy was just Chuen's favorite fighter, because of his brutality.

One day, he thought, *I'm going to reach out to Cowboy, just not yet.* He knew Cowboy was currently working for a farang, the owner of a go-go bar outside his district, the Dizzy. He thought Cowboy would make a good co-owner of a go-go bar in his district. It would be a father and son business.

It would be an easy arrangement. For now, he thought it would be best if Cowboy continued to work for the farang until he acquired a little more experience in the bar business. When he felt the time was right, he would reveal to Cowboy who his father was and make him an offer. It would be an offer he hoped his youngest son wouldn't turn down.

35

SHAME

Bopha asked JJ to meet her at the place where she normally met Moon, at the Bangkok Coffee Café. She didn't want to meet JJ at Dizzy. She feared how JJ would react when she told him about Aroon. Dizzy had become a happy place for her, and she didn't want to spoil her good memories of it. If JJ decided to end their relationship, she didn't want it to happen at Dizzy.

JJ didn't argue with Bopha when she insisted on meeting him at the Bangkok Coffee Café. Why she didn't want to come to Dizzy, he couldn't understand. Despite this, JJ was more than happy; in fact, he was ecstatic. He was willing to meet Bopha no matter where. He needed to know why she had stopped seeing him. He wanted her back in his life. It was empty without her.

JJ arrived first. He picked a table way back in the corner, away from the other café's patrons. When he saw Bopha walk in, like she always did, she took his breath away. Like the first time they met, his heart was pounding in his chest.

Bopha was terrified of the man she loved. She was terrified he would reject her after she told him about her life. She didn't see this ending well. She forced herself to enter the café and found JJ already sitting at a corner table. He got up from his chair to greet her. For the first time in her life, she felt ashamed. She didn't offer him her hand like she wanted to do. Instead, she walked up to him and placed both her hands near her forehead and gave him a very deep wai. He returned it, feeling a little baffled, *why is she acting this way?*

JJ had so many questions to ask her, but the first words out of his mouth were, "I've missed you so much!" Tears were now rolling down Bopha's face as she replied, "And I have missed you, my Love."

They sat down and JJ took hold of Bopha's hands. She had always loved the feeling of his strong hands holding hers. The café's lone waiter came to their table to give them menus. He knew Bopha and was disturbed to see that she was crying. The waiter asked her in Thai, "Ma'am, are you okay?" The polite waiter was one of the reasons Bopha liked meeting Moon at this café. Bopha took a napkin off the table, wiped her tears away, and answered, "Don't worry. I'm fine." She tried to give the waiter a reassuring smile.

Bopha requested, "Let's leave this place and go to Dizzy. I'm afraid I may embarrass you if we stay here. This place is too public for what I need to tell you." Bopha regretted picking such a public place to meet JJ. She was not thinking rationally at the time.

Chuen had started to keep an eye on Bopha. He had informants all over the city. He had learned that Bopha often meets people at the Bangkok Coffee Café. The waiter at the Bangkok Coffee Café, the one Bopha liked, was one of Chuen's many informants. Unfortunately for Chuen, the waiter was not a particularly good informant. The waiter was very selective in what he told Chuen and didn't tell Chuen everything, only what he thought was important.

Chuen was concerned about his brother's total infatuation with Bopha. His bother seemed to forget, that she was just a whore. She killed her old boss and countless others. Aroon didn't seem to care as long as she gave him what he hungered for, her golden cunt; he was completely addicted to it and blinded by it. Something Chuen could totally relate to. From the first time Chuen saw Bopha, he wanted her, and he wanted her badly! He was totally infatuated with her; *she acts as if I didn't exist. Someday, I will let her know that I do.* Unfortunately, his brother refused to share her. Aroon had told him, "I will not share her with anyone, including you, brother."

The waiter had seen Bopha meeting with an attractive younger lady. At first, he suspected that Bopha had a lesbian lover but then decided that was not the case. The waiter overheard Bopha calling the young woman her little sister. They did look alike, and they didn't have the body language of lovers; he knew the signs. He was gay himself; he smiled while thinking about his ladyboy lover.

He didn't bother telling Chuen about the young lady. *What would be the point of that?* He assumed that Chuen already knew that Bopha had a younger sister. However, when he saw Bopha with a farang, who had made her cry, he thought, *this might be something that Chuen might be interested in.*

They decided to have their private conversation on JJ's private balcony. Bopha didn't want to go to his house. She didn't want to feel the ache in her heart by seeing the bed she made love to JJ in. Removing her high heels, she started climbing up the steps. A sign hung on a chain at the beginning of the stairway. The sign read, "The balcony is closed." JJ placed the chain across the first step of the stairway, blocking its entrance.

The balcony had curtains that could be drawn to block its view from down below. JJ drew the curtains closed and pulled out a chair for Bopha to sit on. They looked into each other's eyes. Tears again ran down Bopha's face, breaking JJ's heart.

JJ took hold of one of her hands and stated, "You know I love you. Please tell me what is going on." He could feel her hand shaking in his. "I will love you no matter what you tell me." This statement gave her the hope and strength that she desperately needed.

Bopha told JJ everything, her whole life story. She didn't hold back anything. During her telling, JJ didn't utter a single word. He just looked at her. When she had finished, she tried to read JJ's face.

It was a face of stone, but then a tear appeared in the corner of one of his eyes. He quickly wiped it away. He got up from his chair, walked over to Bopha, offered her his hand, and beckoned her to stand directly in front of him. They were now facing each other, less than a foot apart, looking into each other's eyes. Bopha stepped in closer, and JJ could feel her breasts up against his chest.

JJ remained silent. Then, like the time when he told her he had killed Pinky, he wrapped his arms tightly around her, embracing her. He made her feel like he would never let her go, and she didn't want him to.

She heard him sob softly; she had never heard him cry before. In her ear, he whispered, "I love you, more than ever for having the courage to tell me." Again, another small part of her brilliant, shattered mind became mended. Unfortunately for Bopha, her mind will never be completely mended.

Bopha's and JJ's love for each other had morphed into another stage. It was more mature. They have become soulmates. But their love for each other would remain as hot as molten lava; it is a love that will never cool.

They left the balcony for JJ's house. After they finished making love, Bopha went back to her compound. JJ went back to his balcony, to be left alone. He couldn't stand the thought of another man touching her, much less having sex with her, with a man she loathed.

JJ's thoughts became focused on Aroon. What was he going to do? If Aroon found out about them, Bopha said he would have him killed. She didn't know what Aroon would do with her, but she knew it wouldn't be pleasant.

Aroon's ego wouldn't allow her to get away with it. JJ didn't want Bopha living in fear of anyone. Bopha asked JJ to leave Aroon alone. She said she had a plan to deal with him. *If Aroon isn't out of our lives soon, JJ* thought, *I'll remove him.*

Bopha was in Aroon's bedroom, about to do something she had come to despise, *for the very last time.* JJ had asked her to stop seeing Aroon. JJ wanted her to tell Aroon she wasn't feeling well, *but that would only post-pone the inevitable.* She was afraid if she didn't take care of Aroon soon, *JJ would.* It was time to act.

Bopha was unaware of Aroon's suspicions. Chuen had told Aroon that Bopha was seen in a café, with a farang. That was not too suspicious, but she was seen crying. *What could a farang possibly say to Bopha that would make her cry in public? Why was she meeting a farang in the first place?* It made him wonder if Bopha was cheating on him. *Was the farang a secret lover?* He was determined to find out.

Bopha came into the bedroom carrying two extraordinarily strong drinks. She added something special to Aroon's drink from her Visine eye dropper located in her purse. She added nearly enough clostridium botulinum toxin into Aroon's drink to kill a horse. Though, Aroon wouldn't die until the next morning.

Clostridium botulinum is a slow-acting toxin, but deadly. There were masking agents added to his drink, as well, to ensure he would sleep soundly all night before feeling ill the next morning. When they got around to determining his cause of death, botulism poisoning, she hoped they would think the toxin came from something he had eaten. Aroon was normally gentle in his lovemaking, but not tonight.

She asked him to stop. He replied, "Why, isn't my dick good enough for you? Do you now need a large farang's dick to satisfy you?" Bopha was scared that Aroon had found out about JJ. "What are you talking about?" Aroon could see the surprise on her face. "You were seen with your farang lover inside a café."

"What makes you think he is my lover? Have you been spying on me?"

"You were seen crying while you were with him. Did your farang boyfriend tell you he was leaving you?"

Bopha was relieved. Aroon was basing his assumption on someone seeing her cry while she was with JJ in the Bangkok Coffee Café, and hopefully, he knew nothing else. But it didn't matter because Aroon would be dead by the next morning.

"Don't be silly. He is not my lover. He is one of the mercenaries I hired to attack the Saudi. You don't remember?" Aroon didn't know that JJ was the owner of Dizzy. Bopha never told him.

"I remember, but why were you with him? And why were you crying?"

It's a good thing his informant didn't mention they were holding hands and left the restaurant together. With anger showing on her face, she again lied, "I hired him because I wanted closure."

"Closure?" asked Aroon.

. . .

"Yes, closure. Khen killed my parents, and I have no idea what he did with their bodies. I wanted to find them so that I could have them cremated. The farang, whom I met at the café, had just returned from Cambodia. He told me he and his partner were unsuccessful in finding Khen and locating my parents' bodies. That is why I was crying." Aroon was unaware that Bopha had already killed Khen.

"Why did you hire a farang to find Khen? Why didn't you use your men to find him? asked Aroon."

"I didn't want to use my men, because I don't want Khen to find out that I'm looking for him."

Lucky for Bopha, her weak lie satisfied Aroon. *What was I thinking? What man in his right mind would ever dump Bopha?* He concluded, *no one.* He decided that Chuen was trying to stir up trouble between him and Bopha. He knew that Chuen was still angry because he refused to share Bopha with him. Bopha was his, and his only; Chuen would just have to learn to accept it. *I will never, never, share Bopha with anyone. Not even you, brother. I hope you never force yourself on her because then I would have to kill you.*

Aroon told Bopha he would have someone look for Khen and force him to reveal the location of her parents' bodies. "When they are done with Khen, I'll have him killed. I'll show you photos of his dead body."

Bopha then gave him a happy ending for the very last time. Uncharacteristically, he fucked Bopha only once that night. Afterward, she told Aroon, "I'm still angry with you for doubting me and your false accusations. You are lucky I allowed you to touch me tonight. I'm leaving."

Aroon felt very sleepy and didn't want a fight with Bopha. She didn't mind that she wasn't going to spend the night with him. "I'm sorry. I promise I'll make it up to you." She then left his bed.

Bopha carried two empty glasses to the sink, washed them, and placed them into her purse. Aroon was already snoring, sound asleep. Like her very first visit to Aroon's penthouse, she left with a smile on her face.

The next morning, when Aroon woke up, he suffered from acute abdominal cramps, blurry vision, and nausea. He barely made it to the toilet before throwing up. He wondered, *what the hell did I eat last night?*

After he got back to bed, he called his brother Chuen. He told him that Bopha had hired a mercenary to find her parents' bodies, and he failed; that was why she was crying at the café. This led to a brief argument. "Don't trust her! Why didn't she use her men to find Khen? She didn't need to hire a mercenary to find them. That doesn't make sense!" Chuen didn't believe Bopha's story, but he knew it was useless trying to convince Aroon otherwise. Aroon would believe whatever Bopha told him.

"She had her reasons for not wanting to use her men. Stop trying to stir up trouble between us. I know what you're up to. You want me to dump her so you can have her. That's not going to happen. You can never have her. She's mine, and only mine!" Aroon was finding it increasingly difficult to think clearly and talk. He was running a high fever. He told Chuen, "I'm not feeling very well. I think I must have eaten something bad last night at that new restaurant you have been raving about. I think I better call a doctor."

By the time the doctor arrived, Aroon was already dead, lying in his own excrement. The botulinum toxins Bopha had placed into his drink had blocked the release of acetylcholine at the neuromuscular junctions. This caused the muscles in his lungs to become paralyzed. He died in his bed, unable to breathe, a victim of Bopha's fatal bite.

The sloppy autopsy performed on Aroon determined his cause of death was severe food poisoning. Chuen wrongly concluded it was the fault of the restaurant he had recommended to his brother. He didn't bother to see if other restaurant patrons had become ill on the night Aroon ate there.

Chuen ordered the restaurant to close. Its executive chief was arrested and sent to the notorious Klong Prem Central Prison; there, he became the personal chef of the prison's warden. During the chef's incarceration, the warden gained over thirty pounds. The chef's cooking was the best the warden had ever eaten, and he became the warden's personal chef.

Unlike most of the prisoners incarcerated in the Klong Prem Central Prison, the chef's life in prison was not all that bad. The warden arranged for the chef to have a private cell with female companionship. After the chef's release from prison, together the chef and warden opened a phenomenally successful Bangkok restaurant.

Immediately following Aroon's death, Bopha started transferring the money from Aroon's accounts to her own hidden accounts, leaving no trail. She had become incredibly good at hiding money transfers. If she had stopped there, likely, she would have been okay. But she didn't. Like Bot often did, Bopha let greed get the best of her. The money she obtained from Aroon's secret accounts only whetted her appetite. She wanted more, much more, billions more.

She started going after the assets in Aroon's shell companies; Aroon was not listed as the owner of any of them. Taking control of them was tricky. Selling the shell companies' assets was even trickier. She couldn't avoid leaving a trail, even though it was a very small one. But it was a trail that a well-trained forensic accountant could follow.

One of the two surviving brothers needed to take over the Network. Aroon's good-for-nothing playboy son was out of the question. Aroon's son was lazy and lacked the brains to run the Network. Aroon's son was content with his monthly allowance from the Network. He felt that letting one of his uncles run the Network was perfectly okay with him.

Chuen had no interest in running Network. Chuen was quite happy with his current employment and had no plans to retire from the Royal Thai Police any time in the near future. He wasn't ready to slow down his whoring, and he didn't want to do anything that would interfere with it, such as running the Network.

It was decided that Samak would run the Network. Samak would retire from the Royal Thai Army, as a brigadier general. He was one of the youngest men to ever attain that rank in the modern history of the Thai army. He was the logical choice.

Samak is low keyed, but confident. When he speaks, people listen. Of the three brothers he is the most intelligent and the Network would be in good hands when he takes over. He is a Jet Li look-a-like, with short cut black hair and dark eyes. He is easy to talk to. However, when he becomes angry, he is someone to avoid. He uses Buddhist prayer beads to reduce stress and meditate, while reciting the mantras he learned as a child. And like Jet Li, in the movie Lethal Force 4, he carries his prayer beads wherever he goes.

Aroon had a safe in his office. His brothers had been instructed to open it upon Aroon's death. Inside the safe, they found an external hard drive containing instructions on obtaining access and controlling the Network's assets. Samak found approximately a third of the Network's bank accounts had been closed. The funds in those closed accounts had been transferred to untraceable accounts. To his dismay, he also discovered that a number of the Network's shell companies had been sold off; the money from these sales had disappeared as well. All this occurred shortly following Aroon's death.

The Network had been compromised. Where was the money and who had stolen it? The brothers were determined to find out. So, Samak hired one of the best Asian forensic accountants available, known for her discretion. The accountant found a trail leading to Bopha, Samak's mistress. There was surveillance footage showing Bopha leaving Aroon's penthouse on the night just before his death.

The brothers turned their full attention to Bopha, determined to find out everything about her. They knew she killed her old boss, Bot, and taken over his gang. They learned she had a connection to a Bangkok go-go bar named Dizzy. She had often been seen going to the bar and meeting with the owner. They would find out why.

One of Bopha's informants, inside the Network, warned Bopha that the Vaskik brothers were investigating her, and they knew about her interest in Dizzy. Bopha decided to develop a cover story explaining her interest in Dizzy, hoping the brothers would not discover the truth.

36
THREE STRIKES

The Vaskik brothers now believed they knew Bopha's connection to Dizzy. The brother's sources told them that Bopha had become a silent business partner of Dizzy to launder her gang's illegal proceeds. To them, it made perfect sense. It was just what Bopha had hoped for.

Chuen suggested to his brother that he place an informant in Dizzy to keep a lookout for Bopha. Samak liked the idea. They decided Dizzy would be a good place to capture her. Chuen had a person he thought would be perfect for the job.

He decided that Janta would be the right person for it. She would have dual purposes. As well as being his spy in Dizzy, Chuen wanted the incredibly attractive informant to seduce his son. Chuen had plans for Cowboy, and with the help of Janta, he hoped to draw Cowboy into those plans.

Janta was one of Chuen's favorite call girls. She was in her early thirties and the prettiest whore in his repertoire. Janta no longer worked in go-go bars, instead she was a high-end escort.

Her work came from repeat customers and referrals. Unlike the other whores Chuen utilized, he always paid Janta for her services. Besides being great in bed, she provided him with invaluable information on her customers. She was a valuable tool.

Chuen convinced her to leave the escort business to become a dancer at Dizzy. He would compensate her. After discussing the amount of her compensation, she agreed to take the job. With her good looks and personality, she would have no problems getting a job at Dizzy.

Janta had ice in her veins and was very manipulative. Chuen had used Janta in the past to get information on rivals. She could make a man act the fool, telling her things that he would later regret. He even had to be careful when he was with her; he had to be careful not to reveal information she had no business knowing. Her female persuasion made it extremely easy for a man to forget who he was with.

Janta was the daughter of a retired prostitute, following in her mother's footsteps. Like Cowboy, she had never met her father. Her mother, Dara, told her that her father was a handsome American. He was a businessman who came to Thailand hoping to import Thai goods to America. When his business deal didn't work out, he left without saying goodbye.

Dara had been a waitress at a café when she met Janta's father. It didn't take long for Janta's mother to fall in love with the handsome American. Before he left, they spent one night together. On that night, Janta was conceived. When Janta's father left Thailand, he didn't know he was leaving a daughter behind. Without telling Dara that he was leaving, he had returned to his wife and family in the States.

Janta's grandparents were angry with Dara when they found out their daughter was pregnant with a farang's child. Eight months after giving birth to Janta, Dara moved away from her parents and went to work as a dancer at a go-go bar. Afterward, her parents wanted nothing to do with her. As a dancer, Dara was able to adequately support herself and her daughter, without her parents' help. Janta was Dara's only child. She never married; she was done with men, at least romantically, but not professionally.

. . .

Janta didn't start out wanting to be a prostitute, but she had three strikes against her:

1. She was a woman living in Thailand.

2. Her mother was a prostitute; and

3. She had a farang for a father.

The strikes made it difficult for her to find a decent-paying job. However, there was one field of work where she was in high demand. Being exceedingly attractive, men were constantly offering her money to boom-boom.

She was still a virgin when she finally relented after a rich and handsome Chinese Thai man made her a generous offer while she was working as a low-paid receptionist. Her virginity was still intact due to her mother's influence. Why give something away that was so valuable? Why throw money out the window? She had been tempted several times to give it away, but in the end, good sense prevailed.

When she accepted the offer, she was a freshman in college. Janta needed tuition money but didn't want to ask her mother for it. The offer was more than she could make in three years of working as a low-paid receptionist. All he wanted in return was her virginity and one night of boom-boom.

When he broke through her hymen, the bleeding embarrassed her. She told him, "I'm sorry about the blood." He replied, "Don't worry about that. It's okay; it's expected." His first few strokes inside her were painful, but then to her relief and surprise, it started to feel good, really good! Janta's handsome john wasn't the only one who climaxed that night. All-in-all it was not a bad experience, causing Janta to think, *this might not be such a bad career choice. After all, my mother made it exceptionally good living in the Game.*

Janta was hooked on the Game; unlike her mother, she loved almost everything about it. She knew prostitutes who hated pretending to enjoy sex with ugly/fat/old men. There were men she didn't enjoy having sex with, but she always loved the power that sex gave her over them. And she definitely liked the money; she earned more money than most Thai doctors. Fortunately, not all of her customers were old and fat, or even ugly. Some were attractive, like her very first customer. Getting paid to let them fuck her was like having your cake and eating it too. When it came to bewitching a man, no one did it better than Janta.

It had become a game for the dancers at Dizzy, trying to be the first dancer to seduce Cowboy. There was a big pool of money awaiting the winner. Each month, the dancers placed additional money into the pool. No one yet had come close to seducing him, and the pool of money continued to grow.

It took a great amount of willpower on Cowboy's part not to succumb to the dancers' sexual advances. When the temptation became too great, he excused himself. He went to the back office, where he meditated to calm himself. The three years he spent as a Buddhist monk had its rewards.

There was a reason Cowboy didn't want to have an affair with one of Dizzy's dancers. It would have been okay if he wanted just a one-night stand, where there were no emotional ties. But, since one-night stands were no longer something he was interested in, at least with a go-go dancer; he would have found it difficult to watch someone he had a romantic interest in selling herself over and over again.

Seducing Cowboy isn't going to be easy. All the dancers at Dizzy are trying their best to get him in their bed, thought Janta. Instead of taking a direct approach at Cowboy, like the other dancers, she will take an indirect approach. She will act aloof and pretend she has no interest in him.

Cowboy didn't know what to make of the new and very alluring dancer. He tried to talk to her, but she would not give him the time of day. She was the only dancer at Dizzy who wasn't actively pursuing him and flirting with him. She acted as if she was too good for him, and to his dismay, he constantly caught himself watching her.

Then, one day, he saw her stumble while she was dancing on stage, nearly falling. Cowboy happened to be nearby. She had broken one of the spikes on her high heels. He went over to help her.

While grimacing, she said, "I think I've twisted my ankle."

"Would you like for me to help you to a chair," Cowboy asked?

"Please," Janta placed an arm around Cowboy's shoulder, took off her shoes, and, with Cowboy's help, hopped over to a nearby chair. He found himself liking the feel of her up against him. Cowboy got another dancer to bring him an ice bag and a towel. He placed the ice bag on Janta's ankle and wrapped the towel around it. Against his intentions, he found himself admiring her legs.

Janta gave him a pitiful look, "It's too painful to dance; can you please take me home?"

The request caught him off guard. He was about to say, "No." However, what he said was, "Yes." Normally, during working hours, he would call a cab to take an injured dancer home. All the girls at Dizzy were required to wear high heels while dancing, and it wasn't uncommon for one of them to twist an ankle.

It was the policy at Dizzy: if you were injured and unable to dance, you went home alone. You were fired if you were caught cheating or faking an injury to avoid your customer from paying the required bar fine. This type of cheating was seen as stealing, and stealing was not tolerated.

Janta lived with her mother. Their house was exceedingly nice and looked expensive. Cowboy wondered how she could afford such a house. Once inside, Dara brought him a plate of food. Dara had seen Cowboy fight in the ring; she was a huge Muay Thai fan and was a little star-struck by Cowboy. Dara thought that Muay Thai was the perfect sport; a sport where men beat up other men. *What could be better*, she thought. After finishing his meal, Cowboy thanked Dara for the food. Both ladies wai to him, and he waid back before leaving.

Two days later, when Janta returned to work, her demeanor toward him changed. She was now friendly and talkative, but not flirtatious. Cowboy found Janta had a great sense of humor and made him laugh. He touched the tip of his cowboy hat as she pasted by him, and she rewarded him by turning around and gaving him a shy smile.

He found Janta very appealing. She told him how much her mother enjoyed having one of her all-time favorite Muay Thai fighters come into their home. He replied, "I enjoyed talking with your mother. Her passion for Muay Thai surprised me."

Cowboy had never asked a dancer out for a date but now he wanted to. When he finally got up his nerve, he invited Janta and her mother to a Muay Thai match. To his delight, they accepted.

Just before going to bed, that night, he took off his cowboy hat and sat it on top of his dresser drawer. Small silver specks of dust that had settled on his hat went unnoticed; Janta had an unknown ally in her plans to seduce Cowboy, the silvery dust was at work.

37

THE RAID

Bopha stopped coming to Dizzy after she found out that the Vaskik brothers were looking for her. She told JJ, "It's too dangerous for me to be seen at Dizzy." But two days later, she had found a secret way to leave her compound without being seen. For the next month, Bopha and JJ met clandestinely, nowhere near Dizzy. Places where no prying eyes could spot them.

After growing tired of waiting for Bopha to show up at Dizzy, the brothers decided to raid Bopha's compound just as the sun was coming up. Most of her gang would be asleep. The compound was surrounded by two parallel twelve-foot chain-link fences topped with razor wire. There was a six-foot gap between the two fences. The gap was filled with more razor wire.

To enter the compound, you needed to pass through two gates. In the middle of the gates were tire spikes that could be raised up and down. The spikes can be lowered just before a vehicle passes over them or raised to flatten its tires. There was also a large truck that blocked the road leading from the gate into the compound. The truck had to be moved out of the way to gain entrance to the compound.

The plan was to avoid the gates. Four bulldozers would plow through the fences at opposite points. Following each bulldozer would be an armored personnel carrier (APC). Each of the four APCs would carry a team of thirteen heavily armed highly trained mercenaries wearing body armor. The APCs would reach the center of the compound within forty-five seconds.

It was early morning, and Bopha was sound asleep when she was awakened by an alarm going off in her room. There were motion detectors set along the compound's surrounding fence. Something had broken through the fences setting off the alarm. She had video monitors in her room that showed the compound and its surrounding area. On the monitors she saw four APCs headed for the compound's buildings; they had broken through the fences. She had less than a minute before their arrival.

She had discovered a hidden tunnel that led from her bedroom, Bot's old bedroom, to a small shack outside the compound's fences. Inside the shack, she found a motorcycle that had been well-maintained. Since discovering the tunnel, she had been taking lessons on how to drive a motorcycle. Just in case she ever needed to use the escape path, she wanted to be able to use the motorbike in the shack. She had also been using the escape tunnel to secretly visit JJ.

She brought another motorbike inside the compound to practice on. Her gang thought she was nuts, watching her whipping around the compound on the motorbike, "Bopha you are going to kill yourself! You don't drive that motorbike any better than your car."

Bot must have secretly built the tunnel while constructing the compound. No one knew about it. She accidentally found the tunnel's door in her room while hanging a picture on a wall. The doors on both ends of the tunnel were well hidden.

With time running out, Bopha made her decision. She realized the only way she was going to escape this attack was to use the tunnel, immediately. She felt bad about the men she would leave behind. There was nothing she could do for them. She closed the tunnel's door as she left her room, hiding her path of escape.

Once she reached the shack, she placed a helmet on her head, swung a backpack, containing her laptop and satellite cell phone, over her shoulders, and drove off on the motorbike. She never looked back, as she headed for the Cambodian border.

The brothers arrived at Bopha's compound, and after they got word, it was secured. Bodies lay everywhere, but Bopha was nowhere to be found. Her safe was located inside her room and opened by a safecracker. Inside, they found a small amount of currency, diamonds, and artifacts taken from the Saudi. There was nothing in it that would help them recover the money Bopha had pilfered from the Network.

They wondered how Bopha escaped. The compound had been under 24/7 surveillance. Bopha had been seen inside the compound the day before the attack, and she had not left. Failing to find the tunnel, her escape baffled them.

When Bopha had traveled far enough from the compound, safe from any pursuit, she pulled over to the side of the road and took out her satellite cell phone. She was worried about what JJ would do if he found out about the attack. She called him and told him her compound was attacked and overrun. "Don't worry about me, my love. I'm ok and I will call you every night while I am gone." But of course, he did worry. She asked him to contact Moon and to let her know what was going on. Bopha then made another call.

She was going to meet with the new members of her gang. She had clandestinely recruited them from her native country. She was going back home, back to Cambodia. At the border, a jeep was waiting for her.

The border guards had been paid to ignore their crossing. Once in Cambodia, they went to her new jungle hideout. There, she would regroup and determine who was behind the attack on her compound. She already had a good idea: Aroon's two brothers.

~

Janta enjoyed the Muay Thai match that Cowboy took her and her mother to. Her mother had been taking Janta to Muay Thai matches since she was a little girl. Cowboy was impressed with their knowledge of the sport. Janta told him, "You were my mother's all-time favorite fighter. She was sad when you retired. I thought she was going to cry."

After the match, they went out for dinner. It was a restaurant near Dizzy, a place Cowboy enjoyed having lunch. They were served his favorite curry dish, "Kaeng Hangl" a Burmese-influenced curry of stewed pork, peanuts, dried chilies, and tamarind juice. Just before it was served, thin slices of fresh ginger were added. Both Cowboy and Dara downed a few Singha beers, while Janta drank Thai iced tea. After an enjoyable dinner, Cowboy took Janta and her mother home.

"Thank you for such a great evening," Janta said, while giving Cowboy her best smile. *This is my chance.* "Would you like to come in for a while? I know my mother will want to talk to you."

"Thank you, I would like that," answered Cowboy, tipping his hat to her offer.

He followed the ladies into the house, his boots click-clacked through the entrance behind Janta. Dara offered him more food, but he was full. He did accept a cup of tea. Cowboy and Dara did most of the talking.

. . .

"Do you miss fighting in the ring," asked Dara. You were such a great champion. You were the best!"

"Thank you. Sometimes, I find myself missing it, but I no longer have the drive that I used to have."

"Why is that?"

"When I was fighting, I carried a lot of anger. It was that anger that motivated me. It's what drove me to win, and I no longer have it. Besides that, I'm now too old."

Dara's eyes squinted, "How does someone lose such anger?"

"Through meditation and two years in the Sangha."

"Oh! You were a monk?"

"Yes, you sound surprised."

"I am surprised. It's hard for me to imagine that such a violent man in the ring would take the vows of a monk!"

After finishing his tea, Cowboy told the women he needed to leave, and how much he had enjoyed their company. Janta followed him outside, where she gave him a goodnight kiss, giving him a slight taste of her delicious tongue. It made him yearn for more, much, more. He had a hard time falling asleep that night, but when he did, he dreamed of Janta's kiss. It was a dream that lingered with him until the next morning when he turned on the lights.

38

INTO THE JUNGLE

On the day of the attack, three members of Bopha's gang had not spent the night in the compound. They had spent the night in hotel rooms with Dizzy's dancers. While returning to the compound, they noticed a large amount of smoke coming from their compound grounds. They decide to be prudent and take an alternative route to the compound, which was seldom used. It was the same route Bopha used during her escape.

When they got close enough, they saw the compound; nearly all of it burnt to the ground. Four APCs and two utility vehicles were leaving the compound, traveling down the road they had been on. They waited until the vehicles were out of sight, before continuing.

They found the bodies of their dead brothers lying on the ground and charred remains under the smoldering rubble. There were no survivors. They assumed that Bopha was among the dead, but they could not find her body. One of them took out his cell phone and dialed her number. He was surprised when Bopha answered. She was at the Cambodian border.

∼

Bopha was just getting ready to cross the border into Cambodia when she received a call from one of her only two surviving Thai gang members who were not in the compound when it was attacked. They were recruited just after she killed Bot and were completely loyal to her.

She wired them money to spy on Samak and Chuen. More than ever, she *needed* to learn everything she could about the brothers. She left it up to her men to document the brother's daily routines. She would learn where they ate, worked, slept, and even the brothels they frequent. They would be watched 24/7. One day, she would use this knowledge to take them out.

The hideout was in a part of Cambodia close to where Bopha's parents had gone while the Khmer Rouge were in control, near the holy mountain of Phenom Kulen; the home of the Ancient One, an old, withered sorceress. Like Bopha, the Ancient One was a woman of power.

This was not the first time Bopha had gone to the hideout. She had been here several times before, preparing it for its eventual use by one of her gang's lieutenants. But now it would not be one of her lieutenants taking charge of the hideout, it would be her. She would stay here until the dust had settled and she could regroup. The only thing she disliked about the hideout, was being so far away from JJ and Moon. She was surprised when she found that she missed them as much as she missed her deceased parents; she had an acking inside her that would not leave.

In a way, Aroons' brothers did her a favor by killing nearly all of her old gang. Some members of her old gang would have resisted the direction she wanted to take the gang. Now, she could start with a clean slate. That didn't mean she would forgive Aroon's brothers for attacking her. Now that she knew who was responsible for the attack, retribution was coming for them... just as it had for Khen.

The new members of her gang will have a different mission than that of her old gang. They will never be involved with drugs or human trafficking. They will become Bopha's enforcers. She will use them to punish her enemies, her private army. She had chosen her first target. Moon had told Bopha about the Malaysian brothel where Moon's Nay Joy had been sold as a sex slave. It still existed, but not for long.

~

Amir had never forgiven Joy for tricking him into helping her to escape his father's brothel, then deserting him in Bangkok with almost no money. Amir believed Joy when she told him if he helped her escape, she in return would marry him. *How could she have fooled me like that? She loved me, or at least at the time – I thought she did. I loved her, but now I know her love was never meant for me.*

Joy had taught him a hard lesson. Love was just a fantasy. He would never be tricked again. He no longer wanted real love; he was content with the fantasy of being loved. It didn't bother him knowing his fantasy wasn't real. At least - that was what he told himself.

After Joy left him in Bangkok, Amir returned home in disgrace, to be beaten by his father. He still carried scars on his back from that beating. His father sneered at him, "You stupid little stuttering hunchback. How could you let a dumb whore trick you like that?"

After his father's death, he became the owner of the brothel. Amir was even crueler than his father. His father had been motivated by profit; he wasn't quite the sociopath that Amir was. Amir was no longer the shy youth that Joy remembered. He no longer stammered on his words when he talked, at least not often.

Since taking over the brothel, each month, Amir picked one of his sex slaves to be his bride-of-the-month (BOTM). Amir had the BOTM reenact the way Joy had first seduced him. She was required to act as if he were irresistible, unable to get enough of him and his dick. This was no easy task, since Amir was as ugly as a toad, with a hunched back, an acne-scarred face, thin arms and legs, and a bloated stomach. Behind his back, his employees and slaves alike poked fun at him. They called him the "Toad".

After a fake seduction by his BOTM, there was a mock wedding. In Amir's sick mind, it was Joy fulfilling her promise over and over again. When Amir had finished with his 30-day bride, she was allowed to return to the brothel's lineup, working twelve-hour days, six days a week, servicing up to ten men daily. But it was better than being constantly fucked and photographed by the ugly Toad.

Bopha made plans to attack Amir's brothel, free its sex slaves, and kill their captors. The brothel's patrons caught in the attack would be tied to posts and severely beaten with bamboo canes. She would make it extremely dangerous to run or patronize a brothel using sex slaves.

Bopha was sitting in her jungle hideout, missing JJ and thinking about her the new members of her gang, as enjoyed her nightly two shots of Macallan 25 Scotch whiskey, along with a slice of hot Poilâne bread with real butter. The Cambodian members of her gang viewed Bopha as a reborn ancient Khmer deity. They believe she was the reincarnation of the Mahayana Buddhist Khmer King Jayavarman VII. She has special powers; no mere human could be as beautiful and as smart as Bopha.

Her new gang was completely devoted to her and followed her orders without hesitation. They were ruthless fighters. Many of them were former Khmer Rouge or their children. She had taken them out of a very dark place, to a place of light and hope. She had given them a purpose to live or to die for. *"However difficult life may seem, there is always something you can do."*

39

EVERY WHICH WAY BUT LOOSE

It appeared as though Janta would be the first Dizzy dancer to seduce Cowboy. He had been out with her on several dates, and each goodnight kiss had gotten a little longer and a little more passionate. Janta thought, *it's just a matter of time before he will be no longer be satisfied with just my kisses. And as much as I enjoy his kisses, I want more as well.*

Unlike her mother, Janta didn't hate all men. She liked a lot of them. Cowboy fell into the group of men she liked, and the thought of having sex with him excited her. Even if Chuen wasn't paying her to seduce Cowboy, she would have been interested in going to bed with him anyway. Cowboy was very handsome. It would be fun telling her mother all about it, whether or not the man her mother admired so much, was as good in bed as he was in the ring.

Not knowing that Cowboy was Chuen's son, Janta wondered why Chuen hired her to seduce Cowboy. She hadn't learned anything about Cowboy that would interest Chuen. She hadn't learned anything at Dizzy that she thought Chuen would find worth while. She hadn't seen Bopha, whom Chuen referred to as the Khmer bitch, not even once. Bopha's name was hardly ever mentioned.

Everyone was so close-lipped about Bopha. The other Dizzy dancers didn't like talking about her. She suspected they were envious of her beauty. Janta had been shown a photo of Bopha. Even Janta found herself a little envious of Bopha's looks. Yet, she admired her. She admired how Bopha had been able to take over Bot's gang, and how she made fools of both Bot and Aroon.

Cowboy, on the other hand, for the first time in his life, felt like he was falling in love. All he could think about was Janta. He had never been so infatuated with any woman. They had a date coming up, and he was hoping for more than just a goodnight kiss. It had been a long time since he had an intimate relationship with a woman.

Even so, he had reservations. *Can I continue to share Janta with other men? In the Game, she makes way more money than I can ever hope to make. If I asked her to leave the Game, how can I support her in the way she has grown accustomed to? Will Janta agree to leave the Game?* He doubted it, and felt it wasn't right for him to ask her to make such a sacrifice. *What am I going to do?*

Chuen decided he would check out Dizzy and introduce himself to Cowboy. Janta had been giving him updates on the activities occurring at Dizzy. Janta had told Chuen she had been taking it slow with Cowboy. All of Dizzy's dancers were after him, and she didn't want to give him the idea she was intentionally trying to seduce him.

Janta hadn't given Chuen any new information on Bopha. She hadn't been seen in the bar since before the attack on her compound. Chuen suspected that Bopha was a silent owner of Dizzy, but there could be more to it than that. He was not sure. He and his brother had plans to question JJ about his relationship with Bopha. They just hadn't gotten around to it.

Chuen had learned that Bopha had the Royal Thai Police commander for the district where Dizzy was located in her pocket; the commander was often seen at Dizzy. Maybe, he was helping Bopha launder money through Dizzy. Chuen would have someone keep an eye on the commander. Unfortunately, Chuen and the commander of this district are competitors, and they hated one another.

The brothers were hoping that someday Bopha would show up at Dizzy. If she did, they wanted to be ready. The brothers placed informants in all the places Bopha was known to frequent.

Chuen entered the bar on a Thursday night, which was more crowded than expected. It's not as big as his go-go bars, but it was very classy, and comfortable. On stage were some of the most attractive girls he'd ever seen in a go-go bar. In most go-go bars, only about thirty percent of the girls were really hot looking, but in Dizzy, it was one hundred percent! Dizzy's attractive dancers were making him feel like a little boy in a candy store. Trying to pick out the prettiest girl was making his head spin.

Chuen sat down at a small table not far from the center stage. He had an excellent view of the seductive dancers swinging themselves around the stage's poles, but his eyes were focused on Janta. Janta was reminding him just how desirable she could be.

He was tempted to pay Janta's bar fine but decided *that is a bad idea*. He had to remind himself why he came to Dizzy. He was here to talk to his son. It would be a bad way to introduce himself to his son. "Hi, son. By the way, I'm your dad and I would like to take your girlfriend to bed." *That would be a bad introduction!*

A sweet looking go-go dancer came to his table and asked him to buy her a drink and to sit next to him. He should have said, "No." But instead, he said, "I would love to buy a drink for someone as lovely as you. Please sit down."

Old habits die hard. Since Dizzy was not in his district, if he decided he wanted to take her to a hotel room, he would need to pay her bar fine.

She had a great body with a cute face and would be well worth paying for. Again, he had to remind himself why he came to Dizzy. Maybe he would pay her bar fine some other time, but not today.

He spotted Cowboy at the bar talking to the bartender, a farang dam, a Black man. He asked the go-go girl to go over to Cowboy and invite him to his table. When she returned with Cowboy, Chuen stood up to greet him. Cowboy, being the younger of the two, wais first. They then sat down and started to talk.

Chuen cleared his throat while eyeing Cowboy from across the table, "I like your bar. I'm very impressed! How did you get so many beautiful dancers to work here?"

"Our bar's manager only hires the best," Cowboy said while adjusting in his seat.

"Yes, I can see that."

By this time, Janta had spotted Chuen talking to Cowboy. She wondered what Chuen was up to. After she finished her dance on stage, she placed her top and shorts back on. She then walked up to a table next to the one where Chuen and Cowboy were sitting. She wanted to get close to their table, hoping to over hear what they were saying.

Sitting at the table, the farang wasted no time offering to buy Janta a lady's drink. After sitting, she placed her hand on the farang's leg, rubbing the inside of it just inches below his crotch. The farang moved Janta's massaging hand up a few inches up and patted it, "Yes Honey, right there. That's the right spot.," giving her a goofy grin.

Both Chuen and Cowboy were watching her. Cowboy was having a hard time getting used to watching Janta sell herself, but he knew how the Game worked. He would either have to accept it or stop seeing her. He didn't want to stop seeing her.

The girl sitting next to Chuen was being ignored. Both men were staring at Janta. After motioning his head toward Janta, Chuen stated to Cowboy, "What an exquisite creature!"

Cowboy nodded, "Yes she is," while staring at Janta and her massaging hand.

Chuen turned his attention back to girl next to him, "I'm sorry, dear, for being so impolite. I've been ignoring you. Someone of your beauty should never be ignored, please forgive me."

She stuck a pouting lower lip at Chuen, and replied in her squeaky high-pitched voice, "I'll try."

"Please be a good girl and refill our drinks and bring me a bowl of boiled peanuts." When she stood up, Chuen stretched out his hand and gently patted her bottom as she was walking away, "Thank you, Honey." He then turned and faced Cowboy again.

Cowboy normally didn't sit with bar patrons he did not know, but there was something about this man that aroused his curiosity. When Cowboy looked at Chuen, he saw striking physical similarities between Chuen and himself.

Chuen stared at Cowboy and asked, "Do you know why I came here?"

"I would assume, for a drink, to escape the heat, and to meet and watch our lovely ladies?"

. . .

211

"Yes, that is part of it, but that is not the main reason. No, I wanted to meet you." He sat up straight, reflecting almost perfect posture.

"Why? Are you a Muay Thai fan? Have you seen me fight?"

"I am, and yes. I have seen nearly all your professional fights." He then took a deep breath and said, "I'm here because I have something important to tell you."

"And what is that?"

Chuen hesitated, "I'm your father."

Cowboy looked like he had been slapped in the face, "You're my what?"

"I'm your father."

Chuen then told Cowboy a well-rehearsed lie. "I met your mother in a go-go bar, and shortly afterward we had an affair. We fell in love, and I asked her to marry me. I was young then, and my parents couldn't accept me marrying a go-go dancer. They made me promise never to see your mother again. I didn't know she was pregnant. After my parents died, I decided to try and find your mother. I learned she had died years ago." Chuen paused, giving Cowboy some time to digest what he had told him."

When he felt that Cowboy was ready, he continued. "Only after did I found out she had a son. I didn't know you were my son until I saw you, and that removed all my doubts."

Cowboy sat there dumbfounded, unable to say anything.

"You need only to look into a mirror to know you are my son," said Chuen. "By that time, you had already become a young man. I watched you become a Muay Thai champion. I was so proud of you. But I couldn't bring myself to tell you that I was your father. I was ashamed of abandoning you and your mother. Can you ever forgive me?"

A single tear trickled down Chuen's face, which he quickly wiped away; Chuen was a good actor. "It took until now for me to collect the courage to tell you this."

Cowboy felt as if he had been sucker-punched in the stomach. The cute go-go dancer returned to the table with Chuen's drink and peanuts. She was unaware of what was going on, but as soon as she sat down, she sensed the tension between the two men.

Chuen then stated, "I know you need time to think about this. Next week I'll return so we can talk again. I think you've been shocked enough for one day. When I come back, I'll have a business proposition for you. Goodbye son."

Chuen's boiled peanuts and drink remained untouched. After Chuen's departure, Cowboy continued sitting at the table. He was stunned by what he had just heard, watching the back of the man, who had just introduced himself as his father, walk out of the bar without even so much as telling him his name.

Janta was puzzled. She had no idea that Chuen was coming to the club. She wondered what Chuen and Cowboy had talked about. She had seen emotions stirring in both the men's faces; she was surprised to see Chuen wipe a tear off his face. *What was that about,* she wondered.

She couldn't wait to find out what had gone on between the two of them. While both men were sitting next to each other, she noticed the physical similarities between Chuen and Cowboy. She wonders, *why hadn't I noticed this before?*

As soon as Chuen left, she forgot all about the farang she'd been sitting with and abruptly removed her messaging hand from his lap. She got up and left the farang's table without saying a word, joining Cowboy at his table. The farang was about to protest when the girl who had been sitting next to Chuen walked up to his table. She was a petite Thai beauty with long shiny black hair that hung all the way down to her cute butt. She had an innocent smile that hid her bold personality. Nothing pleased her more than to watch the shocked expression on a farang's face when she said or did something they least expected.

She asked him in her squeaky voice, "Will you buy me a drink?"

Before the intoxicated farang complained about Janta's abrupt departure, he had second thoughts. He looked at the cute go-go dancer who had taken Janta's place and thought - *she'll do.* When the dancer saw the desire in his eyes, she reached over and gently squeezed the area that Janta had been rubbing, which was still hard, and with that incent smile still on her face she abruptly asked, "Would you like to fuck me?"

"Hell yes! Call your mama-san so that I can pay your bar-fine, then we can get the hell out of this place and go to my hotel room!"

"Do you want to fuck me only once or for a long time?"

"Honey, I most definitely want to fuck you for as long as I can."

.   .   .

The dancer smiled, "Then Sweetie, you stay right here, and I'll be right back."

~

Janta looked at Cowboy and said, "You look like you have just seen a ghost."

"Maybe I have. The man you saw me with said he was my father."

Janta was as surprised as Cowboy. She had no idea that Chuen was Cowboy's father, but they did look alike. She wondered, *why didn't Chuen tell me he was Cowboy's father. That explains his interest in Cowboy.*

"Do you believe him?"

"I don't know what to believe. But why would he lie about something like that? I guess the only way we can know for sure is through a DNA test. Even if he is my father, he never took care of my mother and me."

Janta thought how she and Cowboy were alike in this regard; *both our fathers were mere sperm donors and not real fathers.*

"What are you going to do?"

.   .   .

"For now, nothing. My mind is solely on our date for tomorrow night," uttered Cowboy. He noticed sparkles of silver in Janta's hair. "When did you start putting glitter in your hair?"

"I didn't put it in my hair. I don't know where this stuff is coming from. I thought I had washed it out, but it keeps coming back. It looks like the same stuff that's on your hat." The magical dust that resided in Dizzy was hard at work on its new targets.

Cowboy took his hat off and looked at it. "You are right. I'm going to have someone clean the air-conditioning vents. Anyway, about our date. I'm planning a special dinner for us, and I hope you'll find it to your liking."

"I'm sure I will. And I have something special for you, as well." She twirled her hair with her fingers and winked at him.

Cowboy reached over and took one of the peanuts left on the table. He removed its shell and popped the nuts into his mouth. He then leaned back in his chair and asked, "Yeah, and what would that be?"

"It's a surprise. You'll just have to wait and see." She then got up and again winked at him, before leaving the table.

Cowboy continued to stare at Janta as she walked away, observing the sway of her hips, her sexy ass, and her shiny black hair that fell just below her shoulder blades. Chuen was right when he said that Janta was an exquisite creature. He silently said to himself, "*I can't wait for my surprise. The anticipation is killing me.*" He then reached for the untouched drink that the man who said was his father had left. He gulped the drink down the way a thirsty man in the desert would gulp a cold glass water.

~

Cowboy went to Janta's house to pick her up. But first, like he always did, he went inside to talk to Dara carrying flowers; these were short but enjoyable conversations, sitting on cushioned rattan chairs. After placing the flowers in a vase, Janta would sit with her elbows propped up on the room's teak table, her head resting in her hands, as she listened to her mother and Cowboy engaged in their conversation. It was fun watching her mother and Cowboy talk. He was one of only a few men Dara seemed to like.

Cowboy had no idea how much Dara loathed men in general. Her contempt for men was well hidden behind her smiling face. Cowboy was an exception. Dara had become genuinely fond of Cowboy. She looked forward to Janta's dates with him.

Dara knew her daughter enjoyed having sex with certain men. She wondered if Cowboy would be one of these men. If things went according to Janta's plan, she would soon find out. After the date, her daughter would tell her all about it. She was almost as anxious as Janta about her upcoming date with Cowboy.

Both Janta and Cowboy shared a common love for American movies. Cowboy had a vast array of westerns on DVDs. His collection was not cheap. He could have collected less expensive pirated movies, but he didn't like their quality. Tonight, he would take Janta to his place for dinner and watch *Unforgiven*, on Blu-ray, starring his favorite actor, Clint Eastwood.

Cowboy was a little embarrassed about taking Janta to his house. In comparison to Janta and her mother's house, his house was tiny and bland. In his living room was a couch with a hideaway bed. There was no separate bedroom.

Next to the living room was a small kitchen and an indoor bathroom. Cowboy felt it was a luxury to have an indoor bathroom rather than an outhouse. What he enjoyed most about his home was the 65" curved screen TV, a Blu-ray player, and a home theater receiver with surround sound, located in front of the couch/hideaway bed.

He planned everything out. Before watching the movie, they would eat dinner. Cowboy had prepared 'Padthai' with steamed white rice. 'Padthai' is stir-fried rice noodles with egg, peanuts, dried shrimp, tofu, bean sprouts, tamarind juice, and squid and shrimp. There was a white linen cloth covering the teak table in his kitchen. He had placed candles on the table, and the light above the table had been dimmed. Cowboy wanted to make this meal as romantic as he could. He hoped to get more than just a taste of Janta's delicious tongue for dessert.

While eating they looked at each other from across the table, in the candlelight, making eye contact like first-time lovers. It made Janta giggle as if she were again a teenager, causing Cowboy to laugh along with her. They shared a bottle of Napa Valley Pinot Noir. It's a wine that Clyde donated to Cowboy for his hot date. By the end of their meal, the wine was all gone, giving Cowboy and Janta good-feeling buzzes.

Before starting the movie, Cowboy made a bowl of buttery popcorn, not cooked in a microwave, but in a deep pan on the stovetop, sprinkled with a special ingredient that he refused to share with anyone. They sat on the couch next to each other to watch the movie.

The bowl of popcorn sat on Janta's lap. Cowboy had his arm around Janta's shoulders, with Janta snuggled up against him. She fed Cowboy kernels of popcorn throughout the movie with her free hand. Occasionally, she popped a kernel into her mouth. *"This is good!"*

When the movie ended, they remained on the couch. The bowl of popcorn was nearly finished and placed on the small coffee table where it was forgotten. With longing showing in their eyes, they kiss. Soon after, the couch was folded down to make a bed. Janta then slowly, teasingly, undresses, to show him her promised surprise. And it was everything that Cowboy had hoped it to be.

And "Yes," Janta told her mother, "Cowboy is one of those special men," which brought a look of satisfaction to Dara's face; "I thought so." Dara was surprised to find the thought of Janta finding Cowboy appealing in bed would make her happy, but it did.

The following week, Chuen returned to Dizzy. He sat at the same table near the dancing platform. Janta was the first dancer who approached him, and he offered her a drink. Janta accepted his offer. This was stupid on Janta's and Chuen's part.

Cowboy was standing at the bar, talking to Clyde, when he spotted Chuen. He became irritated when he saw Janta sitting at Chuen's table. Cowboy felt Janta shouldn't include the man who had identified himself as his father in her Game. He quickly went to their table.

Chuen stood up and they wai to each other. Chuen stuck out his hand, inviting Cowboy to sit down. His mouth moved with a slight smile, "I didn't tell you my name the last time I was here. My name is Chuen Vaskik. I'm the Royal Thai Police commander for District 12." It surprised Cowboy to find out that the man who claimed to be his father was a Royal Thai police district commander." He paused before continuing,

"As I mentioned to you last week, I have a business proposal for you. Do you have anywhere where we can talk in private?" Chuen didn't want to talk in front of Janta and regretted his offer to buy her a drink. *I should have never allowed her to sit with me. That was stupid! The business I have with my son is none of her business.* "What I have to say is for your ears only."

. . .

"We can talk here," Cowboy replied, barefaced.

Cowboy told Janta to leave the table; it was not a request; it was a demand and very impolite. He didn't include "kruṇā" (please) and failed to say "kráp," the polite way to end a sentence.

Janta complied after giving Cowboy an angry look - if only looks could kill. She would express her displeasure with him later, by using an old but effective female get-even tactic; Cowboy will have a long wait before she gave him his next happy ending. Janta believed in the adage that said, "A man may wear the trousers in a relationship, but it's the woman who controls the trousers' belt."

"I want you to join me in a business venture," said Chuen, wasting no time getting to the point.

"What kind of business?" asked Cowboy.

"I want us to have a go-go bar, located in my district. You'll be in charge of running it. We'll be co-owners, but for the most part, I'll be your silent partner."

"Why me? You could find someone more qualified."

"Son, I think you have underestimated yourself. I can see the excellent job you are doing here." Chuen swept an open hand around the bar. "With a little help from the right people, I am confident we can run a successful go-go bar. Besides that, you are my son. We need to make up for the lost time."

. . .

"How can you be certain I'm your son without a DNA test?"

"I'm certain of it, but if you like - we can have the test performed."

"Okay, but even if the test proves you are my father, I have no intention of leaving Dizzy. I'm happy here. The people I work with are more than just my coworkers; they've become my family."

"Don't give me your answer now. I want you to have time to think about this. It's something you need not rush into; just don't rule it out. You would make a lot more money as my partner than you will ever make here. I'll come back next month, and we'll talk more about it."

Chuen knew that Janta had successfully seduced Cowboy and that she believed he was in love with her. He will ask Janta to convince Cowboy to accept his offer so that he can afford to take her out of the Game. This was the main reason Chuen hired Janta to seduce his son. He wanted her to motivate Cowboy to leave Dizzy.

Cowboy will never know I hired Janta, thought Chuen. After luring Cowboy away from Dizzy, he will have Janta killed. *I will make it look like she had been killed by a former jealous lover.* Chuen didn't want to give Janta the chance to blackmail him or tell Cowboy the truth.

Bopha had numerous spies to keep track of the Vaskik brothers. She knew their every move. It had come to her attention that Chuen had made two recent visits to Dizzy, which concerned her. On both of these trips, Chuen met with Cowboy. It made her wonder.

Bopha trusted Cowboy. *But why this sudden interest?* It was a question that needed to be answered. She didn't believe Cowboy would willfully betray JJ. If she thought so, Cowboy would already be dead.

Bopha had also learned that Cowboy was having an affair with one of the newly hired dancers. This surprised her. Cowboy had intentionally avoided having any type of sexual relationship with any of Dizzy's dancers, even though they had gone out of their way to seduce him. Cowboy had always managed to avoid their entrapments.

Bopha wondered how this new dancer had managed to have her way with him. She wanted to know if Chuen's visits and the seduction of Cowboy, were related or just mere coincidences, *hmm…* But Bopha had no clue that Chuen was Cowboy's father.

Bopha directed her spies to get information on the new dancer, Janta. Bopha wanted to learn everything about her. She decided to call JJ using their satellite phones; all her calls to JJ were encrypted end-to-end.

"My Love, something strange is going on with Cowboy - and I do not like it."

"And what's that?" JJ sounded mildly concerned.

"Chuen Vaskik has been coming to Dizzy to see Cowboy, and I have no idea why. And I have heard that one of your dancers, Janta, has seduced him. I know that Janta has worked for Chuen in the past, and that has me worried."

"Why?" asked JJ.

. . .

"If Chuen found out about us, that would endanger your life. You need to talk to Cowboy and make sure he doesn't say anything about our relationship with Chuen and Janta."

"I'll talk to Cowboy. But don't you do anything. Remember it was Cowboy who saved your life when he spotted Pinky going into the hotel. I know he wouldn't purposely betray us. By the way, when am I going to see you? I miss you so much."

"As soon as I can, my Love. When it is safe. I miss you too."

After Chuen left Dizzy, Janta walked up to Cowboy to express her displeasure at the way he dismissed her in front of Chuen. She told him that his rudeness had embarrassed her. "I won't tolerate it! If you wanted me to leave Chuen's table, you could have been polite about it."

Cowboy told her that she should not have come to Chuen's table in the first place. "It's bad enough watching other men paying your bar fine. I want you to stay away from my father."

"You know how I make my living. I didn't think you had a problem with it."

"I don't want you going to bed with my father!"

. . .

"For me, he's just another paying customer. Besides that, I've already been in his bed. Before I became a dancer here, I danced at one of his go-go bars. He's had me in his bed several times. It wasn't personal; it was just business."

Cowboy wondered, *why in the hell didn't she tell me this before, that she knew Chuen? Maybe she was too embarrassed to admit she had gone to bed with someone who is now claiming to be my father. I just do not understand her. I don't understand women period!*

"Perhaps it's just business for you, but not for me. I want you to stay away from him.

"Who do you think you are? Do you think you can tell me what I can and cannot do? Do you think you own me, and that you can just order me around and be rude? Have I broken any of Dizzy's house rules? I don't think so!" *For now*, thought Janta, *Cowboy can keep his hands to himself.*

Shaking her head, Janta got up and left, clearly offended, and upset. Cowboy was angry as well, but he couldn't help watching the sexy sway of Janta's hips as she walked away, dissipating some of his irritation. He'll need to meditate to rid himself of the remaining anger. Her being in the Game was driving him crazy, but he couldn't keep himself from wanting her.

40

KING TOAD

Amir had been working hard since his father's death. The small brothel he inherited had grown. He had nearly two hundred female slaves working for him. The majority of Amir's slaves were forced into performing sexual services, but there were a few who worked as maids and cooks. There were even those who worked as hairdressers, manicurists and pedicurists, and makeup artists for the women who serviced Amir's high-end customers and starred in his porn movies.

There was a huge demand for his girls, and Amir loved all the money his brothel brought him. Recently, Amir expanded his business. He was now selling porn videos on the web and the dark web, which he found very profitable and fun to direct. He tried to place some creativity into his movies, trying to make them into more than just ordinary porn flicks. His movies were even developing a cult following.

Amir didn't have to pay any of the movie's actors or actresses. Plenty of horny males eagerly volunteered their free services to mount the attractive actresses in his movies. The actresses were his property, and they did whatever he told them to do. All the money he was making would have made his father exceedingly proud of him.

What Amir loved most about his brothel was the power. Inside the brothel, he was the absolute ruler. He could do whatever he wanted with his slaves, with impunity. He had no one to answer to but himself. The corrupt government officials were amply paid to leave him alone and did so. In his brothel, the Toad was king.

It was the night of their pseudo-wedding, and Amir had just finished consummating their fake marriage. There was the lingering scent of sweet perfume in the air. The BOTM's white wedding gown and Victoria's Secret lingerie lay discarded on the floor; later Amir would have the wedding gown and lingerie prepared for his next BOTM.

Amir's latest BOTM was a petite, cute seventeen-year-old girl abducted from Cambodia. Leung lay naked on her back with her legs spread wide apart, showing Amir her shaved pussy, as he photographed it. She grimaced as she spread her vagina with her fingers. Amir's recently deposited cum, could be seen oozing it. He snapped another picture.

He continued photographing her as she posed in various seductive positions. These photos will be added to Amir's private BOTM collection. When he's done with her, when it's time for a new BOTM, she will return to service the brothel's customers or star in one of his porn movies. She would remain in the brothel until she was no longer desirable or died, whichever came first.

The brothel never closed; it stayed open 24/7. Bopha's men had already penetrated the brothel, pretending to be customers. It was near midnight, and like mystical ninjas, silent assassins, Bopha's men started slicing throats and shooting their victims with nearly silent guns; they did not stop until all brothel employees were dead. For the first time in thirty years, the brothel was closed. When her men completed their work, Bopha entered the brothel.

Amir was unaware that his brothel had been taken over. He was sound asleep lying next to his BOTM. The BOTM was awake when Bopha entered Amir's bedroom. Bopha motioned with her Sig for the BOTM to get out of the bed and leave the room; she grabbed her clothes and left. One of Bopha's men poked Amir in the ribs with his rattan cane.

Amir woke with a painful stinging on his side and saw an angel of a woman smiling down at him. At first, he thought he was dreaming. He then saw his bed was surrounded by men carrying rattan canes, posed to strike him. *If I'm dreaming, this is a nightmare!* Amir stuttered, "W-w-who the hell are yo-u-u?" just before the men surrounding his bed begin to beat him unmercifully. He begged and screamed for them to stop, but they continue the beating until Amir was a bloody pulp.

After taking care of Amir, it was time to take care of Amir's customers. They had been rounded up, stripped of their clothing, and tied to posts. Each customer would receive twenty-five cane lashes. All of them had an "X" carved into their foreheads, to permanently scar them, to remind them of their crimes, whenever they looked into a mirror.

The customers were then photographed, and their wallets and money were taken. One of the customers was randomly picked out to be castrated in front of the others with a hot knife. The agonizing customers were told that they too would be castrated if they were again caught patronizing a brothel utilizing sex slaves.

Amir's customers were then locked together in a room, left to be discovered by whomever. A sign was hung on the room's door stating, "This is what happens to rapists." Except for the one unfortunate customer, the rest were lucky that Bopha had allowed them to keep their balls.

Now, they had to work on the hardest part of this mission… finding a way to accumulate the former sex slaves back into society. A couple of buses arrived. The women were given the choice to get on a bus or depart on their own two feet.

Some of Amir's victims would return to their families, and others would not. Many of them would be stigmatized for working as sex providers, even though it was against their will. Bopha would need to find some way to help these women, and she planned on doing her best to do so.

Some of these women would join her gang. Bopha was no longer the lone female of her gang.

Before leaving, Amir's seventeen-year-old BOTM returned to take a final look at the dead Toad. She spat on his bloody corpse, then went to the drawer where he kept his camera. She took the camera and left. She didn't want anyone getting hold of the photographs the Toad had taken of her. Before boarding the bus, she handed the camera to Bopha. Bopha would ensure the images on the camera's SD card were destroyed. In time, Amir's former seventeen-year-old BOTM would become a valuable member of Bopha's gang.

JJ knew Bopha was a killer, but so was he; he had killed in war. In war, you either kill or be killed. There were no in-betweens. Bopha was fighting a war. She intended to win her war regardless of the cost, willing to sacrifice everything. *Perhaps even me* thought JJ. Like Moon, he understood. Bopha's motive was pure, which was one of the many reasons he loved her.

Like the Riders, the rogue Oakland police officers, Bopha chose vigilantism over legal means to fight her war. JJ didn't care. He agreed with Bopha's approach to fighting sex traffickers, to take them down in the most expedient way possible.

JJ was willing to do what he could to support Bopha's fight against sex slavery. He pondered on why the world's two largest religions' holy books, the Bible, and the Quran, didn't speak out against slavery. By not doing so were they condoning slavery? As far as JJ was concerned, there was no worse sin. He believed that Bopha was fighting a holy war.

It had been months since JJ had seen Bopha. The Vaskik brothers would need to be taken care of before she could safely return to Bangkok. Only

Kat, Cowboy, Clyde, and Moon knew JJ's and Bopha's true relationship. JJ was worried about Cowboy accidentally saying something to Janta, but Cowboy assured him he had nothing to worry about. But JJ was concerned.

JJ thought that Janta had Cowboy right where she wanted him; he would do anything for her. For a while, JJ thought they had broken up. For nearly two weeks Cowboy and Janta hardly spoke, but they were now back together and thicker than ever.

JJ saw the hurt in Cowboy's eyes when Janta was in the Game, selling herself to customers. Cowboy had told him about Chuen's offer. Accepting his offer was the only way Cowboy believed he could afford to remove Janta from the Game. JJ knew Cowboy's days at Dizzy were numbered.

Janta, the manipulator, didn't know what to think about her relationship with Cowboy. She wasn't supposed to fall in love with her mark. *This is a first*, and she pondered how it happened. When she told her mother that she was in love with Cowboy, her mother just laughed at her. Dara called her daughter, "Silly girl." Her mother hadn't fallen in love with any man, since Janta's father. Janta was having a hard time reading her mother. She didn't know if her mother liked the fact that she had fallen in love with Cowboy, or not.

Even if Janta didn't mean for this to happen, it did. Now what? Cowboy wanted her out of the Game. He was seriously contemplating Chuen's offer, thinking it was the only way he could ever afford to take Janta out of the Game. Janta was uncertain about whether she wanted to leave the Game. In many ways, she enjoyed being in it. She didn't want to be financially dependent on anyone.

41

HIS RIGHTFUL PLACE

Chuen finally told his brother about Cowboy. Samak wondered why Chuen hadn't told him earlier. He remembered Chuen taking him and Aroon to watch nearly all of Cowboy's fights. They knew Chuen had an interest in Cowboy, but Chuen had never hinted that Cowboy was his son.

Now that he thought about it, he should have known. *I should have noticed Cowboy's resemblance to Chuen.* He proudly thought *Cowboy is definitely a Vaskik; he has those Vaskik's men good looks.* Samak began his plans to induct Cowboy into the Network. It was time for his nephew to take his rightful place in the family business. Cowboy running a go-go bar wasn't part of Samak's plan for his nephew. He had another job in mind. The job he had in mind for Cowboy would likely make Chuen angry, but he would get over it. The Network always came first.

He had waited long enough. Chuen decided it was time to return to Dizzy. Janta had told him that Cowboy wanted her out of the Game, something Cowboy couldn't afford unless he accepted his offer. It was just as Chuen planned with one exception.

Janta had recently told Chuen that she wanted out of their deal. She had fallen in love with Cowboy. Chuen told Janta it was too late to back out. And if she tried to renege, he would have her killed. Chuen didn't plan on Janta falling in love with Cowboy. The thought of Janta falling in love with Cowboy hadn't even entered his head, after all, she was a professional. This was not supposed to happen.

Chuen entered Dizzy and decided to sit at a table way in the back. Janta saw him come in. She intentionally stayed far away from him. She didn't want to repeat her argument with Cowboy the last time Chuen came to the bar.

Chuen turned down a dancer's offer to sit with him; he too had learned from his previous mistake. Cowboy saw Chuen enter as well and walked over to his table. After waiing to each other, Cowboy sat at Chuen's table.

"Have you considered my proposal?" asked Chuen."

"I have, and I'm still thinking about it. Can you give me an idea of how much I would be making? I need to know that before I can entertain your offer."

"Initially we'll split the bar's net profits 60/40. I will receive sixty percent because I'm paying for the bar's startup costs. You'll get forty percent for running the bar. That will be at least ten times more than you'll ever make working here. After three years, we will then split the bar's net profits 50/50. And after ten years, you will receive sixty percent."

. . .

"When do you need my answer?"

"The sooner the better. We can have the bar ready to open in two months."

Cowboy sat back in his chair, looking at Chuen. He then looked around the bar for Janta. She was sitting with a beer-bellied farang, who was in the process of paying her bar fine. The thought of the fat farang going to bed with Janta was enough to make up his mind, "I accept your offer."

"Good. It will be nice working with my son. Why don't you come and take a look at the bar, and I'll introduce you to some of the people who will be working for us. Call me first, and I'll meet you there." He handed Cowboy his business card.

"Thank you."

"You are welcome."

~

Chuen planned on not killing Janta immediately. It would be foolish for him to kill her immediately. No, he would allow their little love story to carry on for a short period of time. He wanted Janta to pretend she'd marry Cowboy and leave the Game. After several months, he would have Janta pick a fight with Cowboy and end their relationship before they got married. And then he would have her killed.

By then, Chuen believed that Cowboy would be hooked on the money.

There is no way he'll want to return to his low-paying job at Dizzy! Chuen wrongfully thought that money was always the ultimate motivator.

4 2
USING A MULTIFACETED ATTACK

Bopha's battle with sex trafficking would need to be multifaceted. Using one approach would not work. She planned to attack it on all sides. Her plan consisted of three continuous phases.

Phase One: Attack the businesses forcing women into sexual servitude and punishing their customers. Bopha's gang had successfully raided several prominent brothels and massage parlors utilizing sex slaves. The employees of these establishments were killed, and their customers beaten, with a few of those unlucky customers losing their balls. Her goal was to instill fear in the businesses and their customers, knowing they could be punished at any time.

Phase Two: Go after the people supplying women as sexual slaves to the businesses mentioned in Phase One. One of the common ways the suppliers obtained women was to promise good jobs to poor rural women. For instance, recruiters would go into poor rural areas and promise these women well-paying jobs in the cities. Once isolated, they were forced to become sex slaves. If the women failed to cooperate, they were beaten, raped, and threats were made to harm them and their families.

Amir's last BOTM, Leung, now a member of Bopha's gang, had been promised a job as a hotel maid in a high-end Bangkok resort. The recruiters told Leung she would make enough money to support herself and send money back to her family. An old army troop transport truck arrived to pick up Leung and thirteen other women promised jobs. Leung waved goodbye to members of Bopha's gang, who pretended to be her family, and in many ways they were.

The women climbed into the back of the truck to set on hard wooden benches; they were nervously excited. With a cloud of thick black smoke belching out of the truck's tailpipes, and the grinding of gears, the truck lunged forward, launching them on their way.

This was the first time many of them had left home. They thought they were going to Bangkok, but that was not where this truck was taking them. Leung was carrying a GPS transmitter, allowing Bopha's gang to keep track of the truck at a distance. After the truck had traveled for approximately three hours, it came to a stop.

A man appeared at the back of the truck. He told the women to get out and stretch their legs. After they were all off the truck, the women were told they would take a break, use the restrooms, and eat. Another man asked the women for identification papers so that he could prepare their working and traveling documents. They were then herded into a building.

A nice-looking woman, with a boyish haircut, entered the building and walked to the front. "Good afternoon ladies, my name is Rosie. Soon, you will be taken to a room where you will shower. I know you would like to remove all that road dust and sweat you have accumulated from traveling in the back of that truck. Afterward, you will be interviewed and will be informed about your new job."

· · ·

One of the women asked, "Why are we being interviewed again?"

"The reason for these interviews is to obtain additional information for your travel visas. I promise you that you will have a job. Just cooperate and do as you are told, and everything will be okay."

Each of the fourteen women is escorted to individual rooms, by a female servant who instructs them to undress and take a shower. Strangley, each small room contained a bed and a doorless bathroom with a shower and toilet. The confused women did as they were told.

While showering, their female escorts left the rooms. After finishing their showers, the women were surprised to find men in their rooms. The men order the naked women to the rooms' beds; a place where the women would find out all about their new job. And if they refused, they were beaten until they complied.

The cold water felt good, as Leung washed off all the sweat and dirt. After drying herself, Leung exited the bathroom. She found two unknown men waiting for her, and one of them immediately grabbed her towel and tried to yank it away; a tug-a-war ensued.

"Who are you?" screamed Leung.

"Let go of the towel and get on the bed," one of the men shouted at her.

"No, you get out of here!" sneered Leung.

The man slapped her face, leaving her left cheek red. He then pulled the towel away from her and threw it to the floor. She tried to cover her private parts with her arms and hands.

. . .

He pointed to the bed, "Go."

"No, leave me alone."

He grabbed her arm and again slapped her hard across the face; this time much harder, and it felt as if her jaw was nearly broken. The hard slap left a red impression of his hand on her cheek. The other man then punched her in the stomach, causing her to double over. She was again ordered, "Stop trying to cover yourself and get on the bed. If you don't, I'll make sure you regret it." He held his hand back, ready to slap her again. She did as she was told, to avoid the slap.

The men removed their trousers and underwear, leaving on their shirts, and joined Leung on the bed. One of the men was preparing to mount her, spreading her legs apart, while the other man was pinning her arms when an intruder entered the room. The intruder was carrying a Glock 17 pistol equipped with a sound suppressor. The would-be rapists were ordered off the bed and double-tapped, two rapid shots to the chest and one to the head. Just before the man with the Glock left the room, he handed Leung her clothes. She told him, "Orkun Chruen," meaning many thanks. He replied, "Min ei te," you are welcome.

Leung quickly got dressed. Bopha was waiting for her outside. The other thirteen women, who were nearly raped, were placed back on the truck and taken home. Bopha ordered the execution of the recruiters and all the others involved in the operation except Rosie. Rosie's entire complex was set on fire, sending bright flames, smoke, and sparks into the night's starry sky.

Bopha examined the bruise on Leung's face, shook her head, and said, "I'm sorry you had to go through that."

Leung looked at the burning complex, and whispered, "It was worth it." They hugged each other and went their separate ways.

Before setting Rosie's compound on fire, they found her safe and made Rosie open it. Like the Toad, Rosie didn't believe in banks. Inside the safe were the profits Rosie had saved from trafficking women. This money would go toward helping the victims of sex slavery.

Rosie was a child of the Khmer Rouge. While with the Khmer Rouge, at the age of twelve, she was forced to kill her parents. After leaving the Khmer Rouge, Rosie found one of the few fields of work in her country where she could successfully compete against men.

Rosie was taken back to Bopha's jungle hideaway where she was roughly interrogated. She provided information on other people involved in sex trafficking. They were all added to Bopha's hit list.

After her interrogation, Rosie was taken outside. She was ordered, "Get on your knees." Rosie was resigned to do as she was told, knowing what would come next. Bopha placed the muzzle of her Sig to the back of Rosie's head and fired a single round. The bullet exited through the front of Rose's face. Her body was then tossed into a nearby river.

Phase Three: This will be the most important of the three phases, and the most difficult to implement. The phase's goal would be to provide economic equality to Southeast Asian women. In Bopha's native country, Cambodia, birth certificates were not issued to most of the women born in the country. They were second-class citizens and were expected to work at menial jobs for their entire lives.

Many women in Thailand and Cambodia turn to prostitution, because of a lack of economic choices. Bopha wanted to change this. She wanted gender equality, something that would not happen overnight. It would be her crowning achievement if she succeeded, even just a tiny bit.

43

SECOND THOUGHTS

Cowboy had given JJ notice that he was leaving Dizzy. He decided to help JJ hire and train his replacement. It was the least that he could do. He had someone in mind, one of his former Muay Thai students, who was already working at Dizzy part-time. Chat was a Royal Thai Police officer. When Cowboy left, he planned on resigning from the RTP to work full-time at Dizzy.

Cowboy had asked Janta to marry him, on the condition that she would leave the Game. Unexpectedly, Janta told him she needed to think about it. *Maybe, it was premature to give JJ my notice,* Cowboy thought. If Janta failed to accept his proposal, he would back out of his agreement with Chuen.

He was leaving Dizzy, so he could afford to take Janta out of the Game. Cowboy could no longer stand Janta being in the Game. If she refused to leave the Game, he would end their relationship. He could no longer stand sharing her with other men.

～

Janta wasn't blindsided by Cowboy's proposal. She saw it coming, but what she didn't know was whether she would accept it. Cowboy was the first man she had ever fallen for, and she had fallen hard. She wanted to marry him. It should have been an easy decision to make, but it wasn't.

Janta was indifferent about sex with most men, but there were those customers she thoroughly enjoyed having sex with. What she enjoyed - was the power that sex gave her over them. Men would do just about anything for her touch. She liked the look in their eyes when she knew she had them under her spell.

Before she fell in love with Cowboy, Janta planned to lure him away from Dizzy, a place he loved. She had wanted to make Cowboy believe the only way he could afford to take her out of the Game, was to accept Chuen's offer. She succeeded. Now she wondered, *can I live with myself for manipulating Cowboy like this? But that's what I do; I manipulate men. Something I've always enjoyed, until now.*

Dara could tell that Cowboy was troubled by Janta being in the Game. He would come to the house to visit her when Janta was out entertaining a customer. This was a frequent event since Janta had become one of the most popular dancers at Dizzy, and therefore was always in high demand. Cowboy felt powerless to stop it. Dara knew it was eating him alive. If Janta wanted to keep Cowboy in her life, she would have to leave the Game. It was Cowboy or the Game. Her daughter had to choose. She finally did. To Dara's relief, Janta chose Cowboy. She was glad that her daughter was out of the Game.

Janta decided to accept Cowboy's marriage proposal, with one condition. She wanted half of Cowboy's ownership of the new go-go bar. She wanted to be the top mama-san and help Cowboy manage the bar. She wanted to play the same role that Kat played at Dizzy. Cowboy had no problem with this. He wasn't sure if Chuen would agree to Janta's condition, but he would tell Chuen it was his condition as well. Chuen could take it or leave it.

To both Cowboy's and Janta's surprise, Chuen didn't have a problem with it. When they told him of the condition, Chuen laughed to himself. He was planning to have Janta killed, and *a dead person can't own half of anything*.

44

ON TRIAL

Kat was no longer content being a wallflower. She was determined not to allow another woman to take a man she was romantically interested in without first letting that man know how she felt. It was time she let Clyde know.

Clyde had noticed a change in Kat's attitude toward him, even the way she looked at him was different. Clyde wondered, *is Kat looking at me the way she used to look at JJ, or is it just my wishful imagination?* Kat was nearby and smiling at him. *I wonder what is going on with her,* Clyde thought. She then turned her back and walked toward a customer who was waving her over.

The customer handed her a bar fine. After collecting the bar fine, Kat walked back to the bar and handed the money to Clyde, "Can you please place this into the cash register for me?" After Clyde placed the money into the register, Kat asked him, "When we get off work tonight, would you like to go get something to eat?"

He smiled, "I would love to."

. . .

Like they often did when they went to their favorite nearby restaurant, they both order *naem khluk*, a salad made from crushed, deep-fried ball-shaped croquettes made from sticky rice and curry paste, tossed together with shredded fermented pork sausage, and mixed with peanuts, crushed dried chilies, lime juice, sliced shallots, and fresh herbs, and served with a selection of fresh greens and additional herbs on the side.

After finishing their meal, Kat unexpectedly reached across the table and took hold of one of his hands. She looked directly into his eyes, "Clyde, I want to ask you something." She had Clyde's full attention. With an inquisitive look on his face, Clyde asked, "What?"

"Do you find me attractive?" She knew the answer to this question before asking it.

Clyde studied her face. At first, he thought she was teasing him, but she wasn't smiling. "Are you kidding? I think you are the most attractive woman I have ever met."

Now she was smiling and acting a little embarrassed. She asked, "Do you want to go home with me tonight?" The question stunned Clyde, staring at Kat with his mouth wide open. He had not expected Kat to ask such a question. He hadn't been with a woman in months, the longest time he had ever gone without one in his entire adult life. Clyde answered, "More than you can ever imagine."

Clyde had to wear a hat that night. He was on trial. Kat needed to know for sure if he was her Mr. Right before she allowed him to go without one. Both Clyde and Kat had a very satisfying night.

45

THE NEW INFORMANT

Chuen was not thrilled with Janta, but she did what he had paid her for. He and Cowboy were now in business together. Without Janta, this would never have happened. He hadn't planned on Janta getting part ownership of the go-go bar, but that wouldn't matter, once she was dead. Then, it would be a father and son business, just as he planned.

Janta failed to find out anything about Bopha. Bopha had gone underground and hadn't been seen or heard from since the raid on her compound. That was eight months ago, and her trail had grown cold. Now that Janta was no longer working at Dizzy, Chuen felt he needed a new informant to replace her at Dizzy. He and his brother still had not gotten around to questioning Dizzy's owner; they were nervous that Bopha would find out if they did. They suspected that Bopha was still secretly washing her illegal proceeds through the bar.

With so many dancers to supervise, Dizzy had three full-time mama-sons, and a part-time mama-son. The daughter of Kat's newest full-time mama-san worked as a go-go dancer in a bar owned by Chuen. He would try and turn her into an informant. Through threats and bribes, Chuen was able to persuade her to spy for him, to let him know if

Bopha ever showed up at Dizzy. He suspected one day she might, and that was something he wanted to know -*immediately.*

46

FINDING MR. RIGHT

A date was set for a double wedding. The happy couples were Kat and Clyde, and Janta and Cowboy. The wedding and reception were set to take place at Dizzy. Dizzy's doors were scheduled to be closed for this happy occasion.

Kat was an expecting mother, and it was starting to show. As soon as she discovered that Clyde was her Mr. Right, she wanted him inside her wearing no protection. She wanted his child, and there was no need to wait for the wedding. Kat knew Clyde was committed to her, and only her.

At the age of fifty, Clyde had not considered getting married much less fathering a child at his age. Things had changed since meeting Kat, for the better. He found that Kat satisfied him as no woman had done before her. He was content, with just her. She was carrying his child, and it felt right.

But Clyde was no spring chicken, and he was nervous about having a child at his age. Fortunately, he was in great shape and planned to stay that way. He wanted to be around to see his child graduate not only from high school but from college. If his son or daughter decided to join the Marine Corps, he wanted them to go in as an officer. *I want to be the one who pinned the yellow lieutenant bars on their collars.*

Joy and Moon are ecstatic about Kat and Clyde's upcoming marriage. Neither of them could have predicted it. They were beginning to believe that Kat would never get married. When Kat had first brought Clyde to the house, they had no clue he was to become Kat's husband, her long-awaited Mr. Right.

They were all thrilled when they found out that Kat was pregnant. Joy planned on taking care of the baby while Kat and Clyde were at work. Joy's house was again about to grow. A large additional room would be added to the existing house. Joy, Kat, Moon, Clyde, the baby, and Joy's old three-legged dog would all be live under the same roof as one big happy family.

For the first time since Kat had moved to Bangkok, she planned to return home to introduce Clyde to her parents. All of Kat's family have been invited to attend their wedding. Kat had waited long enough; it was time for her long-anticipated White Wedding.

Bopha was having a special team trained. They had been training for the past two month. Now it was time for her to return to Bangkok, to take care of the Vaskik brothers and their supporters once and for all.

She planned to secretly visiting JJ first before the mission. It had been nine exceptionally long months since she had last seen JJ. She couldn't stand being away from him any longer, longing for his embrace.

Because she needed to hear his voice, each night just before enjoying her nightly shots of Macallan 25, she called JJ on her encrypted satellite phone. During one of these calls, she told JJ, "Soon my Love, I'll be in your arms again."

. . .

"That is all I've been dreaming about," JJ replied softly to her.

Meanwhile, Cowboy, Kat, and Clyde noticed there was something different about JJ. He had been gloomy for the past nine months, and now he was acting as if he had won the lottery. There was again a gleam back in his eyes and a bounce in his step.

They had an idea what was going on, even though JJ hadn't said a thing about why he was suddenly acting so happy. Only one person could have this kind of effect on him. None of them had seen her since she fled to Cambodia.

JJ wanted to make the upcoming wedding a triple wedding, but he wouldn't be able to marry Bopha until the Vaskik brothers were taken care of. Bopha would never be safe while they were alive. She had told him that soon the brothers would no longer be a problem.

$$\sim$$

Cowboy left Dizzy to start his go-go bar with his father and Janta. He had no clue that his father and his uncle were the cause of Bopha fleeing Thailand for Cambodia.

He knew there was trouble between Chuen and Bopha, but he thought that was because of Bopha's illegal activity; his father was a cop after all. What Cowboy didn't know was that his father was a very corrupt cop, and his Uncle Samak ran one of the largest criminal networks in Southeast Asia.

$$\sim$$

Bopha let JJ know she would be secretly attending the wedding. Members of Bopha's team would also attend. Bopha no longer went anywhere without protection. JJ had placed a one-way glass around his private balcony to prevent Bopha from being seen by those down below.

He knew it would be best not to sit with her; except for him, no one would know she was attending the wedding. He had a role to play. JJ was going to be Clyde's and Cowboy's best man. He also needed to be present for the wedding reception. If he disappeared during the reception, it would raise questions.

After finding out that Cowboy was a Vaskik, Samak wanted to know more about his nephew's past. Samak found out that Cowboy had been a member of Bot's street gang. This information gave Samak hope that he could use his nephew in the Network.

Samak invited Cowboy to his high-rise suite, previously occupied by Aroon, for a talk. Samak felt it was his duty to convince Cowboy to join the Network. It was part of Cowboy's heritage, and they needed him. He wanted Cowboy to take Bot's place as the leader of a street gang controlled by the Network.

When Cowboy arrived, he was impressed with his uncle's building. The building was sixty stories tall and located near the heart of downtown Bangkok. The guards outside the building allowed him in.

Samak had shown the guards Cowboy's photograph and instructed them to point him to the elevator. He rode it to the 60th floor. The elevator opened to an Italian granite hallway leading to a massive teak door. He used the door's large brass knocker to announce his presence.

Samak got up from his desk to allow Cowboy into the suite. After waiing, Cowboy sat in the same overstuffed leather chair used by Bopha when she first met Aroon.

"Would you like something to drink?" asked Samak.

. . .

"Do you have a bottle of Singha beer?"

"Yes, that sounds good. I think I'll have one as well." Samak walked to the bar's refrigerator and took out two bottles of Singha. He reached into a drawer for a bottle opener and popped the caps off. After handing Cowboy his bottle, Samak said, "Nephew, would you like to hear something about our family history?"

"Yes, I would love that."

"Good. Our family has worked hard to get where we are. We are not afraid to do whatever it takes to continue our success. Our family's business had recently come under attack. Just after your Uncle Aroon died, a substantial amount of our family's wealth was stolen."

"By whom?"

"By a Khmer bitch named Bopha. I believe you may know her."

This surprised Cowboy. *How could Bopha have done this?* "Yes, I know her, but I have not seen her for months."

"Please, tell me what you know about her."

. . .

Cowboy wasn't about to betray JJ, so he told him the cover story that JJ had given to him. "JJ was forced to sell part of his bar to Bopha, to launder some of her gang's money. She doesn't come to the bar anymore. She now sends a Royal Thai Police district commander to Dizzy to conduct her business. That is all I know," declared Cowboy.

"You haven't seen her because we raided her compound. Unfortunately, she managed to escape. She is now hiding in Cambodia, but we will eventually get her," Samak confidently stated before sipping his drink.

Cowboy lied, "I hope so."

"We will. It's just a matter of time. I'm glad you came to see me today. I have a job for you that would be good for you and our family business."

"Uncle, I don't think it's a good idea for me to take on a new job right now. I'm pretty busy getting the go-go bar ready to open. I don't think my father would be happy if I took on another job at this moment."

Samak knew that Janta was helping Cowboy. Chuen wasn't much help, which didn't surprise him. Janta was smart and knew what she was doing. She was a good asset. He was trying to persuade Chuen not to kill her. Besides that, he had plans for Cowboy, and running a go-go bar full-time wasn't one of them. As long as Janta remained alive, she could run the bar.

Samak loved Chuen, but he wished Chuen was a little smarter. Samak also resented the fact that Chuen wasted so much of his time whoring. Chuen thought too much about his dick and not enough about important matters. Smirking, he returned his gaze back to Cowboy, "Why don't you get your go-go bar started, and then we'll talk about this later."

~

Chuen, Cowboy, and Janta, finally came up with a name for their new go-go bar; they decided to name it "The Cathouse." Chuen even came up with a slogan for The Cathouse, "Come to The Cathouse where you can stroke your favorite pussy." When Chuen thought up the slogan, he chuckled to himself, thinking that he was very witty.

Janta was put in charge of hiring the dancers. In some ways, she was even better at it than Kat, and in no time, they had dancers who could rival those found at Dizzy. Hiring attractive dancers was critical to achieving a successful go-go bar. Even Chuen was impressed by Janta's selection.

Janta knew many of the dancers she hired from the escort business. Being a dancer had its advantages over being an escort; it's steady work. There were too many days when escorts had no clients at all. This was okay for college girls wanting a little extra money, but not for full-time working girls. Janta even managed to get some of the cutest college girls in the escort business to work part-time at The Cathouse.

Samak was trying to talk Chuen out of killing Janta. Samak told Chuen he did not need to worry about Janta. She wasn't about to tell Cowboy that Chuen had hired her to seduce him. Janta wasn't stupid. She would be cutting her own throat if she said anything to Cowboy.

Chuen decided he would take a wait-and-see attitude on Janta. She was doing an excellent job at The Cathouse, and her percentage of the profits came out of Cowboy's share and not his. And it was obvious that Cowboy was deeply in love with her, and happy. Most importantly, she did not interfere with his growing relationship with Cowboy. He would hold off from killing her, at least for now.

Cowboy had invited JJ, Clyde, and Kat to the Cathouse's opening. They found the bar charmingly decorated, larger than Dizzy, and the dancers were superb. Kat recognized a few of the dancers who had previously worked at Dizzy. It wasn't unusual for dancers to switch bars.

Customers liked looking at fresh faces. Kat would talk to Janta; Kat hoped she and Janta could agree to rotate dancers from The Cathouse to Dizzy and vice versa. It would be a win-win agreement for both bars.

The Cathouse's opening week was a huge success. The place was packed with farang and Thai men. Some of the customers who came to The Cathouse knew Janta. They tried offering her drinks. She disappointed them by turning them down and telling them she was no longer in the Game. She was now part-owner of The Cathouse.

The customers told Janta she was way too young and desirable to leave the Game. No matter how much money they offered her to spend the night with them, she was determined to stay out of the Game, even though she found it hard to refuse some of her former customers, that is …the attractive and well-paying ones.

While in the Game, Janta enjoyed having sex with many of her customers; a time when she could have sex with as many men as she wanted, which she found exciting. She had become a sex addict, not just liking sex but craving it. *As much as I enjoy being in bed with Cowboy*, she questioned herself, *in the long run, will he be able to keep me satisfied?* Like any addict, she had to resist the temptations that would draw her back into this addictive lifestyle.

Cowboy liked running The Cathouse with Janta. They worked well together. He treated the dancers and his other employees with respect until they showed him that they didn't deserve it. And those who didn't deserve his respect were fired. He was happy with the way Janta was doing her job. He could see she was enjoying herself, which made him happy. Her management style reminded him of Kat's. Most of all, he was happy because Janta was no longer in the Game.

Cowboy sold his little house and moved in with Janta and her mother. He brought his TV and vast Western movie collection with him. Dara didn't mind having Cowboy move in with her and Janta. There was plenty of room in their spacious house.

Dara was rather pleased having Cowboy live with them; he was always hanging around the house anyway. And then there was the bonus that Cowboy brought with him, his TV, sound system, and extensive DVD collection.

JJ hired the person that Cowboy recommended to replace him. Chet had been a Muay-Tai fighter before joining the Royal Thai Police. Cowboy had been his trainer, and after he quit Muay Thai, they remained friends. Chet had grown tired of the corruption in the Royal Thai Police. The officers in the Royal Thai Police were encouraged by their peers to accept bribes to supplement their low-paying salaries. Cowboy told Chet he would enjoy working for JJ and Kat, and he did.

Like Cowboy, Chet was very protective of Dizzy's dancers, and he made sure they were not physically abused by their customers. All the dancers liked him, and like Cowboy, he was very good-looking! Now, the dancers' have changed their focus from Cowboy to Chet.

Unlike Cowboy, the dancers knew that Chet had no experience in meditation. Chet had never been a Sangha monk. The mischievous dancers believed he would be an easy target, a piece of low-hanging fruit to be easily plucked off the tree. And now Chet unknowingly walked around with an invisible bull's eye on his back. The wagering had started.

Doe had been a mama-san at Dizzy for the past six months. Before becoming a mama-san, she was a dancer at Dizzy. All of Dizzy's mama-sans started as dancers. These are usually women who were getting too old to stay in the Game and who were respected by the other dancers.

Chuen's new informant, "Dao," was thirty-eight years old, getting too old to be a dancer. She was grateful that Kat had given her the chance to be a mama-san. As a mama-san, she got a percentage of the bar fines she collected from the dancers she supervised and was paid a steady salary.

Chuen had asked Dao when she had last seen Bopha in the bar. That was about eight months ago before she became a mama-san. Back then, Bopha would come in about once a week. On those occasions, Bopha would visit JJ in his office or while he was sitting on his balcony, and sometimes in his small house, outback. Dao had been told that Bopha had become part-owner of the bar. But she suspected that JJ and Bopha were, in fact lovers. They didn't fool her.

She never saw any romantic contact between JJ and Bopha, but only a blind person couldn't see there was chemistry between them. The way they looked into each other's eyes. They were more than just business partners.

However, she chose not to reveal her suspicion to Chuen. She disliked Chuen and liked JJ. She only agreed to spy for Chuen because he had threatened to imprison her daughter. Chuen didn't realize the tactics he used to create an informant were not very good.

Dao noticed a change in JJ's behavior when Bopha stopped coming to Dizzy. *He is no longer the cheerful person I used to know*, but recently JJ had returned to his old self. He was smiling again, making Dao wonder *why?*

Dao believed it had something to do with Bopha. She would keep her eye out for her, but even if she saw her, she thought, *I'm not sure I'll say anything to Chuen.* He had offered her a huge incentive for alerting him to Bopha's presence, and she could use the extra money, but she didn't want to betray JJ.

47

COLLEGE GIRL

Moon was not your typical college girl. When Moon started college, she was constantly being asked out for dates, which she always turned down. The naïve college boys thought they were all irresistible. They thought they could say something cute; say something that would motivate Moon to drop her panties for them, *yeah right!* The constant come-on lines and flirtation became irritating.

Fortunately, the date requests had slowed to a trickle. The word had gotten out: She was not interested! Some thought she was a lesbian. Moon didn't care what they thought. She was in college to study, not to party or to find a boyfriend.

She quit going to Dizzy on Saturday nights after being abducted. It had lost its appeal. She was happy to go home after school and study, even on weekends. She didn't have to work, because of her full scholarship and Bopha's secret financial assistance. Her only job was to concentrate on her studies and to help Joy with household duties.

Moon did miss going out with her old school friends, yet her studies were more important. Kat and Joy told her she needed to occasionally have some fun, but she didn't have time for fun. Moon was driven and wanted to finish college as quickly as possible. She planned to get her undergrad degree in three years, then start law school. Only after she finished school could she help her big sister and focus on her political aspirations.

Bopha had stopped directly communicating with Moon. She didn't want anyone finding out, especially the Vaskik brothers, about her interest in Moon's affairs. Moon's only news on Bopha came from JJ. She would go to Dizzy for weekly updates on how Bopha was doing.

There was a young man, her age, in several of her classes, that Moon had taken notice of. He was intelligent and good-looking. She caught him looking at her and giving her a big smile. She found it impossible not to return his infectious smile. Later, she learned his name was Atid Vaskik.

Samak had four daughters. Then a miracle happened; his wife, at last, delivered him the son he'd been waiting for. Atid was his only son and the youngest of Samak's five children. Being the youngest and the only boy in the family should have resulted in Atid growing up as a spoiled brat. However, Atid was not a spoiled brat.

Atid was an unusual child. He started reading at the age of four. He had a private tutor, who started homeschooling Atid at the age of three. His tutor continued to teach him, even after Atid was enrolled in a prestigious private school. Atid had a deep respect for his tutor. He was closer to his tutor than to his parents, who were always busy. Before being Atid's tutor, Atid's tutor had been a Buddhist monk for nearly twenty years.

Not only did his tutor teach him reading, writing, and arithmetic, but he also gave Atid lessons in life. He kept Atid up to date on world events, and what was going on in his own country. Most importantly, he gave Atid a moral compass, something his father and his uncles lacked.

Like Moon, Atid had been accepted to attend Chulalongkorn University on a full academic scholarship. He was majoring in pre-law, with a minor in business. One day he would become an attorney as his father wanted. He was an obedient son.

After his uncle Aroon had passed away, his father retired from the Royal Thai Army to take over Uncle Aroon's business, a business that had been in his family for multiple generations. His father told him that one day the business would be handed down to him to run for the family. That was one of the reasons why his father wanted him to become an attorney. In addition, his father expected Atid to get an MBA.

Since starting college, on weekends, his father had Atid join him in his office. His father's office was located at the top of a high-rise building in downtown Bangkok. His family owned the building where the office was located. The building was worth millions of dollars. Atid wondered how his Uncle Aroon could have afforded to buy such an expensive building until his father introduced him to a branch of the family business, the Network.

The Network was worth a little over six billion dollars. His father told him the Network used to be worth even more, until recently, when nearly a quarter of the Network's worth was stolen. Atid was told they were searching for the thief and would eventually find her. The thief had been identified as his Uncle Aroon's mistress. They had no clue how she managed to take over so many of the Network's accounts and assets. They were upset with Aroon for being so careless, allowing it to happen.

To his dismay, Atid learned the Network was involved in all kinds of illegal activities including drug and human trafficking. The Network bribed government officials, police, and anyone willing to support the Network's interests, whether legal or not. It was something he wanted no part of, but he felt trapped. He always did what his father told him to do.

Atid was thriving in college life. He loved academics. He loved all the attention he was getting from the college girls he met. With a lot of effort, he kept the girls from interfering with his studies. Which was difficult because he was very popular with the co-eds.

Recently, he noticed a truly beautiful young woman who was in several of his classes. Now she had his complete attention, making him forget about all the rest of the girls he had been dating. One day, he smiled at her, and she smiled back. It left him feeling happy, almost giddy, for the rest of the day.

Bopha's team was ready to return to Thailand. Before she and her team went after the Vaskik brothers, she planned on attending the double wedding at Dizzy. Only after she disposed of the Vaskiks would she and JJ be able to get married. She planned to arrive two days before the wedding. She needed to spend some private time with JJ before she proceeded with her plans; she started humming to herself in happy anticipation.

The Cathouse was doing better than what Chuen had expected. It had become Chuen's most successful go-go bar out of the five he owned. The Cathouse was making more money than the other four bars put together. Cowboy and Janta made a great team and were running the go-go bar better than he hoped.

Chuen tried to stay out of their way. He wasn't interested in running the bar. The bar provided him the opportunity to get closer to Cowboy, going to the bar whenever he got the chance. He enjoyed Cowboy's company and was glad that Cowboy was now a part of his life. He even found that he was happy with Janta, who would soon become his daughter-in-law. He had decided not to kill her.

He and Janta came to an agreement. They reassured each other it was in both their interests to keep their secret. Neither will tell Cowboy why Janta came to work at Dizzy.

The only thing Chuen disliked about having Janta as a business partner was Janta's mother. Janta had put her mother, Dara, in charge of the dancers. Dara and Chuen were like oil and vinegar. She irritated the hell out of him. He went out of his way to avoid her. But she always managed to find him whenever he came to the Cathouse. She constantly complained about how he was taking advantage of the Cathouses' dancers, not paying the dancers for the off-site services they provided him, causing several of their best dancers to quit.

When Dara found out why the dancers were leaving, she began to pay the women for these services right out of the Cathouse's cash registers. She didn't want to lose any more dancers. This caused Chuen to get upset. Chuen had never had to pay to fuck a go-go dancer who worked in his district, much less for one who worked in his own go-go bar. He expected freebees and got them. If they refused, he would send them to jail. This was the major reason why Chuen had such a hard time getting and keeping good-looking dancers at his other four go-go bars.

Dara scolded Chuen for fouling his own nest. She told him, "If you don't start paying the dancers you take out of our bar, then go elsewhere! You are causing our best dancers to leave!"

Chun finally got tired of arguing with Dara. He reluctantly agreed to pay the Cathouse dancers for their services; after all, he could afford to pay them but didn't like it one bit; it went against his principles. However, he found that paying the dancers was better than arguing with Dara. Anything was better than that!

Wedding plans had been made. The secular double wedding and the reception will be held at Dizzy. Kat wanted the wedding to be like the big American weddings she read about in her romance novels. They would exchange individually composed wedding vows. Janta liked the idea as well. Cowboy and Clyde didn't have much to say on the matter and agreed to do whatever their future wives wanted; both believed in the adage, "Happy wife, happy life."

On the morning of the wedding, each couple would go to their District's Office. There they would give consent to take each other as husband and wife, in front of the Registrar. This will make their marriages legally recognized. The following week after the secular wedding, Cowboy and Janta will have a traditional Buddhist wedding.

JJ was preparing for the wedding and Bopha's arrival. Bopha's team would be staying at the hotel across the street from Dizzy, and of course, Bopha planned on staying with him.

Bopha informed JJ that she was bringing fourteen of her men with her; he wondered why so many. He didn't know Bopha was planning to kill the Vaskik brothers soon after the wedding. If he had known, he would not have objected. He wanted to take out the brothers himself, but Bopha made him promise to leave them alone.

JJ had proposed marriage to Bopha. She agreed to marry him as soon as the Vaskik brothers were no longer a threat. JJ wanted to marry Bopha along with the other two couples. To JJ's disappointment, that wasn't going to happen.

Even though there was little doubt that Cowboy was Chuen's son, they decided to have a DNA test to prove it once and for all, removing all doubt. The test proved they were father and son.

Afterward, Chuen changed his will and had it recorded by the Registrar. Cowboy's last name was now "Vaskik." He would inherit everything in Chuen's estate after his death. Chuen wasn't going to leave anything to his first son and ex-wife; as far as he was concerned, they no longer existed.

~

Atid never missed the classes he attended with Moon. He still didn't know much about her, other than she utterly fascinated him. He couldn't get her out of his head. He dreamed of her night and day. He began to wonder; *is this the woman I was meant to spend my life with? I do hope so!*

He asked one of his friends about her. "Do you know her? Have you talked to her?" His friend replied, "We call her the 'Ice Queen'. Don't waste your time on her. She a snobbish bitch, and besides that, we think she likes girls."

Atid's friend had asked Moon out, and she brushed him off as if he were unwanted lint on her clothing. Because of her rejection, Atid's friend automatically assumed that Moon was a lesbian. He felt that no heterosexual woman could possibly resist his good looks and charm.

While in the college's library, Atid spotted Moon sitting alone reading a book. Her mouth was slightly open, and her eyes were completely focused on her reading. After watching her for a while, he got enough nerve to walk over to her. "Do you mind if I sit at your table?"

Startled out of her concentration, Moon brought the book down a couple of centimeters, her eyes looking over it. There was a frown on her face. She wondered, *who has the nerve to disturb me. There are empty tables all around me.* She saw a boy smiling at her. She recognized him. This was the boy with the adorable smile. But his sweet smile did not stop her from giving him an abrupt reply, "I don't own this table. It belongs to the library. You can sit wherever you like!" She then went back to reading her book. She found herself hoping she hadn't scared him off.

She hadn't. Atid sat down across from her and took a book from his backpack and started reading. After a few minutes, Atid looked up from his book and asked, "Do you mind telling me what you are reading?" Moon again looked up, trying to keep an annoyed look on her face, but instead smiled. Atid had expected her to complain about him disturbing her. The smile he saw on her face was a happy surprise.

"It's a biography on Pol Pot."

"Why are you reading a book on someone who killed so many of his own people? Don't you find that depressing?"

"Actually, I find Pol Pot quite interesting. Who would have guessed that he served several months as a novice Buddhist monk? But I'm reading it for one of my classes. Why are you asking me so many questions? You don't know me."

He stuttered a bit, "Because I would like to get to know you."

Moon looked at him as if he were a little boy bothering her, "Whyyy?"

Atid looked directly into Moon's face and again he showed her the smile that made her stomach tingle, "I find you interesting. You are in several of my classes, and I know how smart you are. A friend of mine calls you the 'Ice Queen.'"

Moon decided to turn into the 'Ice Queen' and send him on his way. *But damn... that smile of his.* "Why does your friend call me the Ice Queen?"

. . .

"Because you acted so cold when he tried to talk to you."

She rolled her eyes, "Maybe I didn't want to talk to him. I don't like talking to strangers."

"Well then, let me introduce myself. My name is Atid Vaskik. I'm eighteen years old, and this is my first year in college."

Atid's last name startled Moon. Vaskik was the last name of Aroon and his brothers. She wondered if Atid was related to them, or did they just share a common last name? She in turn told him, "My name is Moon, and this is also my first year."

Atid looked down at his watch. It was only a few minutes before his next class started and he didn't want to be late. He quickly asked, "Would you be interested in having tea or coffee with me after school so that we can talk?"

Moon was curious to know if he was related to the Vaskik brothers. Besides, *he's so damn cute.* She answered, "Yes. My last class ends today at 5 p.m. You can meet me at the Bangkok Coffee Café." It had been a long time since she had last been at the café. It had been even longer since she had talked to a boy her age to whom she was attracted to.

Atid knew the café, and it was near the campus. "Great, I'll see you shortly after five."

～

The waiter at the Bangkok Coffee Café, Chuen's former informant, was glad to see Moon walk into the café; it had been a while since he last saw her. While he was Chuen's informant, the waiter chose what to tell and what not to tell Chuen. He had never told Chuen about the young lady that Bopha used to routinely meet at the café. He normally informed on people he didn't like, and he liked Moon.

The waiter had learned that Chuen was not only a corrupt cop, but he was also a very bad person. He decided to stop providing information to Chuen altogether. The last thing he told Chuen was that Bopha was no longer coming to the café, which was true.

Moon asked to be seated at a table for two; she was expecting company. As soon as he had seated Moon, a college boy walked into the café. Moon stood up and waved him over to her table. Moon and the handsome young man asked for Thai iced tea.

This time it was Moon asking most of the questions. She asked Atid all about his family. He wondered, *why is she so interested in my family?* When he asked her about her family, she didn't want to talk about them; it was like traveling down a one-way street.

When they finally stopped talking about his family, they talked about what they were studying in school. They were both majoring in the same fields but for different reasons. Atid was studying what his father directed him to study, pre-law, and business. Moon studied what she wanted to study, pre-law, and political science. She didn't tell him about her plans to become prime minister of Thailand. Nor did she tell him anything about her big sister.

She found Atid to be very articulate and smart, maybe as smart as she was. Atid told Moon about his tutor and the things he had taught him, which intrigued her.

"After I finish college, I plan to go into the Sangha for a year, before joining my father's business."

"Why?"

. . .

"I think because of my tutor. He was a monk for many years. He has impacted my life like no one else."

Too soon, it was late, and time to go home. She found herself liking Atid and spending time with him. She agreed to meet with him again for tea and was looking forward to it.

Moon had learned that Atid was Samak's son, which was disturbing. This was something she needed to talk to Bopha about. The next day after school she went to Dizzy to see JJ. She told him about Atid, and that she wanted to talk to Bopha directly. She asked JJ to call Bopha on the satellite phone. JJ normally spoke to Bopha late in the evening, but he thought she would be happy to hear from Moon. He made the call.

Bopha had asked JJ never to share the phone he used to call her with anyone. But when she heard her little sister's voice, it nearly made her cry. She hadn't realized how much she missed talking to Moon and was grateful to hear her little sister's voice.

Moon told her all about the boy she had met in college. That he was the son of Samak Vaskik. She told Bopha that she liked Atid and was planning to meet with him again. Bopha strongly advised Moon, "The Vaskiks are not to be trusted, any of them! Please, listen to me Little Sister, if I'm ever captured by them, they will torture and kill me. To be on the safe side, break your date with him. You need to stay away from him for your sake as well as mine." Bopha paused, biting her lower lip. "It's way too dangerous to have any type of relationship with him."

Her big sister wanted her to avoid Atid, and she would. Moon was disappointed. She thought she might have some romantic feelings for Atid. She thought that the Saudi had completely erased those types of feelings from her. Apparently, he had not. She envied her big sister; she had JJ. Moon saw the love they had for one another. It was something she, too wanted, even though she didn't think she deserved it.

It was early evening. Only a few dancers and one mama-san, Dao, were working at Dizzy. Dao was wondering why JJ was already in the bar. Nowadays, he rarely comes into the bar before nine. JJ was keeping himself busy by rearranging tables, which was again very unusual.

Dao was getting ready to dismiss JJ's odd behavior when Bopha walked into the bar with several men. She recognized her immediately, even though she was wearing a wig and sunglasses; Bopha was impossible to miss.

The men with her sat down at a table to watch the single dancer on the center platform. JJ left the bar to greet Bopha. They didn't wai. JJ took Bopha's hand and led her straight to the back door, going directly into his small house outback. JJ and Bopha were not to be seen for the rest of the day.

Dao's stupid daughter had gotten herself pregnant, by her Thai boyfriend. A big-bellied pregnant go-go dancer didn't attract too many customers. There were a few men who would pay her daughter for allowing them to fuck a pregnant woman, but not many.

There was no maturity leave for go-go dancers. Her daughter had been supporting her good-for-nothing boyfriend, and now Dao had to take over and support the two of them. Dao's loyalty to JJ this time trumped her greed, and she chose not to tell Chuen about Bopha's arrival.

Bopha arrived two days ahead of the wedding. As long as Bopha stayed with JJ, several of Bopha's men would be in Dizzy 24/7. When her men rotated, the fortunate ones would pay the bar fines for their female companions when it came time for them to leave Dizzy. They wanted to blend in with the regular customers. Bopha's men were not anxious about Bopha leaving Bangkok, but they found Dizzy's dancers to be very entertaining.

For the next two days, JJ was missing in action. Kat had to run Dizzy without him; at the same time, she was preparing for the double wedding. JJ made brief appearances for the wedding rehearsals but left as soon as they were finished.

Kat had to tell everyone, who asked about JJ, "He is not feeling well." JJ and Bopha seldom left JJ's bed for the next two days, hardly taking time to eat. After being separated for nine months, food did little to satisfy their hunger.

Moon had surprised Atid the previous day when she agreed to meet with him after school. He had been expecting the rejection his friend had warned him about. He felt his friend was wrong about her. After their conversation at the Bangkok Coffee Café, he believed she was a nice person, someone he would like to get to know better, much better.

At the end of one of their classes the following day, he approached her.

"Good morning, Moon."

"Good morning, Atid."

"I enjoyed our conversation last night. Would you again like to meet for tea after school?"

"I'm sorry, but I am going to be busy. I'm getting ready for several examinations and need to go home to study."

. . .

"How about tomorrow then?"

"Atid, I like you, but to be frank, I don't have time for a boyfriend."

"I'm not asking to be your boyfriend, just your friend."

"I don't have time for any type of new relationship. My next class is about to start, and I need to go." She then got up and walked away, looking upset. And she was upset; she liked Atid and didn't like what she was doing.

Atid didn't know what to think. The other night he was so sure he had made headway with Moon. *Was I wrong? I don't think so.* He didn't believe that Moon was the Ice Queen that his friend had made her out to be. For now, he would back off. However, he was in no way near giving up on her. There were times when he wished he could get Moon out of his head, *but I can't.*

Moon was having difficulty getting Atid out of her head as well. She kept seeing his adorable smile. His smile haunted her sleep, and so did his look of disappointment when she told him she didn't want to meet him anymore. *I wish I could just forget him, but I can't.*

Two days before Cowboy's wedding, his Uncle Samak again invited him to his office for a talk. Samak needed to determine if he could use his nephew in the Network. He needed to fill in the void caused by the loss of Bot's street gang.

Bot's gang had held a critical position in the Network, and it needed to be replaced soon, *by someone we could trust*. Samak wanted Cowboy to form a new criminal street gang to replace Bot's old one. Janta and her mother could run the Cathouse. He didn't bother to ask Chuen for his opinion on the matter. Samak knew what was best for the Network, and Chuen would just have to accept his decision. He picked up the phone and invited his nephew to visit him.

"It's nice to see you again Uncle."

Samak removed two bottles of Singha beer from the bar's frig, and after removing the caps, handed one to Cowboy. He took a swig of the cold beer before he began to talk.

"Nephew, it's good to see you as well. I would like to congratulate you on your upcoming wedding. Your bride is beautiful. Thank you for the invitation to attend."

"You're welcome."

"I asked you here today because I want to ask you about Bot. It is my understanding that you were once part of his gang."

Cowboy was surprised that his uncle knew about Bot. "That was a long time ago, but yes, I knew Bot. Fortunately, I was just an apprentice and not a full member of his gang. I left before that happened. What would you like to know?"

. . .

"Why did you leave his gang?" asked Samak.

"When I met Bot, I was homeless. It was a time in my life when I was just trying to get by. He lured me into his gang. But I wasn't happy and didn't like what he had me doing. Lucky for me, I took an interest in Muay Thai before becoming a full member of his gang. I chose Muay Thai over the gang."

Samak placed a cigarette in his mouth and lit it. He took a drag off the cigarette and blew the smoke rings toward the ceiling. "What would you say if I told you that Bot provided important services to your Uncle Aroon?"

"That would surprise me. What kind of things? Bot was a criminal."

"Yes, that is true, but there were times when your uncle needed his services. Services that were not always legal. Anyway, that is enough about Bot." He extinguished his cigarette after just taking a few extra puffs off it. It was a nasty habit he was trying to quit. "I want to wish you and your bride a happy wedding and a good future together. Both Atid and I will be attending your wedding."

"Uncle, I'm happy to hear that."

Cowboy was curious to know what kind of illegal services Bot provided Uncle Aroon but was too apprehensive to ask his uncle. He decided he would ask his father the next time he saw him.

Samak had hoped that Cowboy would have had a better impression of Bot. After all, it was Bot who had gotten him off the streets. They said their goodbyes and Cowboy left. Maybe Chuen was right, and he should slow down Cowboy's introduction into the Network. But they needed a street gang, and hopefully sooner than later.

Samak's wife had refused to attend the wedding. She looked down on Chuen and his illegitimate son, Cowboy. She had been good friends with Chuen's ex-wife and knew all about Chuen's whoring. She wouldn't be caught dead attending Chuen's bastard son's wedding.

Atid, on the other hand, was delighted to go. He had become friends with his cousin, Cowboy. He met his cousin after his Uncle Chuen dragged him down to his newest go-go bar. At the bar, he introduced Atid to Cowboy and soon they became friends. Atid told his cousin about the girl he met in college. He was surprised when Cowboy told him that he knew Moon and that he too thought highly of her.

"Moon is the niece of Dizzy's general manager, Kat. Kat and I are good friends. Moon will be at our wedding. She'll be Janta's and Kat's Maid of Honor."

Atid was anxious to attend the wedding. He couldn't wait for a chance to try to talk to Moon again. Like an irresistible siren in Greek mythology, Moon continued to beckon him to her.

Chuen disagreed with his brother. He didn't think it was the right time to try to bring Cowboy into the Network. He was just getting to know Cowboy. Because Cowboy was a Vaskik didn't mean Cowboy would automatically want to join the Network; he hadn't been born into the relationship like they were. Chuen wanted time to assimilate Cowboy into the Vaskik family before introducing him into the family business, at least the criminal side of it.

Unfortunately, time wasn't on their side. So, when Cowboy asked him about the kind of illegal assistance that Bot provided to the Network, he told him. As always, the Network came first; its immediate need for a street gang, under its control, had become apparent. They did not want to make the same mistake that Aroon made, by trusting an outsider like Bot. His son running the gang was the perfect solution if he would do it. He came to realize that Cowboy wasn't needed at the Cathouse, Janta and her miserable mother, Dara, could easily run the Cathouse without Cowboy.

Chuen decided to continue the conversation his brother had started with Cowboy. Unlike Samak, he didn't hold anything back. Now Cowboy knew what Bopha had done, why she had fled to Cambodia.

His father and Uncle Samak wanted him to run a Bangkok criminal street gang for the Network. They want him to take over Bot's previous job. However, Cowboy didn't want to have anything to do with the Network. He was happily running the Cathouse with Janta. He needed to convince his father he was not the right person for what they had in mind.

If it wasn't for the Cathouse and taking Janta out of the Game, he would have been tempted to sever his relationship with his father and uncle. Yet, he couldn't stand the thought of Janta going back into the Game. *I can't run a street gang. I'll try convincing them I'm the wrong person for this job.*

JJ was never happier than when Bopha was with him, but he wasn't thrilled about having her attend the wedding. But she insisted on it. It would mean her hiding inside his private balcony for a minimum of five hours until the wedding and reception were over. Bopha would be able to watch the people down below, but they wouldn't be able to see her.

Dizzy was closed for the first time since it was remodeled. A sign hung outside Dizzy announcing its closure for the wedding. It was late morning when Dao spotted JJ leading Bopha up to the balcony. Four of Bopha's men were seated at the balcony's entrance. The other ten were still in the hotel across the street.

During the night, Dao's daughter delivered her baby, prematurely. The baby was placed into an incubator. That meant money, a lot of money. This was not the U.S., where if you couldn't afford the expense of an incubator for your preemie's care your baby would still be taken care of, regardless of whether or not you could pay for it. In Thailand, you had to pay if you did not want the incubator's plug pulled. And that was not cheap. Dao told herself, *I need this money and I need it fast.*

Dao felt she had no choice but to call Chuen. At least, that was how she rationalized her betrayal. Yet, that was not the truth. She earned enough money, working as a mama-san at Dizzy, to pay for her grandchild's incubation. Besides that, she could have asked Kat for financial help, and she would have gotten it. This time her greed trumped her loyalty. Her betrayal didn't come cheap. Chuen had agreed on the price she had asked for, a considerable amount.

Dao told Chuen that Bopha was attending the wedding, and she would be watching it from JJ's private balcony. Doa also told Chuen she believed that Bopha and JJ were lovers. Now, all the pieces fell in place; at last, Chuen knew Bopha's true connection to Dizzy.

The story that Bopha was part owner of Dizzy was just a smokescreen. It made him wonder if Cowboy had known this all along but kept quiet about it. He would talk to Cowboy later. But for now, dealing with Bopha was his top priority.

Cowboy and Janta were getting married in less than two hours. He was getting ready to leave for Dizzy. Since Janta did not have a father to give her away, she asked Chuen to walk her down the aisle. He agreed to do so, over the fervent objections of Dara.

Dao told Chuen that Bopha had brought four of her men with her. Chuen had to avoid a gun battle in front of such a large crowd. Over a hundred people will be attending the wedding and the following reception. However, this was a golden opportunity they couldn't squander; they started making plans.

~

Samak thought that Chuen had finally done something smart by placing a new informant into Dizzy. If not for Chuen's informant, they would not have known that Bopha had returned to Dizzy. As promised, the informant will get paid, but not with money; she'll get a bullet to her head. It was the only way they could be sure Dao remained silent.

Chuen and Samak wanted to get back the money Bopha stole from the Network. To do that, they need to capture her alive. It wouldn't be easy to capture Bopha at the wedding with guests present. Luckily, the stairway leading to JJ's balcony was located near the bar's front entrance. They would use a distraction, one that would draw everyone's attention away from the stairway.

When the distraction went down, they knew Bopha's men would position themselves around the balcony's stairway to block access to the balcony. This would make them easy targets. They would be surprised and killed with guns equipped with sound suppressors.

Three men would run up the balcony's stairway with tasers. Bopha would be tased, and a rag soaked in diethyl ether would be placed over her mouth and nose. If she happened to yell, no one would hear her. Any yell would be muted by the noise of the distraction and by the glass enclosing the balcony. She would then be extracted out through the front door to an awaiting van. If everything went well, it would be over in sixty seconds.

Chuen thought about contacting Cowboy, to tell him he needed to find someone else to walk Janta down the aisle, that he was feeling ill. But he decided that was a bad idea. He didn't think Bopha would try killing him while the wedding was taking place, at least, he hoped not. He was also worried that if he didn't attend, Bopha would become suspicious of why he wasn't there. He was expected and he didn't want to spook her by not showing up. Besides, he wanted to see first hand how his plan worked out.

～

For the past two days, JJ had been as worthless as tits on a boar. JJ had been no help at all, and Kat blamed Bopha for that; for now, Bopha had all of JJ's attention. *Bopha couldn't have chosen a worse time to appear,* thought Kat. *Why now? Why did you have to come during my wedding? But no, you are again acting like a boil on my ass.*

Kat had gotten over Bopha for getting JJ's affection; it's what drove her to Clyde, with whom she was happily in love with. But that didn't mean she liked Bopha; she didn't. She tolerated Bopha for JJ's and Moon's sake. She knew how much they loved her. Besides that, she would always be in Bopha's debt for her part in rescuing Moon from the Saudi.

It was a good thing she had Janta, Chet, Clyde, Joy, and Moon to help her, and that she had the foresight to hire people to help decorate and prepare the food. The place was now ready, and it looked beautiful. Soon, her family and childhood friend would arrive.

Upon their arrival, Kat met them at the entrance door. It felt good to be able to hug and kiss her mother and father again. It was so good to see her dear childhood friend and her husband. Her friend no longer wore Coke bottle glasses. She wore contacts. Her spikey hair was bright orange with blue highlights. Her husband looked nothing like the bare-breasted men on the covers of the romance books her friend loved so much. No, he looked more like a hip Asian Pee Wee Herman. While Kat was standing next to her friend and husband, she noticed the way they looked at each other. When her friend noticed Kat staring at her, she whispered in Kat's ear, "He's sweeter than a bowl of jackfruit covered in whipped cream." She then licked her lips and winked. Kat knew her friend had also found her Mr. Right.

Kat was no longer embarrassed about how she had made her living, in the present or the past. She had been a good daughter. Her parents were proud of her; they felt she had done nothing to be ashamed of. Their prosperity was due to Kat's generosity and sacrifice.

Chet was left in charge, to take care of her family and friends. She needed to prepare herself to marry her Mr. Right. She thought to herself, *dreams can come true*. Before leaving, Kat's mother rubbed Kat's slightly bulging stomach and kissed her daughter's cheek. She told Kat, "I'm so happy for you; you deserve to be happy!"

Chuen was nervous, waiting for the music to start; he knew that Bopha was watching. He was hoping that Bopha would do nothing to spoil the wedding, like killing him. To settle his nerves, he took a long look at the two brides. *They are gorgeous in their white wedding gowns.*

When *Here Comes the Bride* started to play, he offered Janta his arm. He resisted the urge to walk fast, intentionally slowing his walk, with Janta on his arm. Kat and her father were walking down the aisle next to them. The guests were up on their feet smiling and clapping as they passed.

When they reached the podium, and the guests were seated, however, Dara, Joy, and Kat's mother and father remained standing. The wedding officiant began, "Dearly beloved, we are gathered here today to witness the union of these two couples in holy matrimony. Who presents these women to be married to these men?" In unison, Dara, Joy, Kat's mother and father answered, "We do," and then sat down.

As Dara sat down, she noticed a silvery dust had settled on her shoes. The enchanted dust had found a new target to work on; even Dara will have little chance to resist its magic. She tried to wipe the dust off but was unable to. Annoyed, she thought to herself, *I'll wash my shoes when I get home*. She then looked up at the two couples at the podium.

After the two couples had exchanged their vows, the officiant stated, "I now pronounce you husbands and wives. You may now kiss your brides." The veils were lifted, and Clyde and Cowboy kissed their lovely wives.

For Kat, this was a dream come true; at long last, she had married her Mr. Right. Janta had not dreamed about getting married, but when Cowboy kissed her, she realized just how much she was in love with him. She felt he was the only man capable of taking her out of the Game.

Bopha was watching Chuen and Samak. Her heart was beating fast. She hated them nearly as much as she hated Khen. They were the ones responsible for keeping her away from the love of her life. Soon they would be dead, but for now, they were safe. She would not kill them here and tarnish this wedding. Bopha felt a certain amount of anguish, wishing she could be at the podium with JJ, but that would happen soon enough.

Atid became excited when he saw Moon. Moon was the maid of honor for both brides. She was standing next to a tall farang, the best man for both grooms. She looked so alluring in her maid-of-honor dress. He wishfully imagined how Moon would look in a wedding gown, standing next to him. Atid would try and talk to Moon at the reception. *Maybe she'll be in a good mood; at least, I hope so.*

Moon was not surprised to see Atid. She knew he would be attending. Before the wedding, she had looked at the guests' list. She did not know how she would react when she saw him. He looked so handsome in his light blue suea phraratchathan shirt and black trousers. When Atid saw Moon approach him, he gave her his best smile. They exchanged wais and traditional Thai greetings.

· · ·

"It's good to see you, Moon."

Bopha spotted Moon talking to the young man whom she assumed was Atid. The young man had been sitting next to Samak, who had left his chair to talk to his brother. Bopha saw why Moon was attracted to him. He was quite a handsome young man. She had hoped that her little sister would have had enough sense to avoid him, but apparently, that was not going to be the case.

Moon returned Atid's smile, "I'm glad to see you as well." And she was glad to see him. She couldn't help herself; she knew she shouldn't be ignoring her big sister's advice.

Moon and Atid stayed next to each other for the next hour talking. They were enjoying each other's company until Atid's father returned and abruptly told Atid, "We need to leave."

Atid angrily objected, "I'm not ready to go!" His son's strong reaction surprised him. This was the first time Atid had ever talked back to him. *I'll need to talk to him later about this,* thought Samak.

Atid wanted to know why they were leaving before the reception was over. But his father insisted, "It's time to go!" and Atid reluctantly did as he was told. Before leaving, Atid asked Moon if she would like to have tea with him the following day. Again, she ignored her big sister's advice and answered, "Yes."

When Moon walked over to greet him, Atid felt it was one of the happiest moments of his life. He had told his tutor that Moon was the woman he wanted to someday marry. It was love at first sight, but Moon appeared to be avoiding him. His tutor just smiled but offered him no advice. He was wise enough to know that in matters of love, Atid needed to figure things out on his own.

After the Vaskiks left, a group of drunken men, at the back of the bar started to shout at one another. Dao had allowed these uninvited guests into the bar through a side door. As planned, the noisy argument drew everyone's attention. Then a fight broke out. Chet tried to separate the combatants, but there were too many of them. JJ came to assist Chet.

Like in a Western movie, a free-for-all broke out. In no time, it became a complete cluster fuck, with yelling guests and combatants with flying fists and feet. JJ was knocked to the floor, after being struck on his back by a chair. Cowboy and Clyde joined the fray, even though Janta and Kat tried to keep their husbands out of it. JJ quickly got up. The man who struck JJ with the chair was getting ready to hit him again, when Cowboy delivered a hard roundhouse kick to the side of the man's leg, striking the common peroneal nerve. The man dropped the chair and collapsed to the floor.

Bopha had a radio to communicate with her men. Her men were equipped with earpieces. Bopha instructed two of her men to assist JJ and Chet, in breaking up the fight. Her other two men remained at the entrance of the balcony's stairway.

Chuen's and Samak's men entered Dizzy wearing black hoods and masks. They were equipped with M4 Carbine assault rifles with sound suppressors. The two men guarding the balcony entrance were taken by surprise, as they watched the fight. They were shot and killed before they could get off a single round.

Three of the attackers silently ran up the stairs to the balcony, where they found Bopha. She was distracted by the mayhem below. She didn't hear the men coming up the stairs. It was too late when she finally saw them. One of the men shot a Taser dart into her chest as she turned around to face them. Another man placed the rag soaked in diethyl ether over Bopha's face, knocking her unconscious. She was then taken to an awaiting car parked in front of Dizzy's entrance.

Chuen was pleased. *The distraction worked as planned!* The masked men went nearly unnoticed. Several of the female guests, near the entrance door, yelled when they saw the masked men carrying an unconscious woman out the door. However, they were not heard due to the commotion.

$\sim$

When the fighting was over, JJ happened to look in the direction of the balcony. He was wondering what Bopha was thinking about all of this. He then spotted two of Bopha's men on the ground. He shouted out, "Fuck me to tears! What the hell is going on?"

He motioned to Bopha's men, the ones helping him break up the fight. After he got their attention, he pointed to the men lying on the ground. They ran up the stairway to the balcony. Bopha was not there. They learned what had happened from a female guest who witnessed Bopha being carried out the entrance door.

JJ noticed that Chuen and Samak had left just before the fighting began; he didn't think this was a coincidence. The fight was a distraction. They must have found out that Bopha would be watching the wedding from the balcony, *but how? Chuen and Samak must have an informant working at Dizzy, but who?* JJ spotted one of the men who started the fight. He was captured and taken to JJ's office.

Bopha's men easily persuaded the captured man to talk. They used techniques JJ wouldn't have used, but he didn't interfere. He knew if Bopha was going to be rescued, it had to be soon. He didn't want to think about her being tortured and killed; if that happened, he would personally kill both Chuen and his brother. And not with his M40. No, that would be way too quick. *I will kill them slowly.*

The captured man admitted to being hired along with a group of other men to start a fight. He didn't know the name of the man who hired him, but he had been paid well. The man didn't know Chuen by name; the first time he had set eyes on Chuen, was when Chuen hired him off the street that morning.

After the men described the man who hired them, JJ and Cowboy had no doubt he was describing Chuen. The man then described the woman who allowed them into the bar; Dao fitted the description. Dao was brought to the office, and the man stated, "Yes, that's her." Dao admitted to being Chuen's informant. The man and Dao left the office with Bopha's men, never to be seen again.

Ten of Bopha's team were in the hotel across the street when she was abducted. Two of Bopha's men had been killed. The twelve surviving members of her team would be looking for her.

Bopha had an electronic transmitter located in the heel of one of her shoes, with a range of eight miles. Bopha's transmitter was constantly being monitored by one of her men. When her tracking signal became steadily weaker and then disappeared, they knew something was wrong. Bopha's men at Dizzy met up with those who were in the hotel, and the search for Bopha began. JJ, Clyde, Chet, and Cowboy joined the search.

Bopha's idea of having her men watch the Vaskik brothers, 24/7, paid off. The brother's car had a long-range electronic tracker placed on it. The brothers were located at Samak's residence, where Atid was dropped off.

After dropping off Atid, the two brothers then proceeded to an isolated house located on the outskirts of Bangkok, where several of Chuen's men were waiting for them. When Bopha's team arrived at the house, they again had a strong signal from Bopha's heel transmitter.

Bopha woke up to find herself naked, except for her black nylon stocking and high heels. Her clothing had been cut off and discarded on the floor. She was on her back. Her arms and legs were handcuffed to the posts of the bed. She was spread-eagled.

Chuen walked up to her and placed a hand between her legs. He ran his fingers through her dark pubic bush and then gently patted it as if he were petting the head of his favorite dog. "So, this is the golden cunt that Aroon was so in love with. I'll just have to find out for myself if it is as good as Aroon bragged it to be." Chuen had wanted to fuck Bopha since the very first time he set his eyes on her. He was angry with Aroon for refusing to share Bopha with him, unable to figure out why his brother was so possessive of his whore.

Bopha didn't reply. She was waiting for Chuen to get closer so that she could spit in his face. She was confident her men would soon arrive. And after they rescue her, she would personally cut off Chuen's balls and shove them down his throat, before killing him.

Samak was irritated with Chuen. He wanted to immediately torture Bopha, to get the information they were seeking. However, Chuen insisted on raping her first, and Samak gave in. After all, she was incredibly beautiful. It would be a shame to allow such beauty to be wasted. Samak decided, *"I'll have a go at her as well."* He wrongly thought, *there is no need to be in such a rush.*

Chuen took a jar of Vaseline out of a dresser drawer next to the bed. He dipped two of his fingers into the greasy gel, and then inserted his fingers, with the gel, into Bopha's hole. He didn't want to fuck a dry pussy. He then inserted a ball gag into Bopha's mouth, not wanting Bopha to try to bite him or spit at him.

She was now ready to be fucked, and he wiped the remaining Vaseline off his fingers. He took off his shoes, removed his trousers, and then pulled down his underwear. He was fully erect. He thought to himself, *finally, I'm going to get my chance.* Bopha was wiggling and trying her best to get out of her restraints. This excited Chuen, as watched and licked his lips. Just as he was getting ready to mount Bopha he heard gunshots coming from outside.

Samak went to the bedroom window to see what was going on. While Samak was looking out the window, Chuen saw blood exploding out of the back of his brother's head, and a small round hole in Samak's forehead as he fell backward to the floor. Clyde was outside, looking through the scope of an M40. He had just placed a bullet into Samak's forehead. *One brother down and one to go.*

Chuen immediately pulled his pants back on. He heard someone call out, "We have you surrounded. The only way you'll get out of this alive is to surrender Bopha to us." The offer was too late for Samak. "If you give us Bopha, we will allow you to leave unharmed." *That is not going to happen,* Chuen thought to himself. *There is no way they were going to allow me to leave this place alive.* He didn't want to end up dead on the floor next to his brother.

I need to think fast! My only chance is to fight my way out of this. But I'll need a distraction. There was a can of lighter fluid, used to refill his vintage sliver flip lighter, in the drawer where he obtained the Vaseline. Before covering Bopha with the sheet on the bed, Chuen took one last longing look at her. He exhaled a deep breath, *what a shame! I'm never going to get my chance to enjoy you.* The thought made him once again angry with Aroon for his refusal to share her.

Lighter fluid was sprayed on the white sheet he had covered Bopha with. He pulled the ball gag from Bopha's mouth; he wanted the people outside to hear her screams. Chuen took out his lighter and set the sheet on fire. And Bopha did scream! *Her screams will give me the distraction I need, and the Khmer bitch will get what she deserves.* He knew better than trying to use Bopha as a human shield, with snipers around; in all likelihood, a sniper would put a bullet in his head, and he would end up dead like his brother.

Three of Chuen's men were in the living room. The two men he had waiting outside have been killed. He and his remaining men exited out the back door, where his car was parked next to the door. They come under fire. His men, with their M4 Carbines on fully automatic, provided him with cover fire while he made his way into his car, parked next to the house.

While driving away, he saw Cowboy running after him. Cowboy yelled for him to stop. He then fired a single round, from the pistol in his hand, at the moving car. The bullet shattered the rear window, but the bullet missed Chuen by inches. A feeling of sadness came over Chuen; *how could I've been so wrong about you?*

The men who had been providing Chuen with cover fire dropped their guns and placed their hands above their heads to surrender. They were shot and killed anyway. JJ and Bopha's men ran into the house.

They were more concerned about Bopha than trying to capture Chuen, just like he hoped they would be. When they entered the bedroom, they saw a squirming figure on the bed, covered by a burning sheet. The burning sheet was thrown to the floor and extinguished.

The cuffs were removed, and Bopha was carried to a waiting car. Very carefully, they cover her naked body, afraid the covering might stick to her burnt flesh. Not all of Bopha's body was burnt, just the left side, including the left side of her face.

Bopha was taken to the nearest hospital. The hospital wasn't equipped with a burn unit. They treated her burns the best they could and started an IV to keep Bopha hydrated. A helicopter arrived and took Bopha to the hospital with the best burn unit in Thailand.

The only time JJ left Bopha's side was to relieve himself. Most of the time he was holding Bopha's unburnt hand and thinking, *Thank God, you're alive.* He loved her more than anything he had ever loved in his life. The happiest day of his life was the day she told him, "Yes, my Love, I'll marry you."

This was personal. *This is something I need to do for myself and by myself. How could Cowboy betray me like that?* Just when he thought he had a son he could be happy with. *Maybe he was never truly a Vaskik. After all, he is also the son of his little rice whore mother, a heroin addict. What was I thinking?* He was here to correct his mistake. That was why he found himself outside the house where Cowboy lived with Janta and Dara, in the middle of the night.

He found an unlocked window, allowing him access to one of the house's bathrooms. He exited the bathroom into a hallway. The hallway had two-bedroom doors. Chuen tippy-toed to the closest door and opened it. He found Dara in bed; sound asleep. In his right hand was a Colt .45 Gold Cup, a pistol he dearly loved. He was tempted to fire a couple of rounds at Dara, but as much as he wanted to, he didn't; that would wake up Cowboy and Janta. He slowly closed the door and went to the next room.

Chuen quietly opened the bedroom door and found Cowboy and Janta fast asleep. He stood at the door watching Cowboy for a moment, feeling sorry it had come to this.

As he pointed his forty-five at Cowboy, he felt a sharp pain in the middle of his back just before he could pull the trigger. He turned around to see Dara staring at him. She had buried an eleven-inch butcher knife into his back that pierced his heart. Chuen collapsed to the floor. His last thought was, *I should have killed that bitch when I had the chance.*

Cowboy called JJ telling him that Dara had killed Chuen, and they do not know what to do with his body. JJ informed Bopha's men, who were out looking for Chuen. They removed Chuen's body from the house and dumped it in an area of Bangkok that was filled with feral dogs. The dogs would either piss on Chuen's corpse or eat it; no one seemed to care, with one exception.

Cowboy was still the sole beneficiary in Chuen's will. All Chuen's considerable wealth and property, including his five go-go bars, would go to Cowboy. Cowboy will also inherit part ownership of the Network, which Cowboy wanted no part of.

48

GREEN MANGOS

Before the bandages were removed from her face, Bopha was transferred to another hospital. This happened while JJ was getting a couple of hours of sleep, and no one was willing to tell him Bopha's new location; Bopha didn't want JJ to know. She was frightened of what she would see in his eyes, when he looked at her scarred face, now that the bandages had been removed.

After her relocation, Bopha learned something that completely took her by surprise. She's pregnant! The doctors had been wrong. Like her mother, it was difficult for her to get pregnant, but not impossible. During those two days, just before the wedding, she hardly left JJ's bed; they had copulated multiple times, and that was during that lovemaking when this child was conceived. She was lucky that she didn't miscarry when she got tased.

∼

A week passed before Moon saw Atid again. She had learned how his father had been killed. She found herself worrying *if he finds out all the details about his father's death, and my relationship with Bopha, will he still want me?*

After their last class together, Atid invited Moon for tea at the Bangkok Coffee Café. She found herself anxious to meet with him. Again, she completely ignored her big sister's advice to avoid him.

At the café, sitting next to each other, Moon asked, "Where have you been? You haven't been attending any of your classes."

"My father was killed last week. I've been helping my mother with the funeral arrangements."

Moon moved closer to Atid and hugged him quickly, "I'm sorry. How are you holding up?"

"As good as can be expected."

He was taken aback by Moon's hug and tried to smile but couldn't. Finally, Moon reached over, took hold of one of his hands, and squeezed it. This time, Atid succeeded in giving Moon the smile she was aching to see.

"Do the police know who killed your father," asked Moon, still holding his hand.

Shaking his head, Atid answered, "No, they don't have a clue."

. . .

"Do they know why he was killed," asked Moon, biting down on her lower lip.

"No, but I have some ideas," answered Atid, looking down.

She then placed her free hand underneath Atid's chin, raising his head so that they were looking directly into each other's eyes. "Have you told the police?"

"No. My mother would be furious with me if I told them my hunch."

"Why?"

"Would you think less of me if I told you the truth? I care about what you think."

"That depends. There is one thing I can't stand, and that's someone who is deceptive. *Even though I am,* she thought to herself. Just tell me the truth, and then I'll tell you how I feel."

"I think it had something to do with my father's business. He was involved in illegal activities. I think his death is connected to those activities. Now that I am going to be inheriting his business, I do not know what I'm going to do with it. I want any part of it."

Moon removed her hand from underneath Atid's chin. There was a startled look on her face. She had not expected him to be so frank. Atid didn't know why he was telling her this. But he felt he could trust her. Atid hadn't even told his aging tutor about the Network's illegal activities. Moon was wondering the same thing, *why is he telling me this*, but she was relieved, relieved to learn that Atid wanted no part in his father's illegal activities.

"Atid, why are you telling me all this?"

"Because you asked, and I felt a need to tell you. You are the only person I have told this to. I'm in love with you." While smiling at her, he said, "The first time I saw you, I knew you were the woman I wanted to marry."

"I like you too, but I'm not in love with you," causing the smile on Atid's face to vanish. This wasn't quite true. She more than just liked Atid; she had strong romantic feelings for him. But she was still dealing with self-hate for the things she had done to win the Saudi's affection, and for not telling Atid the truth, about how his father was killed.

Moon felt she wasn't ready to be in love with anyone. *How can anyone be in love with me?* Still holding Atid's hand, she told him, "If you trust me, I can introduce you to someone who can help you."

"How can anyone help me with this problem," asked Atid.

"Please, just trust me," whispered Bopha.

Moon arranged for Atid to talk to Bopha. Her feelings for Atid proved to be right. He was trustworthy, and a good person. She wondered if she was a good person like Atid believed she was. She wondered if she deserved his love.

After leaving the hospital, Bopha went back to her jungle hideout. She no longer drank fine Scotch whiskey. Instead, she listened to classical music, Mozart and Beethoven, before going to bed. Over the following months, the baby began to kick, and she rubbed her belly trying to soothe him. She loved to hum him Cambodian lullabies. They were the same lullabies that her mother would hum to her when she was a little girl.

Slices of sour green mango covered in pink fermented salty shrimp paste had become her favorite food. Nearly every night she would cry when she thought about JJ; she missed him so much. Even though she wanted JJ at her side when their son was born, the fear of what she might see in JJ's eyes, the startled look when he saw her scarred face, was enough to keep her away from him.

In her jungle hideout, Bopha had become a force to be reckoned with. No one entered her area of control, including government troops, without Bopha's permission. She had become the most powerful warlord in Cambodia.

Her private army had antiaircraft missiles that could down any plane in the Cambodian armed forces' arsenal. Her antitank weapons were capable of destroying any armored vehicle fielded against her. She had the best trained and equipped private army that money could buy. Her men and women were battle-tested-hardened warriors, willing to fight to the death for her. There would be no repeat of what happened to her compound in Thailand. She would never again be taken by surprise.

JJ received a call from Bopha telling him she was okay. She didn't want him to see her scarred face. She would undergo plastic surgery to repair it, which would take a while. She could afford the best plastic surgeons in the world, but there was only so much they could do. She told JJ, "My

Love, when they are finished, my scarred face will no longer scare small children."

JJ tried convincing Bopha he didn't care how she looked, that he could not stand being away from her any longer. But his pleas were of no avail. Bopha was unable to tell JJ that she was pregnant. She knew he had a right to know. Much of the surgery she needed would be delayed until the birth of their baby, prolonging their separation. She planned to tell JJ, but not today.

~

Just before leaving Cambodia for the double wedding, the ancient Khmer sorceress who resided near Bopha's compound had a vision of Bopha delivering a son. As a young sorceress, she had prophesied the coming of a man who was destined to do great things. She believed Bopha's son would grow up to be that man.

When Bopha was told of the sorceress's vision - she laughed and then cried. *How could a sterile woman give birth to a son?* The prophecy had brought tears to her eyes. Nothing would have pleased her more than to give JJ a son, something she believed to be impossible.

Now that the first part of the sorceress' vision had come true, her son's conception, she would pay closer attention to the Ancient One. Maybe the Ancient One was someone she could learn from. Perhaps, she could convince the sorceress to share some of her powers with her. Then maybe, with these powers, she could give JJ the illusion that her face was not scarred.

~

Bopha was taken aback when Moon asked her to talk to Atid. Not even in her wildest dreams did she expect the results that occurred from that conversation. The Network was no longer involved in illegal activities.

The Network will grow and prosper under Atid's leadership, more than ever.

Atid will assist Moon and Bopha in their fight against sex trafficking, but Atid disagreed with their methods. Atid didn't believe in extreme violence and refused to use it. He will bring legal pressure against corrupt officials who assisted sex trafficking and will not allow sex traffickers to remain hidden; they'll be exposed as the cockroaches they were.

The Network will assist victims of sex trafficking by giving them job training, and financial and psychological help. These victims will also be provided with good-paying jobs. Thailand and its neighbors have a long way to go to bring their women gender equality. Presently these countries are not motivated to break the glass ceiling. Atid will try his best to change this, but using violence was not part of his plan.

Atid's wish to see Moon, in a wedding gown, standing next to him will come true, just not yet. They will complete their college education. After graduating, Atid will enter the Sangha for a year. He will need to obtain merit for his father, for all the evil his family had committed in the name of the Network.

While he was in the Sangha, Moon, with the help of Bopha, will run the Network. They have promised to keep the Network out of any illegal activity including vigilantism. Moon would make sure Bopha keeps her promise.

Atid had taught Moon there were times when she needed to stand up to her big sister. Atid had made Moon a stronger person, and Moon had made him stronger. In this case, the whole was greater than the sum of its parts.

Atid had a feeling that there was something in Moon's past that still haunted her, but she would not talk to him about it. He could sense that it was something terrible, and it acted as an invisible barrier between them. Maybe when he had won her full trust, he'd be able to tear down that barrier. He was as thirsty as a man stranded on a hot desert day without water. But it's not water he thirsted for. He thirsted for Moon's love and trust.

At first, Atid's mother didn't like Moon, but that did not last long. She saw the effect she was having on her son, and she approved. Her son had grown confident in himself and took over the family business without missing a beat. Atid's mother knew little about the illegal business the Network had been involved in. She never questioned her husband.

Atid was no longer a boy; he had become a man she was proud of. She knew that Moon had a lot to do with it. Atid's mother's opinion of Moon's extended family even changed. She had become friends with Joy, Kat, Clyde, JJ, Janta, and even Cowboy, but she wasn't a fan of Dara. Dara rubbed her the wrong way, but Dara rubbed nearly everyone the wrong way.

Atid had become the man that his old tutor hoped he would become. He was proud of his student. The old tutor was aware of Atid's father's illegal activities, but he never told Atid what he knew. He had hoped that Atid would reject and weed out the corruption found in the Network when it came to his turn to take over the family business.

He tried his best to lead Atid down a path that would allow Atid to know the difference between good and evil - to do the right thing, even when it went against Atid's self-interest. He wanted Atid, as an adult, to choose his path. He believed his student had chosen the right one.

Recently, he was offered a new job, tutoring a young child. A child as bright as the sun. He looked forward to becoming her tutor and mentor. When he looked at his new student, she looked back at him in a familiar way. He suspected that she was the reincarnation of his old abbot, a man he deeply respected. It made him wonder, *in the end, who will be the teacher and who will be the student?*

A person shows different parts of their personality to different people. There was the part you show to strangers. There was the part you showed to close friends and family, and then there was a part that you showed to no one. No one ever knows everything about another person, no matter how close they are to that person.

There were a lot of things Atid didn't know about Moon. Moon didn't want Atid to know about the Saudi. Those few months she had spent with the Saudi, had killed something inside her. But perhaps, not permanently. She was not yet willing to share such personal secrets with him or anyone. Not even her big sister knew all her secrets.

After her rescue, she viewed the child that the Saudi had placed inside her womb as a parasite; she rejoiced when it was aborted. Now she grieved for that innocent child. She prayed it would be reborn into a loving family.

She had come to love Atid. Yet, she felt something was missing. She may never love Atid the way Bopha loves JJ, but she hoped to. Regardless, someday she'll marry Atid. If she could love a man with all her heart, it's Atid; she knew this would only happen if she learned to trust Atid as thoroughly as she trusted her big sister. The day would come when Atid knew Moon even better than her big sister.

Moon still planned to become the prime minister of Thailand. With Bopha's help and Atid's help, she will achieve her political ambition. Unlike Pu, when she becomes the prime minister, she will never allow Thai generals and corrupt politicians to chase her out of Thailand like a scared dog with its tail tucked between its legs. It's an accomplishment that will make Bopha very proud of her little sister.

The sun was setting, when Moon found herself alone, next to a riverbank. The water here was moving fast and was muddy. She reached into her pocket and pulled out a golden wedding band, the one the Saudi made her wear on her left hand. She looked at it, rotating it in her fingers; it glittered in the fading light of the setting sun. Moon then threw the ring at the river with all her strength. The ring hit the murky water and quickly sank.

Again, she reached into her pocket, and in her hand, she pulled out a broken golden chain; the chain she yanked off the dead Saudi's neck. She had every intention of throwing the chain into the murky water but instead placed it back into her pocket. Moon then turned her back to the river and walked away.

A new life had been introduced to Joy, Kat's baby girl, Mai. Joy took care of Mai while Kat and Clyde were at work. Mai would become the joy of her life. Joy would become Mai's most cherished Nay, even though Mai would also love Kat's biological mother.

Joy's three-legged dog had died of old age. He had followed Joy home as a pup. He lost his right rear leg after being hit by a car. His injured leg was still barely hanging on when he followed Joy home. Joy took him to a vet. The vet removed the injured leg, and afterward, Joy adopted him. For the next sixteen years, he lived a good life with Joy.

Recently, an emaciated expecting mother dog followed Joy home, and of course, she adopted her. She quickly fattened her up. Soon after, there was a litter of pups to entertain Kat's baby girl. Joy will find good homes for the pups and have both mother and her pups fixed.

One of the new pups had taken to Moon and followed her wherever she went. If he could, he would jump up on her bed, but he's too small. At bedtime, he would whimper until Moon picked him up and sat him on her bed. They would snuggle up next to each other and fall asleep. He was a good boy, and would whine whenever he needed to do his business and she would take him outside.

Joy had heard that every child should experience the grief of losing an old beloved dog and the joy of witnessing the birth of puppies. Though Joy was a far cry from being a child, these experiences held something special for her; they were examples of the cycle of life.

Clyde couldn't be happier. His little girl, Mai, melted his heart every time she looked at him. Mai had him wrapped around her little chubby baby finger. He couldn't imagine his life without her.

All those years before marrying Kat, Clyde knew he was missing something, but he couldn't figure out what. He believed no woman in the world could satisfy him for more than just a moment. He was trying to fill a void that couldn't be filled. It took Kat and Mai to fill it.

Before marrying Kat, he thought he could hear his grandmother's voice whenever he looked at Kat saying, "Honey, she is the one!" If only his grandmother were still alive. He wished she could have met Kat and Mai before passing away. He hoped that his grandmother had gone to the place she believed she was going to, and that she knew he was happy and at peace with himself. He hoped she was staring down at him with a big smile on her face.

Clyde wondered, *why does a man decide to go down a path without first having a rational reason for doing so. Are you being pushed by destiny, by fate, by God? At the time, I thought that JJ was foolish when he told me that he was going to buy a go-go bar in Thailand. I felt foolish when I asked JJ for a job but thank God I did. I was wrong to believe that there was no one out there for me.*

Kat, at last, had found her Mr. Right. A Mr. Right, who came right out of one of her paperback novels and gave her Mai. She couldn't have asked for a better husband or a sweeter daughter. Clyde, Joy, and Moon all adored Mai. Even Joy's new dog tried to lick Mai's face whenever she got the chance.

Her mother and father now routinely come to Bangkok for visits. Kat wasn't the main reason for their visits. It was to see Mai. Mai is a special child. She's as bright and as pretty as her Auntie Moon. Atid's aging tutor was now tutoring Mai.

As a wedding present, JJ gave Kat and Clyde half ownership of the bar. He told them they deserved it for all their hard work. JJ told them he wanted to spend less time at the bar, and more time with Bopha. He was planning to move to Cambodia to be with her; a plan that Bopha knew nothing about. Dizzy was still one of the most successful go-go bars in Bangkok and will remain so for many years to come. Its enchanted dust would continue to ensure its success.

The mysterious magical slivery dust that resided in Dizzy had found a home it was reluctant to leave. Dizzy was the perfect place for it to work its magic. Glittery-silver-colored dust, floating in the air, ready to land on a selected lucky few.

Cowboy didn't know what he was going to do with the five go-go bars he inherited, so he sold four of them. All but the Cathouse. The Cathouse was enough to keep Janta happily busy, and out of the Game.

The size of Chuen's estate surprised everyone, making Cowboy a very wealthy man. He had come a long way from being a homeless orphan on the streets of Bangkok. Chuen's ex-wife and his first son tried to contest Chuen's will but lost in court. Bopha had hired Cowboy one of the best attorneys in Bangkok, and she motivated the judge to rule in his favor.

Cowboy had become familiar with his father's side of the family. They weren't all bad. Most of them were good. He had become close friends with his cousin Atid. Atid was making the Network into a family business the whole family could be proud of. Cowboy was now willing to do his part to help continue the Network's success. It will stay a family business for many generations to come.

Cowboy was now looking for his mother's side of the family. Hopefully, he will find them soon. When he does, he'll need to decide what he'll tell them about his mother. Someday, he planned to ask Janta if she wanted to search for her father in the U.S., yet Cowboy was nervous about how Dara would react if Janta said, "Yes."

Cowboy didn't know how to handle all his inherited wealth, but he was getting help. Janta, at first, did not approve of Bopha's help. But when the inherited assets steadily increased their value, she knew that Bopha was the right person to be advising her husband. She would learn from Bopha and would someday manage the assets for Cowboy and herself.

Cowboy wasn't stupid. He knew Janta manipulated him. He believed women were hard-wired to manipulate men, and they started learning the craft at a very young age; it was a female basic survival trait. As long as Janta wasn't being malicious and was following an agenda that was beneficial to both of them, he thought, *so what's the problem?*

Janta had no regrets. Her marriage to Cowboy was a happy one. It was easier leaving the Game than she had thought it would be. There were times when invisible strings tried to draw her back, but so far, she had always managed to cut them. She had to resist because it would destroy Cowboy if she ever went back into the Game. And she loved him too much to allow that to happen.

She no longer had to worry about Chuen telling Cowboy that he hired her to seduce him. Cowboy might not even mind if he knew the truth, but she didn't want to take that chance. In a way, she was grateful to Chuen. If not for Chuen she would have never met Cowboy. Even though Chuen had tried to kill them, when Chuen died, she lit joss sticks to Buddha and prayed he would be reborn to become a better person. After street cleaners found Chuen's body, and the dogs had their way with it, no one wanted to claim the body – with one exception, Janta. She had his body cremated. With her mother at her side, she sprinkled his ashes on blooming flowers.

Kat talked Janta into routinely rotating their dancers from one go-go bar to the other. The dancers like it, and it's a win-win for both bars. Kat and Janta have become close friends if not best friends.

Every Thursday was movie night at Janta's and Dara's house. Clyde, Kat, Joy, and Mai never missed movie night, watching classical movies on Cowboy's TV. On movie night, Cowboy made the best buttery popcorn in all of Bangkok, sprinkled with his secret ingredient.

Kat asked him for his secret ingredient, but Cowboy refused to share it with her. Then Janta intervened, using her special female persuasion; Cowboy quickly gave it up. Janta had not forgotten how to loosen a man's tongue.

For the most part, Dara was behaving herself. She still hated most men, but she was getting better at liking some of them. She had even met a man near her age, at the Cathouse of all places, with whom she enjoyed going to Muay Thai matches. This was how they met.

Dara was talking to a dancer, when she heard someone behind her call out in a loud voice, "Hi good looking!" Both she and the dancer assumed the comment was meant for the dancer, and the dancer started walking toward the man.

"No, not you, the other one," pointing directly at Dara. Dara turned around to face the farang. She then pointed one off her fingers at her own chest.

"Yes, I'm talking to you!"

Dara frowned at the farang, "Do I look like a dancer? Am I wearing a skimpy outfit and wearing high heels?"

"Does that matter? You do work here?"

"I do, but I'm not here for your entertainment."

"I didn't think you were. I just want to talk to you. Do you mind if I buy you a drink?"

"Yes, I mind," she turned on her heels and started to walk away.

The man then said in a loud voice, "I hear you like Muay Thai. As it happens, I have two front-roll tickets to the Muay Thai championship match tonight, and I would like for you to go with me."

It's a match that Dara wanted to watch. Janta and Cowboy said they were too busy to go, and she didn't want to go by herself. The farang had done his homework. The day before, he had asked one of the dancers what Dara liked to do when she wasn't working. He learned that Dara loved going to Muay Thai matches, and so did he.

Dara became curious. And because she wasn't wearing her eyeglasses, she walked back to take a better look at the farang. She was startled to see he looked like an older version of Janta's father! The same good looks. The same carbon-colored eyes and dark hair that was starting to turn grey. She had mixed emotions; she didn't know if she wanted to talk to this man or to flee from him. However, she decided to stay.

"You can buy me a Singha beer, and we'll talk." She took a seat at the farang's table.

The farang turned out to be an American, a retired Green Beret, who was now living in Bangkok. He spoke Thai, exceptionally good Thai for a farang. Dara wanted to know why he was interested in her and not one of the young dancers.

"They are nice to look at, but they are way too young for me. I have nothing in common with them. I'm looking for a woman I can relate to. I came in here yesterday at the urging of a friend, and I spotted you. I watched you for a good hour, and thought to myself, what a lovely woman and so confident! I'd like to get to know her. That is why I came back today."

"Really! Do you have any idea what you are asking for?"

"I'd like to think so. I know you like Muay Thai, and so do I. And I would like your company tonight."

He had such an uncanny resemblance to Janta's father. She found she was unable to stop herself from saying, "Okay, I'll go with you. We'll meet here."

As it turned out, she liked his company. The farang was direct, uninhibited. He said what was on his mind, something that Dara could appreciate. And most important - he knew his Muay Thai.

Cowboy and Janta laugh at her and call Dara's new friend her "boyfriend," which angered her. When Dara got really angry, she cursed them in broken English, making Janta and Cowboy laugh at her even harder.

Janta thought her mother deserved to be teased; she remembered the way Dara had teased her about Cowboy. Tonight, Dara had invited her new friend to their house for dinner. She warned Janta and Cowboy, "Behave yourselves, and do not embarrass me in front of him!"

The first time Dara saw her new friend, up close, he startled her. He looked so much like Janta's father, just older. At first, she had hoped that the man who had deserted her and their daughter so long ago had return to say, "I'm sorry." This was not that man, and that is okay.

Besides Cowboy, she hadn't liked being around a man in a long time. As she stared at the mysterious silvery dust, still stuck on her favorite shoes, she thought, *I really like this man*! The magic dust was hard at work.

Bopha was recovering from the recent surgery on her burnt face. Little by little her scarred face was beginning to return to its original beauty. She felt her burnt face and body were the result of her karma catching up to her for all the people she had killed.

She had deserved a bullet to the head, like the one she put in Rosie's, for trafficking women while working for Bot. On top of that, she was still enjoying her memories of Khen's screams when she burned him to death and the screams of the old gentleman as she inserted the iron rod up his ass. Their screams sounded like instant karma.

One day Bopha will look pretty again, but she will never again be able to compete for the most beautiful woman in a room filled with tens. She couldn't stand the thought of JJ seeing her scarred face. She was trying to convince herself that her scars didn't matter, yearning to be surrounded by his arms. She couldn't understand why she loved a man who owned a go-go bar; however, she did. *I love him more than my own life*, she thought.

49

I SWEAR

JJ is sitting on his private balcony in his favorite location in the world. He's not drinking iced tea. He needed something stronger, a tall glass of Wild Turkey on ice with very little water. He felt he was in a quagmire. He loved Bopha with all his heart, but at this moment, he was angry with her.

He missed the small things about Bopha, such as the feel of her hands in his. The way she smiled at him, and how her eyes sent flaming arrows into his heart whenever she looked at him. He missed her perfumed body and their passionate embraces. Most of all he missed her sweet whispers of love, while he hugged her. *Why is she being so hard-headed?*

She had recently told him she was pregnant with their child, something he didn't think was possible. Her doctors had told her she couldn't get pregnant, but her doctors were wrong. He needed to convince her to return to him before their child was born.

Bopha was the most beautiful woman he had ever seen, and if the truth be told, that's what drew him to her; it's what drove Beth from his mind. However, their relationship had grown way beyond that. Bopha was now his spiritual partner, his soulmate, and he was lost without her. Not having her near him felt worse than losing a limb.

He had never thought of Bopha as being vain. She had always said she valued her intelligence over her looks, but that was not the way she was acting now. The world's top plastic surgeons had reassured her that they would be able to repair her scarred face and body. She told him; she didn't want to return to him until those repairs were made. JJ had grown tired of waiting; he wanted her now, scars and all! *How am I going to convince you to return to me sooner rather than later?* He then decided, *if you won't come to me, then I'll go to you. If the mountain wont' go to Mohammed, then Mohammed must come to the mountain.*

Members of Bopha's new gang had been in contact with JJ. They knew how badly Bopha needed him. They heard her cries at night. They knew that if JJ was not in Bopha's life, she would become mentally unstable. They would meet JJ in Cambodia and then take him to her.

Bopha didn't need to worry about how JJ would react the first time he saw her scarred face. He will kiss her face, with a loving tenderness that couldn't be faked. He wanted to hold her hand as she delivered their child. And like in the lyrics "I swear," JJ though, *I'll love you with every beat of my heart, and like a shadow, I'll never leave your side. I swear!*

JJ had removed the glass enclosing his balcony. The glass that he had put up to keep Bopha hidden during the double wedding was gone. He didn't want glass interfering with his senses as he watched and listened to the crowd below; the noise had a hypnotic effect on him that caused him to reminisce.

The song playing below caught his attention. It's a song he has never heard played before at Dizzy. A melancholy song, rather than an upbeat one. It's Toni Braxton's song, *Un-break My Heart*: "Don't leave me in all this pain / Don't leave me out in the rain / Bring back the nights when I held you beside me..." More than anything in the world, JJ wanted to hold Bopha next to him. Only that would relieve his pain.

~

And for now, we'll end this story where it began, with JJ sitting alone on his private balcony, sipping Wild Turkey on ice, listening to Toni, deep in his own thoughts, at 'Dizzy,' a Bangkok go-go bar. A place like Disneyland – a magical place – a place where dreams can come true.

The End – for now!